RED DARKLING

L. A. Guettler

cover art by Jason Kemp

DEDICATION

To Vladmir V.

May the Fourteen bring him peace.

And here we stand, at the edge of reason, hands entwined, about to leap.

Exaius, *The Seven Discourses*

Baby baby, gimme your, gimme your love monkey, baby, yeah.

Pink Chenille, "Love Monkey"

CHapteR 1

The night was hotter and stickier than the inside of a clomis after a couple kilos of garlic yozzies.

Red Darkling wiped her forehead with her arm and eyed her target: a shiny new Air Skimmer LX. She twiddled a knob on the side of her visor, scanning for the ultraviolet glow that would spell disaster for the mission. Nope, no glow. No glow meant no shield generator, and no shield generator meant no shield.

Game on.

Grownups were so stupid. They didn't deserve such a nice ship. They should thank her, really, for finding all these holes in their security. Maybe they'd learn to take better care of their stuff. They probably didn't even lock the manual controls to their palmprint.

A croaking sound floated through the air. Red froze for a second, then relaxed and rolled her eyes. Was that supposed to be an orl? Idiot. She'd told Buck a hundred times to pick a different signal. He couldn't do an orl cry to save his life, and besides, orls didn't even live on this planet.

She stuck the visor into her bag and darted out from the bushes, crossing the grassy verge to the pad where the ship was parked. She moved quickly and silently in her broken-in sneakers. Her black clothing blended into the deepening shadows as she ducked under the ship. She paused to send her own signal (a double flash from her pocket light) back at Buck, who was somewhere near the main house.

She swiped at her forehead again. This was the tricky part. It was unshielded, but starting up a ship of this size was a noisy, flashy business. True, these surface-restricted models didn't need gravity modulators, but they still had perimeter lights and it's hard to dampen the sound of thrusters.

Red glanced back at the main house. It was mostly dark and looked empty. Buck thought it *was* empty. Still . . .

Eh.

She pulled on a pair of mismatched gloves and punched the hatch button. The hatch slid open with a whisper. She yanked the short ladder down, sent another double-flash signal, and climbed in. A minute later, Buck Landers stuck his head through the portal. He was sweaty and out of breath from the short jog across the lawn.

"Wow, this thing is nice! I think this is the nicest one yet. Right, Red?"

"It's great. C'mon, Woodman's waiting for us to pick him up."

"Okay, sure thing." Buck closed the hatch behind him and the interior lights came on automatically. The cockpit was easy to find. The ship wasn't that big, only a few steps up from the 'hopper Red got for her last birthday.

Sure enough, the manual controls had no palmprint lock. Idiots. Red dropped into the cushy captain's chair and surveyed the controls. She located the ignition panel and flipped on the engines. The perimeter lights came on, and the thrusters began to hum through their warm-up cycle. Cool air flowed from the vents over Red's sweaty skin, raising goosebumps.

"Hold on," she warned. "I don't know how much kick this thing has." Buck grabbed the arms of his copilot's chair, a crazy grin on his round face.

Just as the ship began to lift, the lights come on in the house and the door flew open. A man ran out, robe flapping, waving his arms and shouting. Red smiled and waved. Then she banked the ship sharply and sped away over the trees.

"Holy moley, Red! That guy saw us! We're busted!" Buck grabbed her arm.

"Dude, you want us to crash? Cut it out." She shook off his hand. "We're not busted. Let's get to the rendezvous point."

"Rondy what?"

Jeez. Buck was only ten, a couple of years younger than she was, but that didn't mean he had to act like such a baby. "Rendezvous. It means where we meet Woodman."

"Oh. Right."

They flew in silence over the city, heading toward the old aqueduct. Buck kept checking the scopes, but no one was following.

It was full dark when they arrived. Red landed the ship among the crumbling concrete and ragged weeds without even a wobble. Buck ran back to open the hatch. A minute later, Mark Woodman strolled into the cockpit, a lit cigarette dangling from his lips, Buck immediately behind.

"Nice landing, *Mild*red." Woodman went to give her a high five, but she scowled and punched his arm instead.

"I hate when you call me that."

"It's your name, innit?" Red crossed her arms, and Woodman sighed dramatically. "Fine. I'll call ya whatever you want. Just let me fly this baby."

"No way. I did all the hard work. I'm doing the flying."

"Hey, I was lucky to get out of the house. I'm still grounded from the last time. Had to use the last of my Pergolian sleep tea on my mom. You owe me. Now scoot and let me show you some real flying."

"No."

"Hey, I'll tell you what—you let me fly, you can have the rest of my cig. Swiped a pack from my dad."

"Fine. Jerk. Gimme." She stood up and snatched the cigarette out of his mouth. After fumbling it in her fingers a bit, she took a drag. "So fly already," she said, smothering a cough.

He plopped down in the seat and grabbed the controls. "No palmprint locks? Sheesh. No one saw you?"

"Oh, they saw us," Buck said eagerly. "I thought for sure that we were busted but Red just waved and took off. It was so cool."

Woodman shot Red a look. "Someone saw you?"

She rolled her eyes. "It's no big deal. No one followed us. Buck was watching the scopes the whole way over here."

"Yeah, man, I totally did. There wasn't even a blip. Not a blip."

Woodman looked out the viewport and grinned. "Well, we'd better make this good, then."

~ ~ ~

4

They left the ship outside the abandoned warehouse where they had stashed their 'hoppers earlier. The ship was intact except for a ding near the left thruster. That'll be the last time they let Buck talk them into taking a turn at the controls. They were all lucky it was just a vid tower and not another ship or something.

Before splitting up to head home, the three bumped fists.

"Remember: not a word to anyone." Woodman pointed at Buck. "Right?"

Buck laughed nervously. "Yeah, sure, not a word, don't worry."

"All right. Red, you doing the market tomorrow?"

She shrugged. "Probably. I spent my last credits on that pizza yesterday."

"Cool. I'll see you there if I can sneak out again." He winked. Her stomach did a weird twingey thing. It did that sometimes when Woodman was around. It was annoying.

"Whatever. I gotta go." She climbed into her 'hopper and flew off without looking back.

After the joyride in the Air Skimmer, the 'hopper was tame and boring. Red landed it a block from her house and walked the rest of the way. She went to the back yard and scuttled up the homona tree that conveniently grew outside her bedroom. She slid along the branch until it began to bend, lowered herself onto the roof of the dining room, and slid through her open window.

Her parents, Lacey and Richard Darkling, were sitting on her bed.

Crap.

"Mildred." Her mom didn't sound angry. She sounded sad. Her eyes looked like she'd been crying.

"Red," she mumbled, staring at the floor.

Richard stood up and pointed his finger at his daughter. "I don't care what you call yourself, this has got to stop."

"Look, I can explain. There was this—"

"We don't want to hear it, young lady," he interrupted. "There's no excuse for sneaking out, especially at night. Anything could have happened to you."

"Dad, I'm fine!"

Lacey wiped her nose with a wadded-up tissue. "Honey, we're trying to give you space. I remember being your age. You're so full of feelings and you want independence and I get that. *We* get that. But you're only twelve years old, and we're still your parents."

"I know, mom! Jeez, enough with the lecture."

"Mildred, that's no way to talk to your mother."

"Sorry." She shoved her hands into her pockets and kicked the carpet with the toe of her shoe.

"Sorry's not enough anymore."

Her mother stood and reached out to touch her arm. "We were just so worried about you, honey."

Red pulled away. "I said I was sorry. Look, whatever. Am I grounded or what?"

"It's late. We'll talk about this tomorrow. Now, go to bed. Come on, Lacey." They left, pulling the door shut behind them.

Red flopped on the bed. It wasn't fair. They treated her like a criminal and nothing even happened this time. Well, if they were going to get mad no matter what, she might as well do whatever she wanted. She'd show

them. She scrubbed her eyes with her fist and pressed her face into the cool pillow.

I'll show them, she thought until sleep overtook her.

Chapter 2

A loud crash woke her. Light streamed through the window—more light than usual. Blinking and yawning, Red got up to see what was going on.

The homona tree lay in pieces. Leaves, branches, and sawdust littered the lawn. Three men in hard hats and stiff leather gloves were dismantling the trunk, which lay prone among the debris.

To be honest, she was surprised it had taken them this long to get rid of that tree. Good thing she still had the basement window propped open a crack.

She threw on some clean clothes, leaving the dirty ones on the floor, and headed downstairs. She found her mom in the kitchen drinking coffee.

"Don't go anywhere today, Mildred. We're going to talk as soon as your dad gets home."

Red silently grabbed a zuranfruit from the fridge and stalked out of the kitchen. She wandered into the living room and switched on the vidbox. She munched her fruit and waited to see if her mom would follow.

She didn't. Red left the vidbox on and dropped the zuranfruit peel on the sofa. She went into the front hallway and eased open the door under the stairway. Thank the Fourteen gods of Penthus she had fixed that squeak. She closed it gently behind her and descended into the basement.

Red loved the basement. Her parents hardly ever went down there, so it was a perfect place to store her private stuff. Plus it had the window so she could come and go without anyone knowing. It was harder at night, because the basement didn't have lights and it got super dark. One time, she had come back from a late-night community improvement project (drawing obscene things on lawns with grass killer) and had tripped on an old suitcase. She still had a scar on her knee from that one. But, with the homona tree cut down, it would have to do.

Right now, the room was dimly lit from the late morning sun filtering through the dirty window. A small grid of light cut through the dusty air from the vent grate near the ceiling. Red had moved a sturdy box over there to stand on so she could see and hear everything that went on in the kitchen. It was the perfect way to listen to her parents talk about stuff they didn't want her to hear. Mostly, that meant stuff about her.

She climbed on the box and peeked through the grate. Her mother was still at the table with her coffee.

Perfect.

Red hopped down and grabbed the beat-up grumskin bag that had all her props in it. She rummaged through the contents. Yep, all there. She crossed the room to the window, where a chair was shoved up against the wall. She climbed this, pushed the window open, and checked the yard. No one in sight. She tossed the bag up first, then shimmied through on her belly. She crouched, squinting in the bright sun, but no one appeared. She quickly slid the window down, making sure that the brick was there to keep it from closing all the way and locking her out.

She stood, stretching her legs and brushing the dust and dirt from her clothes. Ew. Well, it never hurt to look a little dirty for the market. She picked up the bag and slung the long strap over her shoulder. Ducking under the windows, she made her way to her 'hopper. One of the tree guys saw her climb in, but she just acted normal and he kept dragging branches around.

The market was only a few miles away. Red landed the 'hopper near the far end of a lonely alley that ran behind a string of shops. She took a cap from her bag and pulled it low over her eyes. She also dug out an oversized photo of a dog. She checked her reflection in a broken window. Cool, time to work.

Red moved through the crowd. She clutched the photo in her hand and put a worried look on her face. She scanned the scene, looking for an opportunity . . .

There, that woman with the two little kids outside the candy shop. Her purse had slipped down around her elbow and she was distracted by the kids, who were jumping around and pointing at a display of FlinkBars and Tootsie Froots.

Red ran up to the woman and pushed the dog photo in her face. "Have you seen my dog? He's lost."

The woman sputtered but had no choice but to look at the photo. Red dipped her hand into the dangling purse and took the wallet.

"I'm sorry, no, I—JESSICA!" the woman shouted at her daughter, who was busy sticking her fingers into her brother's nose. She pushed the photo aside but Red had already slipped the wallet into her own bag.

Red mumbled a thank you and moved on.

She used the lost dog story a few more times, then switched to the "oops I spilled my soda" routine. After a couple of hours, she caught a policeman giving her a weird look.

Yep, time to take a break.

Winding her way between the stalls and down a few side streets, she found a piece of curb mostly hidden by a display of brightly-colored robes. She sat and started poking in her bag to see what she had gotten.

"Got a match in that ugly bag?" It was Woodman. He sat next to her and pulled a cigarette from his shirt pocket.

"Maybe. You got a cigarette for me?"

"Maybe." He grinned. Red felt that weird stomach thing again. She turned away and dug in the bag until she found a slightly soggy book of matches advertising some bar in Septimal City. She passed them to Woodman. He managed to get a match going and lit two cigarettes with it. He passed one to her and tucked the matches into his pocket.

"How'd you do? Let's see what you got."

Red held the cigarette in her teeth and the bag in her lap as she sorted through the wallets.

"About fifty credits."

Woodman somehow managed to whistle without dropping his cigarette. "That's it? Who've you been working?"

"It's not my fault there's no one good here today."

"Well, you must not be looking too hard. I'm going to find someone for you." He stubbed out his cigarette on the road and stood up. "C'mon, people are already starting to go home."

Red dropped her half-smoked butt on the ground and ground it out with her shoe. Stupid Woodman. Like she needed *his* help. He'll probably get her busted. Pick a cop on his day off or something.

She followed him through the market. He was right; the crowds were thinning out. They walked past a food vendor trying to get rid of his last few yozzies before packing up. The greasy smell made Red's mouth water and stomach grumble. She was about to lift one when Woodman nudged her with an elbow.

"Hey. Check it." He nodded toward a vidscreen booth on the other side of the yozzie stand.

Two guys in black suits were standing next to the booth, having a tense conversation. The tall one had the brilliant green skin and skeletal fingers of a Glorreen. The other was a short, fat human with the biggest eye bags Red had ever seen. Seriously. She could have packed a lunch in each one and had room left over for dessert. Her stomach rumbled again.

"Those guys? Why those guys?"

Woodman shrugged. "Their suits look expensive. And I've never seen a Glorreen before. You know, in person."

"I dunno . . ." Red didn't like it. These guys looked like serious business.

"C'mon, we'll do a little pushy-pushy." He shoved her and backed away. "You calling me a liar?" he said in a loud voice, putting up his fists.

Oh jeez, he was doing this whether she wanted to or not. She walked over and got up in his face. "Yeah, I called you a liar. A big, fat, grum-sucking LIAR." She pushed him hard in the chest. He stumbled back a few steps.

They were almost on top of the two guys in suits. Woodman winked at Red and roared, "I'M NO LIAR!" He took two handfuls of her jacket and slung her around behind him. His foot flew out as if to trip her. Red faked a stumble and ran head-first into the guy with the eye bags.

"Oof!" he grunted, flailing his arms. The Glorreen grabbed her roughly and pulled her off his companion, but not before she had lifted the contents of Eye Bags' pocket. It was a weird shape for a wallet, but she didn't spend time looking. She dropped whatever it was into her bag as the Glorreen pushed her away, shouting a string of alien words in a voice like broken glass. She didn't understand a word, but his hand gestures made it pretty clear what he saying.

Woodman had already disappeared into the crowd, so Red ran off, taking the back ways to her 'hopper. He was, of course, waiting for her.

"Woo, did you see that green dude's face? He was pissed! I had to skate cuz I thought he was gonna come at me, you know? Man, I haven't done a pushy-pushy in ages! It was fun! We gotta do that again sometime." Woodman paced around the alley, practically bouncing, waving his arms all around.

"Didja get the fat guy's stuff?"

Red tossed her bag into the 'hopper and looked nervously over her shoulder. "Hey, we should get out of here. You wanna come? Maybe we can grab Buck and Frankie and those guys and get some pizza at Shellchucker's."

"You buying?"

Sigh. What a mooch. "Yeah, sure. But I want nintha on it."

"You and your nintha." He climbed into the 'hopper's second seat. "Well? You wanted to go, so let's go."

Double sigh. Red got in the pilot's seat and made sure to blast her favorite band on their way to the pizza joint. The Poly Torrents. Woodman hated The Poly Torrents.

Chapter 3

Several hours and an extra-large nintha and onion pizza later, Red landed the 'hopper in her usual spot down the street from her house. It was late and dark. She went around back and was surprised to remember the tree was gone. The house looked naked without it.

Basement window, then.

She slid it up and lowered her bag down. Then she got on her belly and wiggled through, dropping feet-first into the basement. Through the vent grate, she could see light from the kitchen. She took off her boots, padded across the room in sock feet, and climbed up on the box to look through the grate.

Her parents were sitting at the kitchen table. Her mom was crying. Her dad stared off into space, patting her on the back like a robot. Red felt a stab in her chest and her eyes prickled. She swallowed hard and sat on the box. Her sock had a string sticking out near the toe. She picked at it for a while until the tears stopped. There was no way she could go up there now. She swiped a sleeve across her face.

Might as well look at her take from the day, what was left of it anyway. She got her bag from under the window and sat on the floor in the patch of light from the vent. She pulled out assortment of wallets, loose credits, and other junk. She flipped through the wallets, checked for any cash hiding behind family photos, and tossed the rest into a pile to be dropped in the sewer later. She counted the cash. Ugh, only sixteen credits. She should have made the other guys chip in for the pizza.

Most of the rest was stuff like bottle caps and food wrappers. This all got dumped into the sewer pile. One odd thing caught her eye, a flat square disk that fit in her hand. She held it up in the light to get a better look. It was black plastic, maybe a quarter inch thick with rounded corners. One side had a metal strip, also black. There were no markings on it at all. This must be the weird thing she picked up from Eye Bags. It didn't look particularly valuable. Maybe Woodman would know what it was. She shrugged and dropped it on top of the sewer pile.

The kitchen light was still on, so she took a quick peek. Yep, her mom and dad were still at the table. They didn't look like they were going anyplace. At least her mom had stopped crying.

Red couldn't deal with this scene now. She'd wait until morning. It wouldn't be the first time she'd slept in the basement. She kept a pillow and blanket down here just in case. She pulled them out from behind a box, shook off a few spiders, and got herself settled on the old sofa with the wobbly leg.

Her mind wandered as she stared into the gloom. She didn't like seeing her parents upset, but it wasn't her fault, not really. If only they'd just stop worrying. She hated that they were so strict. All her friends could be out after dark without their parents barking at them like rabid fazzers. It wasn't fair, she'd never even been caught, not once. It was just having fun, that's all. Just having fun.

A bright flash startled her awake. She didn't even realize she'd fallen asleep. She blinked a few times, not real sure where she was. Another flash and her eyes flew open. It was coming from the vent. From the kitchen!

She heard some voices. One sounded like her dad, but the other she didn't know. It was hard to make out the words, so she crept over to her makeshift stepstool and looked out.

The Glorreen from the market held Lacey, one long green hand across her mouth, the other one pinning her arms behind her back. Eye Bags was there too, pointing a blaster at Richard. There was a smoking hole in the kitchen table, another in the cabinet behind her dad's head.

"Richard—may I call you Richard? Richard, I don't think you understand the situation here. We tracked the data chip to this location. It *is* here. Now, we can go about this in a civilized fashion. Or, I can let Limey Jim here disassemble your lovely wife. It's entirely up to you."

Red's eyes got wide. She darted a glance at the flat square thing on top of the sewer pile.

Richard held up his hands. "I have no idea what you're talking about. I don't have any data chip. I don't understand why you think it's here, but it's not. I swear, it's not."

Eye Bags looked at Limey Jim, who tightened his grip on Lacey. Her eyes were wide in terror. The Glorreen croaked something unintelligible.

"No! I don't—please, maybe if you told us what this data chip looks like, we could help you."

"You're trying to tell me that you have the data chip, but don't *know* you have the data chip? Oh, Richard, I am inclined to agree with my colleague. That story is just not believable." He leveled the blaster at Richard's face. "I'll ask one more time. Where is the data chip?"

"I don't know, I—" The blaster flared and Richard's body slumped to the floor. Red's hand flew to her mouth to smother a scream.

"You see, Mrs. Darkling? Joey Pockets is not to be taken lightly. In fact, I think it is fair to say that I should be taken very seriously indeed. Wouldn't you agree, Limey Jim?"

Lacey moaned and twisted under the Glorreen's hands. Tears streamed from her eyes. Behind the vent grate, Red's did the same.

Joey Pockets nodded at his companion. The green fingers released their grip on Lacey's mouth, and she let out a loud sob.

"Mrs. Darkling. I am hoping you will be more cooperative than your husband. My employer is anxious to have this data chip returned. He may be willing to make certain . . . concessions if it is returned unharmed and, of course, unopened. I encourage you to consider your answer carefully."

Red watched her mother sink to the floor and touch her husband's face. She brushed the hair away from his forehead and kissed him. "Okay. Okay. The data chip . . . it's upstairs. In the bedroom. I'll show you."

Lacey stood up and start walking out of the kitchen. Through the grate, Red saw her mother's bare feet pass by, followed by a pair of men's shoes.

Suddenly, there was a scuffling and thumping. Something crashed, and Limey Jim shouted in his alien language. Someone snarled, and there was another sickening flash. Red's mother fell to the kitchen floor with a thump, landing so she could look straight down the vent grate. Her eyes met her daughter's for an instant before they went blank.

Chapter 4

"Well, Limey my friend," Joey Pockets sighed. "There's nothing else but to search this house until we find that data chip. The boss will not be happy if we come back empty-handed. Shall we start right here in the kitchen?"

The Glorreen said something and seemed to laugh.

"Fine, but if there's any fried juta, save it for me. Deal?" Then there were sounds of cabinets opening and dishes breaking.

Red scrambled back behind the sofa. Pain and panic threatened to overwhelm her, but she fought against it. She needed to get out of there before they got around to searching the basement. She tried to focus on making a mental inventory of what she had in the basement that she could easily take. It helped her avoid thinking about the way her mother had kissed her father's face. Or watching the life disappear from her mother's eyes.

She couldn't wait any more. Cautiously, she eased herself out from behind the sofa. She pulled on her boots and picked up her grumskin bag. She took out all the props and replaced them with her meager pile of credits, her blanket, and an old jacket with a hole under one arm. She grabbed the data chip too. No way those guys were going to get it.

The window was still open. It was full dark, but the moons were big and bright. Again, the bag went up first and she followed. She didn't bother closing the window behind her. Tears welled up in her eyes, but she blinked them back. She made her way to the front, keeping low and close to the house and moving fast. She stuck to the deepest shadows and got to the 'hopper. She started it up and took off with no plan. She just needed to get away.

Where should she go? Woodman's? Buck's? Her brain scrambled but there was really only one place that she could go. But first, she needed to get rid of that data chip before they could track it to her again.

Red headed to the lakefront. The 'hopper couldn't travel over water, so she landed on an industrial pier. She didn't power down all the way. She climbed out and stood at the very end of the pier, booted toes poking over the edge. The data chip filled her palm.

"Screw you, Joey Pockets, and screw you, Limey Jim." She pulled her arm back and let the chip fly, horizontal to the water. It skipped along the surface four times before sinking. She wiped her eyes and nose with her sleeve and got back in the 'hopper.

~ ~ ~

Granny heard the bell ring. She groped for her glasses on the bedside table and checked the clock. Why, it was after midnight! Who could it be so late?

She got out of bed, slid her feet into her slippers, and wrapped her robe around her aged body. The bell rang again.

"I'm coming!" she called out. She turned on the hallway light and made her way down the stairs, clutching the railing under her bony knuckles. Her legs didn't cooperate very well these days. It was better to be safe than sorry, and that was the truth.

When she made it to the door, Granny put her eye to the peephole. She gasped and fumbled with the doorknob until it finally turned and the door swung open.

Standing on her porch was her darling little Mildred. Her face was pale and she was shivering, though the night was warm.

"Granny," she cried. The tears and pain she had held back for hours broke free in a flood. She ran to her grandmother and crushed her face into her shoulder. Granny held her tightly. As she felt the girl's body shaking and her tears soaking through the thin robe, she realized she had been expecting this for a long time.

Oh, Johnny. What have you done now?

Chapter 5

Fifteen years and several light years' worth of scuttling around the galaxy later, Red leaned back in her captain's chair of the *Pit*. (The ship's official name was the *Cherry,* but Red and most law enforcement agencies felt this name was far more accurate.) She lit a thin Crolinian cigar. Smoke swirled around the cockpit as she stretched out her legs, thumping her battered boots on the console. A dusty can of Old Wo'hall'a dripped condensation onto the sub-light panel, threatening to short it out again.

Life wasn't bad. It had been weeks since she had a paying job, sure, but she hadn't crossed blasters with any bounty hunters either. Good thing, too. That guy on Albicon 8 got a little too close for comfort. She still had bruises and her hair would probably never grow back the right way. Bastard.

The work thing needed attention. She was down to her last case of beer. She was lucky to find it, hidden under some long expired duoofish in the back of the main storage compartment. She took a sip and grimaced. Lucky? Nah. It was the last beer on the ship for a reason.

"Okay, then," she said to the nobody in the copilot's chair. "Let's see what's on the scanner."

Red clenched the cigar between her teeth and sat up. She flipped a few switches. Static flared. She twiddled a knob and the noise resolved into the familiar background chatter of the low-res bands. She doodled in the water left by the can and listened with half an ear.

It was the usual boring bullshit. Kids looking to score some off-world dope, business owners arranging for "accidental" fires, pimps claiming that their chicks were the hottest thing since anti-grav handcuffs. Red stifled a yawn and took a deep draw on her cigar.

She was about to turn off the scanner and take a nap when she heard it: an irregular series of static buzzes between transmissions. She turned the volume up and leaned forward. Yep, there it was again. Red could never mistake that pattern.

It was Granny's code.

Red switched off the scanner and sat back in the chair. She hadn't seen or heard from Granny since . . . jeez, it had been months. Red flooded with guilt. Last time she'd been at Granny's was the night cops came pounding on the front door. They caught her with her pants down—literally. She was getting good and shagged by that bastard Woodman when the galactic gestapo showed up. She had to bail out the window with nothing but that ridiculous blaster she had stolen when she was twelve.

Heh. Woodman. She had managed to see *him* a few times since then. The guy was an arrogant, crude asshole who couldn't be faithful for a week if his johnson depended on it. But damn she'd still have a go every time the opportunity came around. He was a pretty good shot, too. Someone you'd want at your back in a tight place, pun definitely intended.

Red stuffed her cigar into the beer can. Quit thinking about Woodman, dammit. The code. Granny sent the code. Something's wrong.

"Granny," Red whispered to the silent scanner.

She had to go. It was risky. But she had to go. She'd have to be careful. But after so long, her chances of getting in and back out again without being detected had to be decent. Or at least not catastrophically low. If only she could find out what the situation looked like from the ground, talk to one of the old crew.

But who? Red considered the possibilities. It didn't take long—there weren't many. The few people from home she had actually got along with were either dead (Frankie) or in prison (Buck). Being a fugitive from justice and several minor criminal organizations makes it hard to keep up with childhood friends. You tend to forget birthdays and miss bavit shavah ceremonies. It can be a problem.

There was only one person who might be able to give her the scoop.

"Woodman." She cursed and spit on the floor. It always seemed to come back to Woodman. His parents still lived on Sept Magossii, and he was a huge mama's boy. He probably still did those vidchats with her every week and went to dinner on holidays. If there was still heat for her there, Woodman would know.

She pulled up his name on the vidchat. Her finger hovered over the call button for a few seconds before tapping it. Well, that's it. Now to wait for his pingback. If she was lucky, he might respond in a few—

The vidscreen crackled to life and there he was, in all his scruffy, tattooed glory. "*Mild*red! Are you ever a sight for sore eyes," he drawled.

"You ever gonna get tired of calling me that?"

"Nope." He scratched his chest in a way that pulled his thin shirt tight against his abs. "You are lookin' mighty good, though, I must say. To what do I owe this particular pleasure? Lemme guess. You're missin' me, ain'tcha, babe?"

Red ground her teeth. This was such a bad idea. "Look, I was going to ask you a favor, Woodman, but if you're going to be like this, just forget it." She reached for the off switch.

"No no no, now, just hold on. Let's start over." He placed a hand on his chest and gave a little bow. "'Hello, Red, it is ever so nice to see you again. How may I be of service to you?' Now your turn."

"I wouldn't even ask except you're the only person from back home who can help." She took a deep breath. "It's Granny. She's sent the code through the scanner, like we always talked about. Something's wrong. Really wrong. I need to get back there."

Woodman's grin fell away. "You sure it was the code?"

"Yeah. I'm sure."

He rubbed his neck. "Well shit, Red, what do you think it is?"

"I don't know, dude, that's why I need to go back. Do you think the cops still watching her place?"

"Maybe, maybe not. It's been what, three, four months? And you're not exactly on anyone's most wanted list. Except mine, of course."

Sigh. "Can we just stick to the problem? What do you think I'm dealing with when I get there?"

Woodman looked vaguely off screen. "Well, I don't really know. I haven't noticed any uniforms hanging around the place lately, but it's not like I've been looking. Could be they've decided you're not coming back for your toothbrush. Or they've gotten way better at the plainclothes thing."

"Ha! Not likely. Remember the guy who followed us into that bar on Ophesus? His sunglasses!"

"Right! They were worse than Ephrasia Pfeff's in that movie. And he was trying so hard, the poor bastard." Woodman chuckled. "We sure have seen a lot of shit together, babe."

Red looked at Woodman's face on the cracked and dirty vidscreen and felt that old stupid twinge in her stomach. "Yeah, we sure have."

He cleared his throat. "So. When are you going?"

"Right now. Unless you know some reason I should wait?"

He looked off screen again. "Nothing I can think of, babe. You taking the *Pit*?"

She threw up her hands. "Are you stupid? It's the only ship I've got!"

"Calm down, it was just a question." He paused. "I'd use the western approach, fly in over the lake. That way you should be able to see them coming, if they're coming. Drop down on that strip where we used to hang with the old gang. Frankie's gone, of course, but a few others still around who'll watch your ship and keep the sniffers busy until you can get back."

He met her eyes through the vidscreen. "Do it right. Do it careful. Do it smart. You got me?"

Red allowed herself a little smile. "Yeah. I gotcha."

"Good." Woodman snorted. "See ya around, *Mild*red."

The vidscreen went black before Red could sputter a reply.

It took Red just a few minutes to program a course to Sept Magossii. She heard the thrusters kick in and felt the ancient gravity modulator catch after a brief struggle to compensate for the sudden yaw. She checked the travel time and headed for the storage compartment. It would be a little over an hour before she came out of sub-light speed, and by the looks of the mess, she would need every minute to find what she was looking for. She shoved aside a pile of potentially virulent pants and made a mental note to tidy the place up.

She grabbed every portable weapon she could find: blasters, holoknives, even a suspiciously sticky mini faze cannon. It all got strapped to her body or snapped into a pocket. She found the comm blocker inside an empty cracker box and its battery pack behind a blonde wig she once wore during a particularly dodgy month. She considered the wig, but close inspection revealed a well-established colony of dugger mites. Gross. She needed a cat.

On the way back to the cockpit, Red drained another Old Wo'hall'a as she stretched her legs and swung her arms to limber up. The full complement of gear felt odd, but comforting. It had been a while since she'd purposely walked so openly into danger, and never this much. She couldn't decide if her hands were shaking from nerves or excitement. Or maybe the beer had actually gone over.

The nav beeped, signaling her arrival above Sept Magossii and the beginning of the descent to the planet's surface. Red sat in the captain's chair and checked the scopes. Nothing suspicious, but it was early in the game. She would know more when she got closer to the surface.

A few minutes later, another beep told her that the ship was ready for her to take over the driving. Red took the flight controls and checked the scopes again for anomalies. Still nothing. She aimed for the large lake that appeared on the horizon through the viewport. Woodman was right; from this approach, she'd be able to see straight into Granny's bedroom, if she had the right magnification. She didn't, but that wasn't the point.

Red forced herself to slow down to a virtual crawl and merge into the required altitude with the other ships going about their business. Do it right, do it careful, do it smart. Scopes still negative. Standard traffic patterns, no unusual thermal signatures, no hinky blips on the long range scan. The city emerged in the distance, and Red angled her flight path toward the deserted landing strip on the outskirts. Just a couple minutes and she'd set foot on her home world for the first time in years.

"Come on, come on," she muttered at a slow air skiff blocking her way. She officially regretted the beer that now sloshed around in her gut like bilgewater.

Her eyes flicked over scopes again. If this guy could just move his ass...

The air skiff stopped dead in the air.

Red had only a second to enjoy the sinking feeling of doubt before the water exploded upward around the *Pit*. Half a dozen cruisers burst from beneath the lake. Within seconds they surrounded her, faze cannons bristling from their dripping hulls.

"Damn you, Woodman!" she screamed. Then the concussion blast hit and she lost consciousness.

CHAPTER 6

There was someone shaking her. Red's vision swam as she struggled to make sense of the situation. She was sitting, ankles and wrists tied, a grimy rag shoved deep in her mouth. She couldn't feel any of her weapon harnesses cutting into her skin, which meant they were gone. Duh. Of course they were gone.

This shaking was really getting old. She managed to open her eyes fully and focus on the face in front of her.

It was Woodman, wearing the black uniform of the Guild.

She twisted her body and tried to scream, but her restraints held and she almost choked on the rag.

"No no no, now, just calm down, Red, you've got to calm down," Woodman whispered. "I can explain. Can I explain?" He pulled the rag out of her mouth.

Red lunged forward to bite his backstabbing nose off, but he jerked out of the way. Her teeth clicked together, hard.

"What could you possibly have to say to me?" she hissed.

He put his hands on her shoulders. Her skin crawled but she was helpless. "Red. You know me. I would never rat you out. But I had no choice. It's Sloane. He got my mother." His voice cracked. "He got my mother, and your Granny, he got her too. I got them safe for now but . . . I dunno what you did to piss off the Guild, babe, but Sloane's itching to get his teeth into you. This whole thing was a set up just to get you here."

Red's mind spun. Sure, she'd lifted about sixty crates of supplies from one of the Guild's freighters, but that was ages ago. Job didn't even pay that well. Turns out, the cargo was mostly foodstuffs. Not much of a black market for jams and biscuits, not even in the outer systems.

"Look, I've had a string of luck you won't believe but it won't last forever. We're gonna have company pretty soon. We need to move. I'm gonna cut you loose. Please, trust me." Woodman used her own holoknife to cut through the ropes on her ankles, then went behind her to free her hands.

Red stood up, rubbed her chafed wrists. She turned to face Woodman and smiled. A relieved grin spread across his face. A moment later he was on the floor, her boot at his neck, the holoknife in her own hand.

"You never were any good with this thing," she said, pointing the knife at his eye. "Now tell me, where's Granny? WHERE IS SHE, WOODMAN?" She pressed with her boot.

"She's outside, in my ship," he choked. "My mom too. I got them both out already. I swear. Please, Red."

She didn't have much choice. Snarling, she removed her boot, holoknife still pointed at his face. "I'm not saying I trust you. But I need to see Granny safe. Let's go."

Together, they crept to the door of the holding cell and peered into the hall. Two men in Guild uniforms slumped against the wall, holding cups and covered with a sticky-looking yellow liquid. Pergolian sleep tea. Classic Woodman.

They slipped through the corridors and stairways and encountered no trouble. At the hangar door they stopped. Woodman's ship, the *Chopper* (yes, he actually called it that), was out in the landing area, only fifty yards or so of empty concrete away. They'd be prime targets for any passing thug looking for a promotion.

There was nothing for it but to go, and fast. Red caught Woodman's eye and nodded. He winked. His arm slipped around her waist and he drew her close. Her brain screamed in protest, but his lips felt so good on hers, warm and firm and familiar. She retracted the holoknife and let it slide up into her sleeve as she wrapped her arms around his neck.

"My, my, what have we here?" a silky voice crooned.

Red spun around and saw Alistair Sloane in his crisp Guild uniform. The golden insignia on his cuff caught the light as his hand shot forward and found her throat. He began to squeeze.

"Ah, tut tut, my dear Mr. Woodman," Sloane said, shaking his head. He pulled a blaster from a holster inside his jacket. "This is none of your concern. This is between me and Ms. Darkling. You just go back to your mother, now, there's a good boy." He waved the blaster toward the ship.

Woodman growled, but Red could barely hear over the blood pounding in her head. She writhed and clawed at Sloane's hand, but she couldn't break his grasp.

"Why, Ms. Darkling!" Sloane laughed. "You've turned a lovely shade of purple! Perhaps now you can see that no one steals from the Guild."

Red's vision began to narrow. In desperation, she beat at Sloane's chest with her draining strength. She felt a strange hard shape bang into her arm.

Instantly, Red dropped the arm to her side and caught the holoknife as it fell from her sleeve. With a flick of her thumb, the glowing blade extended. She slammed it into Sloane's abdomen. His eyes widened and his grip went slack. Red used both hands to drag the blade up to his neck, then stepped back. She heard Woodman whistle as Sloane's blood poured onto the floor.

CHaptER 7

On the ship, Woodman excused himself to the cockpit. Red hugged Granny and totally didn't cry at all. Mrs. Woodman tsked over Red's stained clothing and bustled off to find something fresh.

"Granny, I—it's so good to see you."

Granny took Red's blood-drenched hand in her own cool bony ones. "It's good to see you too, Mildred. I've missed you."

"Granny, I've told you. Call me Red."

"And I've told you. You'll always be my little Mildred."

Red rolled her eyes, then gave Granny another hug. "I've got to talk to Woodman."

Granny smiled and patted Red's cheek. "Of course, dear. I'll help Viola with the clothes, then put together a little something to eat."

In the cockpit, Woodman was slumped in the captain's chair. Red watched through the viewport as they left the atmosphere at bat-out-of-hell speed. There was a copy of some Orgullan porn mag on the copilot's chair. Red wrinkled her nose, kicked it to the floor with her boot. It fell face down, thank the Fourteen. An ad for some cheap cat-based tracking system screamed at her from the back cover. Valu-Kat, heh, so clever.

She sat down and looked at Woodman, who had his eyes glued to the *Chopper*'s scopes. "You okay?"

"Yeah. You?"

"I guess so. Pissed about the *Pit*. Bastards probably crushed it to a cube of metal by now." Red stared at the floor and bit her lip. "I kinda liked that ship. It wasn't great, but it was home. You know?"

"Babe, I'm one step ahead of ya." Woodman grinned. "The *Pit*'s at Granny's."

"What! How?"

Woodman winked. "I got the magic, darlin."

"Don't be stupid, Woodman. Sloane wants me dead. He grabs Granny as bait. He knows I'd come to you for help, so he grabs your mom too. That all makes sense, in a twisted, evil way. But what doesn't make sense is how you managed to find me, let alone break me out. Or how we managed to escape without half the Guild firing faze cannons up our exhaust port. And now you're telling me the *Pit* is safe at Granny's." Red's eyes narrowed. "How is any of that even possible?"

Woodman sighed. "I've been trying to figure out the same thing."

Red punched his arm.

"Ow! Normally I'd deserve that, but I'm telling you the truth. None of it makes sense to me either." He rubbed his arm, a frown darkening his features. "When you pinged me for the vidchat, I was in the *Chopper*, parked at my parents' house, with two Guild thugs pointing blasters at my head. I was hoping you wanted to talk about a job or maybe hooking up—"

"What!"

Woodman threw up his hands to block another punch. "Hey, I knew if you brought up Granny I'd have to play along with Sloane and that would go bad for you. And you know what, babe? I was right."

"Hmph."

"Yeah, hmph. Anyway, once I clicked off with you, I had to do something. But I could hardly go racing around Sept Magossii with my new babysitters hanging out in my ship. I had no idea what to do."

Woodman set the nav to auto and started pacing in the cramped cockpit. "That was when it got weird. There was this knock on the hatch. Real quiet, polite, with a rhythm, like this." He drummed his knuckles on the control panel, three slow beats and two short. "My Guild friends must have recognized it, because they opened the hatch."

Woodman paused. "Poor bastards got a blaster to the head. One shot each, real precision work, right between the eyes." He jabbed his forehead with a finger.

Red winced. "Who was it?"

"Dunno." He shrugged. "Never saw anyone. Just this, on the floor next to the bodies."

Woodman dug into his pants pocket and pulled out a small card. He handed it to Red. It was thick, cream-colored, and velvety between her fingers. *Fauas Tea Company* was printed on one side in dark blue ink, like a business card. Someone had written two words on the back: Go now. The handwriting was angular and narrow, but precise, like it too was engraved by a machine.

Red looked at Woodman and raised her eyebrows. "What is this? I've never heard of it."

"I had to look it up. It's a dummy corporation, owned by the Guild, headquarters right there in Magross. It's where I found you."

Red shook her head. "But—"

Woodman held up a hand. "Hang on, let me finish. I had two bodies and a lead, both thanks to an anonymous assassin. First thing I had to do was dump the bodies, so I did. Then I headed straight to this Fauas place. It was over on the edge of the industrial zone, not far from where we used to boost 'hoppers back in the day. You know where I mean?"

Red nodded, still clutching the card.

"I didn't know what would happen when I showed up," Woodman said, pacing again. "I mean, this could have been another trap, right? So I was careful. There were all kinds of Guild people hanging around the front of the building, so I landed in the back. I thought maybe I could sneak into a loading dock or something. But . . ."

"But *what*? Come on, Woodman, just tell me."

"There was a door. Propped open."

Red snorted. "Probably a janitor sneaking out for a smoke."

"That's what I thought too, but there was no one around."

"Okay, fine, the door was open. What was on the other side, an illustrated map to the room they were holding me? Neon arrows pointing to Granny and your mom?"

Woodman chuckled. "No, it was just a storeroom, but look what it was storing." He plucked at the collar. "Dozens of Guild uniforms. I found my size and boom! Free pass to the whole place."

"That was lucky. How'd you find us?"

"It wasn't hard. The place is pretty much just a bunch of offices. And how many offices do you know that need guards posted outside? I found Mom and Granny first, told the guard that Sloane had sent me to get 'em. Idiot believed me. Got them to the ship and went back looking for any sign of you. You know the rest." He dropped back into his chair.

"What about the *Pit*?"

"See for yourself." He tapped a few buttons and a picture of Granny's house popped up on the vidscreen. The *Pit* was parked right outside, dented and scratched halfway to hell and back. Just like she left it.

Red shook her head. "But how did you know?"

Woodman glanced at her. "The coordinates were already programmed into the nav when I got here just a few minutes ago. When I fired up the engine, this picture came on the vidscreen. Another mystery."

"None of this makes any sense." Red looked hard into his eyes. "And you have no clue who killed those Guild guys. No idea who left that card."

"Babe, there was no one there. I mean, I didn't scour the neighborhood or anything. I was kind of busy worrying about you and mom and Granny."

"You'd better not be lying to me."

He took her face gently in his hands. "I don't know what's going on, babe. But it sure seems like there's someone out there willing to kill for you. Be glad they're on your side."

CHAPTER 8

Back on the *Pit*, with Granny safely back home with her knitting, Red set the nav to auto and opened a bottle of Finebock whiskey. She took a deep swig straight from the bottle, then kicked off her boots and fell back onto the bed. She couldn't stop thinking about Woodman's story. The assassin, the card—it made her brain spin. She decided to help it along with another swallow of whiskey.

She was used to having enemies. Sloane wasn't the only one she'd crossed who'd come after her, and he sure as hell wouldn't be the last. There was that groop dealer on Ru'ur, the one who tried to take Red out with a holowhip during a bavit shavah party. And the guy from the poker game, what was his name, the one with eleven fingers. Tony? Tommy? If his ship hadn't blown a thruster, he'd have blown her to fazzer fodder. She took another drink at the thought of a pack of fazzers gnawing at her dismembered parts with their nasty teeth.

Enemies, she had. Enemies, she understood. Friends, though? She didn't have many of those, and she couldn't picture any of them taking out two people and leaving a note. Her friends were more of the "let's get drunk and throw rotten buntling eggs at vid towers" kind.

Of course, Woodman could be lying. Wouldn't be the first time she'd swallowed a load of his grumshit. She'd been doing it her whole life, really. Still, he wasn't a bad guy. Whatever else he was—and she had a whole list—he'd never let her down when it was important. Her gut said he was telling the truth.

Hmph. Her gut said lots of things. At the moment, it was saying it needed some food to soak up the booze.

Red stood up, wobbled a moment, then headed for the tiny, filthy kitchen. "Kitchen" was a generous term for a couple of shelves, dented refrigerator, and possibly even a cooking element buried under the piles of crusty dishes and empty food packages. She poked around, looking for something that hadn't yet accumulated any sentient fungus. She took a close look at a duoofish can, regretted it, and picked up an overturned cup. A giant weevil scuttered out. Red shrieked and threw the cup at it, but it disappeared behind the refrigerator.

That's it, time to get a cat.

Red gave up her search for food and instead programmed the nav for the nearest market.

~ ~ ~

Luminous eyes blinked from the depths of the cage. Red squatted down to get a better look. The cat had one green eye and one golden eye. Cheap Andarian junk, probably a factory screw-up or half-assed patch job. Still, she didn't need a cat with a nine-star warranty. She just needed the pointy bits, which this cat appeared to have.

"You sure this thing still works?" Red stuck her finger through the bars toward the cat and wiggled it. The cat blinked again but otherwise didn't react.

"No poke merchandise." A slug-faced C'longi sat behind the row of cages, seemingly absorbed in a tattered newspaper. His traditional floral headscarf featured an embroidered patch that read *Tom*. Uh huh.

"I'm not poking. I'm trying to see if it does anything but blink." She wiggled her finger more vigorously. "It looks broken."

'Tom' lowered his paper and fixed his goopy-looking eye on Red. "Not broken. No sell broken tings. You hear? Not. Broken." He went back to reading.

"If it's not broken, why doesn't it do anything?"

Down went the paper again. "You not have cat before?"

"No."

The eye rolled. "Cat only go for what programmed, yeah? No go for fingers cuz fingers no programmed."

"Ok, so what's this one programmed for?"

The alleged Tom scratched under his scarf with one tentacle. "All sort of tings. Weevil, gnar, cave mices, buntling—"

"Dugger mites?"

"Yeah, good, dugger mites."

Red stood up and brushed her hands on her pants. "How do I know it'll work? What if I get it back to my ship and it just sits there and blinks? I need a cat that's actually going to cat."

The C'longi chuckled, which made his flabby body ripple in ways that Red would remember every time she saw pudding. "No choice you have. Only cat at market."

Red sighed. "I'll give you fifty credits."

"Fifty? No. You need cat. I have cat. One twenty five."

Half an hour, two threats to leave empty-handed, and eighty credits later, Red lugged the surprisingly heavy cat back to the *Pit*. She regretted not letting Tom talk her into taking the cage for an extra twenty credits. Its semi-grav servos would have been nice right about now. Assuming they actually worked. Why did she park so damn far away? Jeez. Good thing she didn't buy anything else.

Finally on board, Red dumped the cat on the floor and sealed the hatch. "I'll be right back," she told it. "Lemme get us out of here."

She headed toward the cockpit. She flopped into the well-worn captain's chair, flipped a few switches, and pounded on the navbox. Damn thing was getting glitchy. A proper pounding did the trick, though, and the navbox kicked on with a small puff of yellowish smoke. She didn't really have anyplace to go, so she just punched in a few numbers and watched through the viewport as the market disappeared beneath the clouds.

As the ship left the atmosphere, Red noticed a banging sound. It wasn't one of the *Pit's* usual banging sounds—this one didn't sound expensive. She rummaged through the debris under her chair and eventually found an awkward size-D4 screwdriver and a slightly sticky sonic wrench. She sniffed the wrench, decided the sticky part was probably beer and not piss, and made a silent vow to tidy the place up. Right after she dealt with whatever was causing that ominously interesting banging.

It was the cat. It seemed to have decided it should be in the main storage compartment, and could not be bothered with the concept of doors. It kept walking straight at the wall a foot from the open door, again and again, each time accompanied by a metal-on-metal clang.

"Not broken, my fat ass," Red grumbled. She dropped her tools, grabbed the cat around the middle, and hauled it around to the open door. She released the cat and it immediately disappeared into the ceiling-high junk. Muffled squealing indicated the cat had found the dugger mites or, possibly, some neighboring pest whose residence had gone undetected.

Red pretended not to hear the juicy squelch from behind the collapsing crate of rotting homona fruit she hadn't been able to find a buyer for. She shut the door and headed back to the cockpit.

Chapter 9

Red slumped in her captain's chair, trimming her fingernails with her holoknife. Half her mind picked at the Guild mystery for the umpteen trillionth time, while the other half listened to the scanner.

A few job possibilities, but nothing in her quadrant. Her fuel was too low to venture very far, and she had spent most of her cash on the cat. Some other entrepreneur with a full tank would have to deliver that shipment of unmarked (and therefore slightly illegal) data cards to the Plestene militia.

One scratchy message caught her attention: someone in need of a discreet lift from Sector 3 to Sector 7A of the Gambulon nebula. That's practically right next door. Pay sucked, just a hundred credits, but it would be enough to get gassed up for some of those other jobs. Red hit the pingback, scribbling the coordinates on the back of a greasy FlinkBar wrapper. She plugged them into the nav and, after a vigorous pounding, the box spit back an estimated arrival at the pickup point just twenty minutes out. Enough time to take a shower or a nap, but not both. She sniffed herself and decided on the nap.

In her dream, Red chased the cat around the ship in slow motion. She finally dived forward and tackled it, rolling around on the floor. But it wasn't the cat anymore, it was Woodman. He rolled on top of her. She wiggled, trying to escape, but his body was crushing her to the floor, his scruffy face inches from her own, his hands—

She woke with a snort to the beep of the nav. Wiping a thin line of drool from her chin, she peered out the viewport. The pickup point was another ship, slightly smaller than her own, a lot nicer, and clearly disabled. None of the perimeter lights were on, and the gravity modulator seemed to be off as well—Red could see vague shapes floating around inside the darkened ship. No wonder the guy needed a lift. Damn kid probably swiped the ship to skim asteroids and ended up bouncing off one or seven, and now needed to hitch a ride back to mommy and daddy.

A silhouette appeared in the other ship's viewport. With the lights out, Red couldn't see a face, but the silhouette waved and gestured toward the exterior hatch. Red returned the wave and headed back to her own hatch. On the way, she stepped on the D4 screwdriver that was still in the middle of the floor. Pain shot through her ankle as it twisted.

A hundred credits. This job was already not worth it. She kicked the screwdriver across the room and limped grimly to the hatch.

After a few minutes of wrestling with the joystick, Red managed to connect the *Pit*'s walkway with the other ship's hull and make a decent seal. As the hatch opened, the light whoosh of air rushing to fill the walkway's vacuum ruffled the hair hanging around her neck. The opposite hatch opened and the hitchhiker stepped through.

The first thing Red noticed was that there was nothing much to notice. No odd odors, no slime trail, no visible leg restraints with a sawed-off chain dragging behind. The hitchhiker wore some kind of robe with sleeves that covered the hands and a hood that pulled down over the face. That wasn't so unusual, though. Maybe the kid had famous parents, politicians or something. The Gambulon nebula was a bedroom community for the galactic legislature, after all. Red gave a mental shrug. As long as he had the credits—

"You got the credits?"

"Yesss . . . onnne hunnndred creditsss . . . they are heeere." The voice was strange, scratchy, like a bad vidchat connection or good folk music. He patted a small pouch that hung around his waist.

"I'm gonna have to see them, sorry."

He unhooked the pouch. One of the sleeves had pulled up enough for her to see the hand was black with long hooked fingers. Okay . . . weird but not the weirdest thing she'd ever seen. Hell, she'd slept with weirder. Cheap beer was not her friend.

The hitchhiker tossed the pouch across the walkway and Red caught it in one hand. A quick peek inside revealed one hundred neatly folded credits.

"All right, come on over and we'll get going."

As the other ship's hatch slid shut, Red heard a rapid clicking noise, almost a buzz. It sounded like it came from under the hood, but it was probably just a defective latch or something else failing on the disabled ship. The hitchhiker walked past her into the *Pit*. Red dipped a curtsey and raised a finger at his back before sealing the hatch and retracting the walkway.

"Okay, are you gonna need to—" She turned around to see the hitchhiker had dropped the robe to the floor.

Shit.

The hitchhiker wasn't any politician's delinquent kid. This was some kind of giant insect thing with too many body parts that rattled together like castanets from hell. Freed from the robe, the insect stretched its four jointed legs and a pair of veined wings. It had a flat triangular head with curved mandibles that dripped a sickly green fluid that was probably not zuranfruit juice. It chittered at her.

Red's eyes flashed to the screwdriver she had kicked earlier. It was a long shot, but unless dirty socks could be considered a weapon (and hers just might qualify), that long shot was her only shot.

She lunged for the screwdriver but the creature was too fast. A hooked leg shot out and connected with her jaw. She felt the skin tear before the left side of her face went numb. She fell back against the storage compartment door, boots scrambling at the floor, trying like hell to get away from the six foot tall bug that didn't look like it wanted to invite her to a tea party in its blanket fort with a teddy bear named Mr. Fluffybritches.

There was nowhere to go. The creature grabbed her head between its clawlike hands and lifted her until her toes barely touched the floor. Behind her, she heard a thudding noise, like something was trying to get out of the storage compartment.

The cat!

She twisted and thrashed, trying to find the door release on the wall behind her. The pressure of the bug squeezing her skull was almost unbearable. Then her elbow hit something. She heard a scraping noise as the door opened. The bug suddenly dropped her to the floor again. Stars, moons, and a bird or two clogged her vision so she couldn't see what was making that screaming noise. She hoped it wasn't her.

For the first time in her life, she was glad to lose consciousness.

When her head cleared, Red saw two eyes, one green, one golden. The cat sat next to a pile of legs, wings, and body segments, none of which seemed to be connected to any of the others. Red didn't see the head at all.

The cat blinked. It got up and walked back toward the storage compartment. It missed the door by a few inches and bonked into the wall. Again. And again. Red gave it a push and it managed to find its way back to the dugger mites.

"Good kitty."

~ ~ ~

Red squinted into the cracked mirror in the bunkroom, admiring her handiwork: a half dozen irregular stitches along her jawline. Eh, she probably could have done a better job, but at least she'd have a cool scar. As an added bonus, the green thread from the medikit contrasted nicely with the raw red wound. She was nothing if not fashionable.

She tentatively opened and closed her mouth a few times. Yep, it hurt. The sewing had temporarily distracted her from her throbbing head, but now that demanded attention. She tossed the bloodstained towel from her shoulder onto the floor and grabbed the bottle of aspirin. Dosage: two every six hours. Red shook out four pills and swallowed them with a swig of the whiskey bottle that was still next to the bed.

Speaking of bed . . . Red lay down and gingerly rolled over onto her uninjured side. She yelped when she saw the cat sitting on the other pillow, staring at her.

"I'm going to call you Bonk. What do you think about that?"

Bonk's green eye flashed. A bizarre gargling noise erupted from its mechanical guts.

Holy shit, it was purring.

CHAPTER 10

Over the next few weeks, Red concentrated on work. She kept the *Fauas Tea Company* card tucked in her boot, and occasionally she'd stare at it for an hour or two. But mostly she trucked around from one system to the next, trying to lay low and pick low-risk jobs that were at least quasi-legal. Trouble was, no one with any legit business wanted to touch her with a thirty-foot jatball racket.

Bonk concentrated on work too. The *Pit* had enough weevils, gnars, and dugger mites to keep a dozen cats busy for a month, so Bonk had no trouble finding jobs—unless, of course, they were on the other side of an open door.

One day, Red put out a few pings on the low-res bands and decided she was overdue for a shower. She'd caught Bonk staring at her a few times, and realized that she did, in fact, smell a bit like a rodent.

Of course, that's when she finally got a pingback.

Red stumbled into the cockpit, still dripping, a towel twisted loosely around her body. She slapped a button and the screen fritzed to life.

"Well, hello there, darlin." Woodman's eyebrows shot up, practically disappearing under his sloppy shock of hair. "Seems like I've called at the perfect time."

Red tucked the towel tighter under her arms and scowled at the screen. "What do *you* want?"

"I was gonna offer you an easy job, but now . . ." He gave a low whistle. "Now, maybe I'm thinking I'll offer you something else instead."

Ugh. Seriously? The dude was a walking regret.

"I don't have time for this, Woodman."

"What could you possibly be busy doing? Especially dressed like that."

Red crossed her arms. "Look, do you have a job for me or not? I'm getting goosebumps here."

"I can see that."

"Woodman!"

He held up his hands and chuckled. "Okay, I get it, you're all business today. I need a ride."

Red glared at his image on the chipped vidscreen. "A ride? What's wrong with your ship?"

He shrugged. "I had a run-in with some Moldronon assholes over a chick. How the hell was I supposed to know she was their sister? Anyway, let's just say the *Chopper's* got to lie low until they decide to bugger some other slob."

"They'll do that quick enough. Where do you need to go?"

"I'm at my parents' place now. I'm looking to get to Orgulla 5."

Red's mouth flew open. "Dude, that's halfway across the galaxy!"

"That's why I'm calling you and not lacing up my hiking boots."

Red did some mental math. "That'll take a couple days at least. It's gonna cost you. And you should know, I don't work for beer and cigars anymore." Especially not for him.

"Darlin, don't I wish. Nah, I'll pay five hundred plus fuel. I'll even throw in some beer and cigars for the road. You still smoke those ridiculous Crolinian toothpicks?"

Red leaned over the console. Water from her hair dripped on the nav panel. "If I do this, it's strictly business. No fooling around. Got it?"

A smirk crept onto Woodman's face. "Sure thing, *Mild*red."

"Dammit, Woodman, grow up."

"Heh. Ping me when you land here. I'll be ready." The vidscreen went blank.

Red flopped into the captain's chair. Woodman! She'd never get rid of that gnar-biting asshole. Note to self: no more mixing work and personal life, and no more mixing beer and whiskey. Especially around Woodman. Lord knows she didn't need to bite *that* zuranfruit again.

She abruptly got up to get dressed, before her mind took that metaphor to its natural conclusion and she ended up needing another shower.

Chapter 11

Red landed the *Pit* on the private pad of the Woodmans' home on Sept Magossii. Home? Ha. More like estate. This was the sort of place that had gardens instead of a lawn, and where "servants' quarters" didn't mean a ratty couch in the basement where your friends crashed when they were drunk.

As she sealed the hatch, she noticed the *Chopper* tucked back under a stand of flowering aggrippinia trees. The high, spreading branches would easily hide the ship from the air. His story seemed to check out, at least so far. Maybe this was a legit job after all, not just an excuse to shack up for a few days. Not that she couldn't use a little shacking.

No. Not Woodman. Nope. No.

He was waiting at the door, a bulging rucksack slung over one shoulder. He was wearing a shirt at least two sizes too small, and wearing it well. "Babe! Good to see ya." He leaned in for a hug.

Red pulled back. "Just business."

"Yeah yeah, okay." He stuck out a hand. "Shake, at least?"

Red gave his hand a single shake and dropped it. "You ready?" She wiped her hand on her pants.

He frowned. "Hey, babe, what happened here?" He gently touched the fresh pink scar along her jawline.

Red turned her face away. "Nothing," she mumbled. "Picked up a nasty bug. You don't want to know. I'm fine."

"Is that Red?" a voice called from inside the house. Woodman's mother emerged from a doorway, wiping her hands on a checkered dishtowel. "Mark! You didn't tell me Red was coming over!"

Oh my god, Woodman might actually be blushing.

"Hi, Mrs. Woodman." Red couldn't avoid this hug, and she endured it with gritted teeth. Woodman caught her eye and winked.

"It's been months since I saw you last. You're looking so pretty! How's your granny these days? I haven't seen her since that, ah, episode with the Guild."

"She's great. All settled back in again."

"Mom, we have to go," Woodman interrupted. He kissed her on the cheek.

"Mark, don't be rude," Mrs. Woodman scolded. "Now, Red, you keep this one out of trouble, you hear?"

Red shrugged. "I'll try."

"Well, that's all anyone can do." She sighed. Woodman rolled his eyes so hard Red wondered if he had hurt himself. "You two have fun now!"

Woodman grabbed Red by the arm and steered her toward the gardens. "Bye, Mom. I'll stop back in a week or two."

"It's just a business thing!" Red called over her shoulder, but the door had already closed.

She yanked her arm out of Woodman's grasp and stalked across the gardens. He caught up to her and they walked in silence toward her ship. She opened the hatch and gestured for him to go in first. His muscles flexed in a fascinating way as he climbed the ladder. Red bit her lip.

Oh, man. This was such a bad idea.

It wasn't Woodman's first time aboard the *Pit* so Red didn't bother with a tour. She went straight to the cockpit while he dropped his bag in the storage compartment. She had just started up the engines when she heard a crash, followed by a flurry of obscenities. A minute later, Woodman limped dramatically into the cockpit. He brushed a few beer cans and cigar butts off the copilot's chair and dropped into it.

"You got a cat," he groaned, clutching his ankle.

A rhythmic banging started somewhere in the rear of the ship.

"That's Bonk. You closed the storage compartment door?"

"Uh. Yes?"

"I'll open it once we get going. You'll get used to the banging." Red flipped some switches and the ship lifted, tilted, and headed upward on its exit trajectory.

As the landscape disappeared beneath the atmosphere, Red turned on the navbox to calculate their trip to Woodman's destination point. The unit flashed a few times, emitted a faint electrical odor, and went blank. She pounded it with her fist. There was an odd click and the odor got stronger, but the display sputtered to life.

"You sure that thing is working? It seems . . . fried."

Red responded with a single finger.

Woodman grinned his least obnoxious grin. He pulled a slip of paper out of his pants pocket and slapped it on top of the navbox. "The coordinates. You need to fuel up first?"

Red started entering the ridiculously long string of numbers into the nav. "Nah, I'm almost full. You can get the fill-ups."

Woodman got up and limped out of the cockpit. Red's eyes flicked over to watch him leave. The nav let out a harsh beep. Dammit, she screwed up, had to start over. Thanks, Mr. Glutes.

Her second attempt went through. The nav returned a travel time of forty-nine hours. She felt the sub-light drive kick in and leaned back in her chair. Two days stuck on the *Pit* with Woodman. What could possibly go wrong?

He walked back into the cockpit with a six of beer in one hand and a bottle of Finebock whiskey in the other.

Damn you, Woodman.

CHAPTER 12

Red woke up with a screaming headache. She groaned and pulled the scratchy blanket over her head. That's when she heard Woodman snoring away next to her. A quick glance at herself confirmed her suspicions.

Ugh, not again.

She slipped out of the bed and pulled on some relatively clean clothes from the pile on the floor. She staggered into the kitchen, looking for anything resembling coffee. Bonk blinked its mismatched eyes at her from under a broken shelving unit.

"Oh shut up," she muttered, opening a coffee packet and dumping it into a mug that didn't have any visible mold. She filled it with hot water from the dispenser on the wall and inhaled the fragrant steam.

Red wandered into the cockpit and sank into the captain's chair. She was a few sips into the coffee before she realized something was wrong. Like, really wrong. They were moving, but the navbox was dark. Red pounded it, but for the first time, it failed to respond. She kicked it and was painfully reminded that she was barefoot.

She frantically checked the scopes. Nothing looked familiar. That's the trouble with space: it all looks the same.

"Woodman!"

Red slammed open the override box and pulled the paddle. The sub-light drive protested but slowed to a stop. Well, that was something, anyway.

"*WOODMAN!*"

He shuffled into the cockpit, wearing only a slouchy pair of sweatpants and yawning. "What's up, babe? Where are we?"

"You tell me!" Red waved her hand at the scopes. Coffee sloshed out of her mug.

Woodman took the mug from her hand and took a sip. He grimaced and spit it back. "Instant? Really?"

"Shut up and help me."

He put the mug down on the console and tapped a few buttons. The scopes flashed, magnified, switched angles, rotated. After a few minutes, he sat.

"Huh," he said.

"Huh? What, huh? Where are we?"

Woodman shrugged. "I dunno."

Red stared at him. "You don't know."

"Nope. No clue. Can you get any info from the nav?"

"I can't even get it to fire up."

"Lemme try." Woodman wiggled the on-switch for a while, thumped the unit a half-dozen times, and mumbled under his breath. He pried the front panel off the unit to reveal a complex system of circuits and wires.

Something was nesting at the bottom of the unit, next to the main processor. Red squatted down and reached out to touch the furry lump.

A clattering streak pushed her aside. It took Bonk mere seconds to dispatch the rodent with a minimum of blood and noise. The cat blinked, turned around, and walked toward the cockpit door. It missed and hit the wall. Red gave it a nudge and it exited silently.

Woodman picked up the tiny corpse by its tail. "Well, I think we found the problem." He tossed it over his shoulder.

Red met his eyes. "What are we going to do? We're lost."

He scratched his stubbled chin. "Hm. We can put out a message on the scanner. We'll run a systematic scan on all the scopes, look for blips."

"Yeah." Red chewed on a hangnail.

"Come on, babe, it's an adventure! Like the time we ran out of fuel over Ru'ur. Remember? Those hippies picked us up." He took her hand and squeezed. "It's space. We're not the only ones out here, you know."

Red took a deep breath, then grabbed the half-empty mug. "I'm getting more coffee. Want any?"

"Hell no. You got anything better? Sewer sludge, maybe?"

"Ha ha. Start on the scopes. I'll be right back."

~ ~ ~

Several hours and a dozen cups of alleged coffee later, they were no closer to figuring out their location. Once, Red thought the long range scan showed a planetary system where she had pulled a job a few years earlier, but it turned out to be a random magnetic field creating ghosts on the sensor. Their pings on the low-res scanner had also been less than helpful. In fact, the whole scanner was unusually quiet, both high-

and low-res. It seemed that they had managed to find the one unpopulated sector in the entire galaxy.

Red was stuck in the middle of nowhere with a sarcastic sex fiend, a defective cat, and a dead rodent. Could be worse, but not by much.

Woodman slumped in the copilot's chair, staring blankly out the viewport. Red smoked one of the Crolinian cigars he'd brought, idly flipping between the high-res and low-res bands on the scanner. Flip, empty static. Flip, louder empty static.

"You get any anonymous notes lately?" Woodman asked, yawning.

"Nope. You?"

"Nope."

Flip. Flip.

"Figure out who it was?"

"Nope."

"Weird."

"Yep."

Flip. Flip. Flip.

"You sure there was nothing there but that card?"

"Nope."

"Nope, there was nothing there? Or nope, you're not sure?"

"Babe. There was nothing else there. Just the card. I've told you a hundred times already."

"All right, all right, never mind. I just wish there was some way to track it."

Flip. Flip. Flip.

"Oh my god." Red sat straight up, her mouth hanging open.

"What? You got something on the scanner?"

"No no, but I think—hey, you have any Orgullan skin mags with you?"

"I'm right here, darlin."

"Shut up, this is important. Do you have any?"

Woodman shrugged. "I might, lemme go look in my bag."

"Thanks. I'll stay here and keep flipping."

It only took Woodman five minutes to come back with a handful of magazines. "Here you go."

Red eagerly grabbed the magazines and started paging through them.

"Hey, be careful with those, okay?" Woodman sat back in the copilot's chair and put his feet up on the navbox. "Those have sentimental value."

"Jeez, don't worry, I'm not going to rip Ms. February."

"What are you looking for, anyway?"

Red slapped an issue on the dashboard. "This!" She pointed to an ad on the back cover.

VALU-KAT® MEANS VALUE!

Tired of the SAME OLD cat?

Wish YOUR cat could do MORE?

Then STOP WISHING and START TRACKING!!!

Only Valu-Kat® offers SensoTrak* technology, the only fully programmable tracking system on the market that can operate at long distance—up to three light years away!** Simply rub a sample on the SensoTrak* pad*** and your cat is ready to track!

Turn your cat into a treasure-hunting machine!
Amaze your family!
Impress your neighbors!
You won't be disappointed!

Some assembly required.
*Patent pending.
**Actual distance may vary.
***Sold separately.

"So?"

"Don't you see?" Red asked. "With this, Bonk could track the card to its source."

Woodman raised an eyebrow. "Babe, you know this is probably a scam, right?"

"It's worth a shot, don't you think? I'm going to order it."

Woodman picked up the magazine and examined the ad. "It's your money, I guess. Now, can we get back to business here? Or did you forget we're lost?"

"Fine. Thanks for all your support."

Flip. Flip. Ping! Flip.

Red dropped her cigar in a puddle of cold coffee and sat up. She flipped back to the high-res band. There was another ping.

"It's about damn time!" Woodman stretched. "Is there a message?"

Red tapped a few keys and some text appeared on the overhead display.

<<<NOT A GOOD PLACE TO BE LOST. MAYBE I CAN HELP. SENDING COORDINATES.

Then a string of numbers.

Red looked at Woodman. "What do you think?"

"Do we have a choice?"

Good point. Red typed:

>>>NAV OUT. BEACON?

<<<OF COURSE.

Red looked at the scopes. Aha! The beacon appeared on the mid-range scan like a bright orange chemflare.

>>>GOTCHA. HEADING YOUR WAY.

<<<ROGER.

She switched off the scanner and grabbed the manual controls. She pointed the *Pit* at the beacon. "We'll need to go slow. Don't know what's out there." Woodman nodded and set the sub-light drive to its lowest setting. The ship started crawling toward the beacon's source.

They traveled in silence for a long moment.

"Why d'you think they didn't show up on the scope until they lit the beacon?" Red shifted in her seat.

Woodman scratched his armpit. "Maybe your scopes are infested with weevils."

"I'm serious!"

"So am I. This ship ain't exactly plum, babe."

Red shuffled her feet in the debris under the console. Yeah, it was dirty, it was old, it broke down all the damn time. But she loved it anyway.

She thought back to when she picked up the *Pit*. She was called the *Cherry*, but even back then she wasn't anywhere near living up to that name. Red had run some product past a planetary blockade for the ship's Andarian owner, a gnar-muncher named Rolar. The job was trickier than Red had anticipated, and she lost valuable time and cargo getting it done. When she met up with Rolar, she naturally upcharged him. He objected. Worse, he tried to negotiate for some touchy-touchy. Red left him with his offending hand pinned to the wall with a holoknife and his chances of fathering children significantly reduced. She flew off in the *Cherry* as payment on the debt. It promptly blew a grav plate in spectacular fashion, but accepted Red's patchy repair job, which pretty much set the tone for their whole relationship.

"Red? Check it out. We're here."

Woodman pointed out the viewport at the finest piece of spacecraft Red had ever seen. The entire thing was polished so thoroughly that she could see the *Pit* reflected in its hull. Perimeter lights flashed importantly. The ship's viewports (there were several) seemed to shimmer—there must be raycron shielding on the panels. A gilded decal under the main hatch read *Gumdrop.*

Woodman let out a low whistle. "Sweet ride," he said. "I wonder what it looks like on the inside." He stood up.

Red hesitated.

"Well? Are we going?"

"Why didn't it show up on the scope? I mean, that's weird, right?"

Woodman pulled her up from the chair. "Babe, your ship is a broke down, bug infested, filthy piece of junk. Let's go meet our obviously rich friend so we can patch it up and get our asses out of here."

Red punched him in the gut. He made a satisfying oof.

"Put on a shirt already." She pushed past him out of the cockpit.

In the storage compartment, she pulled on her boots and slipped the holoknife into one, discreet-like. Didn't want to offend their new buddy, but she'd be damned if she was walking onto a strange ship unarmed again. Bonk blinked approvingly.

"Be a good kitty. Back soon."

Woodman found a shirt, thank god. This one even seemed to fit properly. He also wore a broken-in grumskin jacket with a half dozen visible pockets and, Red knew, a half dozen more concealed ones. He'd changed into regular pants too, and an ancient pair of once-blue sneakers.

Red gestured to his jacket. "You packing?"

"Darlin, you know I am."

"Seriously. We do this right, we do it careful, we do it smart. Right?"

Woodman nodded and they both went to the hatch. A peek out the tiny viewport revealed that their new buddy had extended a walkway while they were getting ready. It was sealed to the *Pit*'s hull, and the hatch opposite was already open. An elderly woman with long grey hair stood in the opening.

Red stepped aside to let Woodman see. He looked at out the viewport, then at Red. She shrugged and opened the hatch.

Chapter 13

The woman spread her hands. "Welcome, welcome! My name is Haxa. Just the two of you?"

"Yeah, I'm Red, this is Woodman." She nodded in is direction. "Thanks for the pingback."

"Of course! Always glad to meet new people, hm. Come, let's have a cup of tea and you can tell me about your troubles."

Red and Woodman followed Haxa aboard the *Gumdrop*.

"Oh! I almost forgot to seal the hatch." Haxa pressed a button and it slid shut with a clang. "Best to be safe."

The old woman led them through a series of compartments to a small but plush room. Red goggled at the décor. A thick Luforian rug covered the floor. The walls held framed holograms of movie stars, politicians, athletes. Most seemed to be signed. Delicate white carvings of human figures covered every flat surface. Red was examining one when Woodman stuck an elbow into her side. He pointed at a cage filled with redheaded twitterlings. Huh. She thought those had gone extinct when those Zaldroni'i assholes blew up that planet a few years back.

Haxa gestured for them to sit on some kind of leather sofa (grumskin? no, wrong texture) while she busied herself with a tea set on a side table. "So, hm. You say your nav went out?"

Red cleared her throat. "Yeah, we were, ah, busy with something else and when I looked, it was dead."

"Oh, that's such a shame. Milk?"

"No, thank you," Red said. Woodman declined with a shake of his head.

"Then here you go." Haxa handed them each a tiny cup of light green tea. "What series of navbox do you have? X600?"

Red took a sip of tea. "No, it's a Toc, a 137."

Haxa's bony hands fluttered about her mouth. "My! That *is* an antique, hm. But you know, I think I may have a portable contraption that might help. Would you like to see it?"

"Sure! I mean, yes, it would really help us out." Red shot Woodman a look of relief. He raised his teacup to her and grinned. The cups seemed to be made of the same material as the carvings.

"Wonderful! I'll go see if I can't find it for you. No no, don't get up!" She patted Red's arm as she started to stand. "You sit right there and finish your tea, hm. I'll be back in two shakes of a shiq's tail."

She left Red and Woodman clutching their teacups on the sofa. The door slid shut behind her.

"Can you believe this place?" Woodman stood up and looked at the holograms. "Wow, she's got a signed Archie Noligg! I saw him play in the championship last year. He shoulda gotten MVP. Robbed, I tell ya."

Red pointed to the nearest carving, which depicted a child's face. "Woodman, I've seen a lot of fancy shit in my day, but I've never seen anything like that. What's it even made of? And this sofa? Whatever it is, it sure ain't grumskin."

"Hey, Red, come over here and—"

Red dropped her cup. Her body was stiff, unmoving, but her eyes were wide and terrified. Her rigid arm still pointed at the child sculpture. Woodman tried to reach her but found his own limbs unresponsive. He fell to the floor, landing hard on his arm.

The doorway slid open. From the corner of her eye, Red saw Haxa enter. Her eyes were gleaming in a face contorted by a hateful sneer. She approached Woodman, nodded, then turned to Red.

"Oh, you silly little girl! You should have taken the milk! It would all be over by now." She searched Red's clothing. Red could smell the old woman's body, a rank, bitter odor. As she leaned over, Red caught a glimpse of a tattoo on her neck. It looked like a crescent moon with an eye in the middle.

Red recognized the symbol immediately. A baega! The woman was a baega! Red's panic became a hot, living thing inside her.

Haxa found the holoknife and dropped it to the floor. "Naughty, naughty!" she cackled, wagging a finger. "Now let's see what your friend is hiding!"

Red couldn't see what the baega was doing, but she heard rustling and a few thumps. "Ah ah ah, so many naughty things you have, young man! What *were* you planning? Hm."

When Red saw her again, she had gathered up Woodman's assortment of weapons and her own holoknife. She trundled them out of the room.

Red strained against the paralysis, but it was no good. She couldn't even blink, let alone escape. And Woodman was clearly no better off.

Haxa returned. "You've caught me at an awkward moment, I'm afraid. I've just eaten, hm, and won't be hungry again for days. Since you wouldn't drink your milk, you'd just spoil if I carved you now. Hm. There's nothing for it. I'll just have to keep you in here until I'm ready for you."

She poked Red's extended arm. "The tea will start losing effect soon, but you needn't bother trying to escape. No one ever does, hm. I'll see you in a few days!" And she was gone, the door firmly shut behind her.

Red's mind raced. She tried to remember what she'd heard about the baega. Think think think.

Baega were the stuff of nightmares. When she was a little kid, her mom would threaten to sell her to a baega if she didn't behave. She said the baega loved naughty children because they made the best-tasting soup. That was just a story, though. Reality was much, much worse. Baega were cannibals, yes, but they preferred roasting their victims. Alive. With gravy.

ARGH! Those sculptures! They were—

Her arm suddenly felt heavy. The drugged tea must be wearing off. She blinked. It felt heavenly. A few minutes later, she managed to stand up on shaky legs. She went straight to Woodman, who was still on the floor, groaning and clutching his arm. The baega must have taken off his jacket when she searched him, because it was crumpled next to him.

"I think it's broken," he spat.

Red braced herself, then peeled back his fingers. Sure enough, his arm had an odd zigzag a few inches above the wrist. It was swelling up but there wasn't anything poking out that shouldn't be. She tore the bottom half of her shirt into two strips and twisted them together into a crude sling.

"Okay, now, just hang on. This'll hurt." Red eased his arm into the sling and secured it behind his back. He ground his teeth but didn't make a sound. She helped him sit up and pull his jacket over his good arm.

"Thanks, Red." He glanced at her exposed midriff. "Nice abs."

"Woodman, we gotta get the hell out of here. That's a *baega*!"

"I figured as much. Good thing we don't take our tea with milk or we'd be having this conversation dead."

Red started circling the room. "No shit. These sculptures? I'm pretty sure they're bone. Human bone. And the teacups. And that sofa, that's-" She shuddered. "There has to be some way out. There's just got to be. Check those panels for hollow places."

Woodman struggled to his feet. He started tapping the panels with his knuckles. Red was tapping and lifting and pushing everything she could find.

It didn't take long to discover nothing useful. Worse, there was a lens sunk into the wall above the door. Red could feel the baega watching her.

She sat on the floor and played with her bootlaces. She couldn't bear to look at the sofa again, let alone touch it. Woodman paced. He gave the camera a different obscene gesture with every pass. Whenever he passed the cage of twitterlings, they fluttered and chirped loudly.

Red watched him for a while, a glimmer of an idea taking shape. She rolled it around in her head, poked at it. Okay, yeah, it wasn't Vladmir's plot to unseat the Erh, but it wasn't terrible. She stood up and caught Woodman near the twitterling cage.

"Baby," she purred. "You've got to relax." She twined her arms around his neck, being careful not to press on his wounded arm.

Woodman stared at her. "Red? You okay?"

"This might be our last few days together, baby. We shouldn't waste it." She put her lips close to his ear. "Play along," she breathed. "The camera."

Woodman winked. He put his good arm around her and buried his face in her neck. Red checked to make sure he was between her and the camera, then began frantically whispering her plan into his ear. He mumbled responses, lips brushing her skin. The twitterlings' frantic chirping covered their hushed voices.

When they were done, Woodman squeezed Red in the place she liked best to be squeezed. She bit his earlobe in return. They broke apart, flushed, tense. They winked at each other theatrically.

Woodman opened the twitterling cage and ran his finger along the bottom. It came back coated with thick, gooey droppings. One of the birds pecked his hand hard enough to draw blood.

Woodman walked to the door and looked directly at the camera. He smeared the droppings on the lens, effectively obscuring whatever view the baega had of the room. He wiped his hand on his pants and gave Red a thumbs up.

Red picked up one of the carvings and dropped it. Woodman stomped his feet on the rug a bit. After a minute, Red dropped another carving. This one cracked in two.

"Shhhh, she'll hear you!" Woodman whispered loudly. Red grinned and picked up one of the broken shards. She scraped it along one of the wall panels. A few more minutes of silence, a few more thumps. Good god, but this was actually fun. Probably hopeless, but fun. Red felt like a kid again, distracting Granny in the front yard so her friends could sneak cookies out of the kitchen.

"Hurry up!" she hissed, gave the panel a final thump, then nodded at the door. Woodman moved silently across the room and pressed himself against the wall next to the door. Red picked up a heavy carving, refused to think that it was probably from a femur, and crept to the other side of the door.

Now, to wait.

CHAPTER 14

They didn't have to wait long.

The door slid open. From their position, they couldn't see the baega in the corridor, but they heard her gasp at the seemingly empty room. As soon as Haxa's head appeared through the doorway, Red swung the carving. She missed her target, hitting the baega on the shoulder instead of the skull. The baega screeched and clawed at Red's throat.

Woodman's fist didn't miss its target, connecting with the baega's chin, but his broken arm robbed him of some strength. Haxa pushed Red away and turned her fury on Woodman. She was strong, stronger than an old woman had any right to be, and he was injured. Red watched helplessly as she grappled with him, pushed him to his knees. The twitterlings were chirping madly.

The twitterlings!

"Woodman! Look out!" Red grabbed the cage, tore open the door, shook it at Haxa. The terrified birds flew out, straight into the baega's horrible face. Her hands flew up to protect her eyes, but it was too late—they were nothing but bloody pulp. Woodman, his good arm thrown over his own face, shoved her legs with his shoulder. She went down, scrambling and screaming, and crawled away down the corridor under a cloud of twitterlings.

Red dropped the cage and helped Woodman up. Blood was seeping through the sling, and his face was pale, but he managed a weak smile. "Good thinking, babe. Now let's get that bitch."

It wasn't hard to follow the baega's trail of blood through the ship. They found her cowering under the kitchen sink. Red found a carving knife, but Woodman turned away.

"Woodman, we can't leave her like this. Either she'll die slowly, or she'll live to kill again." She held the knife out to him.

In the end, Red did it herself.

~ ~ ~

Red clenched a cigar between her teeth as she finished patching the *Gumdrop*'s navbox into the *Pit*'s system. Woodman watched from the copilot's chair, groaning dramatically every few minutes. Red had set his arm and dug out a proper sling from the medikit, but the big baby was still playing it up.

They had stripped the ship of all its wealth, portable tech, and sundries, including Red's holoknife and Woodman's pocket arsenal. The *Pit*'s storage compartment couldn't hold it all, and piles were stacked around the main room. They agreed, businesslike, to split the profits fifty-fifty. They debated taking the ship itself—it was worth as much as everything else combined—but it felt haunted. Red took grim satisfaction in activating the remote charge that detonated it. She regretted leaving the twitterlings behind, but after two hours and three nasty bites she gave up trying to get them back into their cage. They left behind the sofa and all the carvings.

Red banged the wrench on the floor. "Okay, light 'er up."

Woodman flipped the on switch and the new nav whirred happily. Red didn't realize she'd been holding her breath until it came out in a whoosh.

"Let's get the hell out of here," she said, shuffling through the papers spread around on the console. "You got those coordinates for your dropoff point?"

Woodman sat up with a wince. "Eh, it's not important. Just drop me off at home."

"What about your job?"

Woodman's face spread into a cheesy grin. "It wasn't a job, babe. I was supposed to meet up with this chick." He nodded at his broken arm. "I'm not exactly fit for duty now, am I?"

Red threw her cigar in his face and stormed out of the cockpit.

Woodman chuckled and picked the cigar out of his lap. He stuck it in his mouth as he tapped the coordinates for Sept Magossii into the nav. The thrusters engaged and he sat back, taking a deep draw on the cigar.

"Damn, darlin," he coughed. "How the hell do you smoke these things, anyway?"

Chapter 15

Red's half of the *Gumdrop*'s take was potentially millions of credits. She'd never had such a huge payout before.

Unfortunately, she still didn't.

Before she could even find a buyer for a single Luxorian rug, she got into a bit of a pushy-pushy with some old business associates. Bastards blew out the controls for the *Pit*'s main hatch and stole everything. Not only was she out the cash for the goods, she'd had to replace the entire hatch control panel. That little endeavor ate up a big chunk of her financial resources and split open her knuckles on at least three separate occasions.

While she'd been tits-deep in that project, Bonk discovered a cave mouse making itself at home under her bed. By the time Red noticed, the glitchy cat had dug a hole right through the mattress. Red now slept on the floor among the cigar butts and petrified cave mouse droppings.

Then there was that bitch of a job on Ru'ur. It should have been a simple product delivery, but the client bailed at the last minute, leaving Red holding 2,500 units of prescription hallucinogens and no prescription. Last time she'd do business with one of those flaky Blixic hippies. Red had to scramble to find another buyer before the meds could be traced to her, and took a major hit on the payout.

It had been a long couple of months.

Nothing a drunken binge couldn't fix. Well, that and a good solid shag from a good solid man. Or any man, really. It had been ages and her standards were getting lower by the day. She'd even considered giving Woodman a ping. It was *that* desperate.

First things first: drunken binge. Maybe that would lead to the other.

Red found herself at Chuck's Tap, a scuzzy dive smack in the middle of the Debrayan luxite mines. It was one of her favorite places to drink, primarily because of Chuck himself.

She plopped down on a stool in front of him. He barely glanced at her, and continued wiping glasses with a filthy towel.

She leaned forward. "Hey, Chuck, you got a customer here."

Chuck paused in his wiping and looked around the bar. Apart from Red, it was completely empty. "I don't see any customers," he shrugged. "Just a deadbeat who hasn't paid her tab since I was young and pretty."

"Chuck, you were never young and pretty."

"My point exactly."

"Dude, I've got the credits this time. Just pulled a job out on Ru'ur." Red reached into her hip pocket and pulled out a slim stack of credits. She waved them in his face. "See? Cash money." She slapped them onto the bar. "Now pour me a Finebock. Double."

Chuck eyed the credits. He sniffed. "Don't look like enough to cover your tab, let alone buy whiskey. You'd best head over to the Crud & Bucket." He paused, his eyes momentarily distant. "Wait, never mind, you've got a tab there too."

"Aw, c'mon, Chuck. You owe me."

Chuck raised half of his single shrubby eyebrow. "I do?"

He did? Red frantically tried to come up with something.

She and Chuck went way back. With his oily hair, sallow skin, and sagging jowls, he didn't look like much. But Chuck was some kind of cross-dimensional being who owned and worked at least fifty bars, in dozens of systems, simultaneously. Red had discovered this while barhopping years before. Drunk as she was, she couldn't help but notice the same guy pouring her beer at half a dozen bars on the same night. It was not something Chuck wanted advertised, for what he vaguely referred to as "tax reasons." Red, who had her own secrets, kept his.

They had eventually struck up an informal working arrangement: she would bring him screaming deals on booze, especially rare or illegal vintages, and in return he let her run tabs at his establishments. Since then, Red only drank at Chuck's places. Trouble was, Red liked to drink, and Chuck did eventually expect to get paid, which explained her current predicament.

Hm. Paid. "Did you ever pay me for that case of Tolmarine wine?"

Chuck nodded.

"Are you sure? I don't remember getting paid."

"I paid."

"I'm pretty sure you didn't."

"I did."

Red scratched the scar on her jaw. "Well, okay, what about the time that sniffer showed up at your place on Ulatu? Who distracted it while you hid the blood rum?" Red shook a stern finger at him. "That stuff's illegal, you know."

Chuck glared. He mumbled under his breath, something about ungrateful little fazzers. Still, he put down the towel and poured some cheap Gallard whiskey from a half-empty bottle into a glass. It sloshed dramatically when he shoved it across the bar at Red.

"I'll take that," he growled as Red picked up the credits to put them away. He snatched them from her hand and stuffed them into his own pocket. Red smiled and raised her whiskey to him. He grunted and went back to wiping glasses.

A couple of people wandered in—friends of Chuck's, from the way he punched them on the arms before filling a pitcher. Red sipped her drink and looked around the bar. As always, it was dark, dirty, and smelled like feet.

Red thought it was perfect.

There was something new this time, though. In the corner near the dart board, a shiny chrome-plated box flashed pink and blue lights. It wouldn't have looked more out of place in an Fardic monastery than it did here.

"Hey, Chuck," she shouted, jerking a thumb at the chrome monstrosity. "What the hell is that thing?"

Chuck glanced over. "TuneBot."

"*TuneBot*? You gotta be shitting me."

Chuck shrugged and went back to telling dirty jokes with his buddies.

"TuneBot," Red muttered, throwing back the last of her whiskey. She slid the empty glass down the bar toward Chuck. He frowned but refilled it anyway, sliding it back without interrupting his conversation.

After the second shot, Red felt just fine. Her mind wandered to Woodman as it usually did at this point in her intoxication. Last she'd heard, he was shacked up with that chick on Orgulla 5. Red hated Orgullan women and their ridiculous blue hair that men went stupid over. She examined a strand of her own limp brown mess.

Split ends. Of course.

The bar slowly filled up with the usual crowd, mostly miners fresh from their shift lugging luxite ore. Chuck was busy pouring beer, so Red casually tucked the whiskey bottle under her arm and took it to a table in the back corner. It was her favorite seat in the bar, nearly hidden in the gloom, but with a view of the whole place. As the whiskey did its work, her standards plummeted.

She was even starting to give Chuck the up-and-down when a large, rowdy group of people burst into the bar. Their stylish clothes and glittering jewelry were out of place among the Chuck's drab and dusty regulars. The newcomers all talked at once, waving their hands and laughing as they ordered at the bar. While Chuck mixed fancy-looking concoctions with brightly-colored liquors, the group pushed together several tables and dragged over the few unused chairs they could find.

One of the men walked over to Red's table. He was all generic tattoos and gelled hair and strong cologne, but the whiskey didn't seem to mind. In fact, the whiskey thought he was the hottest thing since Indar Skjov's nude scene in *Dreams of Godaro*.

"Drink with me," she said, pushing the half-empty bottle toward him and kicking one of the chairs out from under the table.

He just grinned and took the chair back to his group. Red picked up the bottle and took a swig. Her eyes followed him up to the bar, where he retrieved an armload of drinks. One of the women put some credits in the TuneBot.

The machine's shrill voice cut through the bar noise. "You've chosen TuneBot! Your selection will play momentarily! While you wait, why not order another round of crisp, refreshing Old Wo'hall'a? It's the official

beer of the Crolinian Psycats! Ok, everybody! It's time to get FUNKY!"
Then the latest pop hit from Pink Chenille blared from the sound
system.

Red took another swig of whiskey to distract herself from the
bouncy synthoboards and skull-splittingly inane lyrics ("Baby baby,
gimme your, gimme your, baby baby, gimme your, gimme your, baby
baby, gimme your, gimme your love monkey, baby, yeah"). Red found
herself missing TuneBot's advertising pitch.

A few songs and a lot of whiskey later, Hair Gel detached himself
from the group and pulled his chair over to sit next to Red. She offered
him the bottle, and he took a drink. His face scrunched up into a
grimace and he coughed.

Red laughed. "Not a whiskey drinker, are you?"

Hair Gel looked sheepish. "I'm more of a beer guy, I guess."

"So, beer guy, do you have a name?"

"Oh! Hunter. Hunter Exley."

"Nice to meet you, Hunter Exley. I'm Red." She dropped a hand to
his thigh and leaned in to whisper. "I'm also a bit drunk."

Hunter put an arm around her shoulders and put his lips to her ear.
"I'm not."

Red felt a thrill head south from her belly. This guy had the worst
cologne in seven systems, but his teeth sure as hell knew what to do
with an earlobe. She moved her hand up his leg and squeezed. "You
wanna get out of here? Find someplace private?"

He squirmed. "Not yet." He gestured vaguely at the rowdy group.
"I'll get us some beer while we wait."

Hunter stood up, adjusted himself, and did just that.

The rest of the night was lost in a haze of whiskey, beer, and bad pop music.

CHAPTER 16

A flock of twitterlings pecked at the back of Red's eyeballs with their stabby little beaks while giant hands tried to crush her skull. Her mouth tasted like the floor of an Orgullan brothel on two-for-one duoofish burrito night. She cracked an eye and instantly regretted it when the light sent a bolt of pain through her head, nearly strong enough to split it in two.

She rolled up in a ball and tried to piece things together. She pulled up flashes from the night before. She remembered ear biting and leg squeezing. Lots of pop music. Red hoped that the image of herself sitting on Hunter's lap, grinding away and singing along with Shugga Mia's "Booty Glow," was a hallucination brought on by too much booze. She definitely remembered beer. It must have been some weird label because it tasted strange. After that, nothing.

The memory loss bothered Red. She'd been sloppy drunk a few times—okay, many times—but she'd always remembered every gory detail. Well, it was probably for the best, if that "Booty Glow" thing actually happened.

Coffee. She needed coffee. And aspirin. And maybe a brain transplant. Red braced herself and opened her eyes again.

She was on the floor of a small room, dingy and grey, windowless, a single door at one end. There was no furniture, only a single bare bulb in the ceiling and a row of rusty chains down the middle of the room. Each chain had one end bolted to the floor, while the other end had wicked-looking cuffs. This did not look good.

At least she wasn't alone.

Hunter was slumped against one wall, his eyes closed. His gelled hair stood up in random spikes. Red eased herself up on her knees.

"Dude," she croaked, shaking his arm. It was cold. His head rolled sideways, blood spilling out of his mouth.

Red scrambled backward until she hit the far wall. Her stomach turned and she vomited. When everything evacuated but her stomach itself, she stood on shaky legs and crept toward Hunter's body. He looked like he could be sleeping. Except for the blood, of course, the blood that made a slowly spreading stain on his white t-shirt.

The smell of his cologne mixed with the smell of her vomit.

The room suddenly seemed to constrict around her. Red spun around, her head throbbing and her stomach threatening to find something else to bring up. She couldn't breathe. She tripped on the chains and landed hard on one knee, but managed to slap the hatch button and stumble out into brilliant daylight.

Red found herself in the parking lot of an abandoned warehouse. She sat down on the weedy pavement and put her head between her knees. She shut off her thoughts and concentrated on breathing.

After several minutes, her head cleared enough that she could take inventory of her situation. Her head was still complaining loudly but otherwise she seemed okay: no broken bones, no missing parts, no unusual bruises. She fearfully prodded her crotch. Oh thank the Fourteen, nothing seemed violated. Her clothing was dirty and torn, but it was always dirty and torn. She explored her pockets and found them empty. She still couldn't remember the night before, but she'd worry about that later. The immediate problem was figuring out where she was.

She stood, weak but steady, and looked around her. She was alone. Nothing was familiar. She could be on Zargon for all she knew. Apart from the empty-looking warehouse with the shattered windows, there was nothing much to see but the ship she had stumbled out of a few minutes before. It was a standard surface-restricted transport, a sad-looking pile of bolts about two days from the scrap heap. It had none of the usual identification codes or markings. Not good, but not surprising.

Red walked around the front of the ship to have a look at the cockpit. It had a separate hatch from the cargo area, which was common enough for these kinds of transports. Red squinted through the glare at the rusty hull panels, kicked one of the dented support legs, peered through the front viewport the empty cockpit.

Then it hit her. The viewport was clean. This was no abandoned transport—this ship was used recently. Someone dressed up to look abandoned, but that someone still needed to see where they were going.

Someone did not want this transport to attract any attention.

Red's thoughts returned to Hunter's body slumped on the floor of the cargo hold, and she shuddered. Hunter was a big problem. She had no idea how long she'd been unconscious. The sniffers could be there any minute and her story sucked. A body and no witnesses? Unmarked ship? Amnesia? Even Granny would have trouble believing that pile of grumshit, let alone the cops. Yeah right, babe, you can't remember, he was like that when you woke up, sure, now get in the cruiser. And for all she knew, they'd be right. Without her memory, she couldn't even be sure *she* hadn't killed Hunter.

She had to get out of there, get someplace safe so she could think. If she could get back to the *Pit* . . .

Shit. Where was the *Pit*? Lost was one thing. Red had been lost before. But lost without the *Pit*? No nav, no scopes, no scanner. She couldn't ping anyone for help, she had no credits, no way of getting any credits. And how would she actually *go* anywhere?

The whine of a distant but approaching sniffer broke through the panic that threatened to overwhelm her. She picked a direction and started walking, not caring where she was headed as long as it wasn't here.

CHAPTER 17

Fifteen minutes or so later, Red emerged from the warehouse jungle and almost collapsed with relief. The familiar yellow sign reading CHU K'S TAP blinked at the end of the road. The *Pit* sat right where she'd left it, next to the door. Its new hatch control panel glittered in the sun.

Red hit the button and the hatch slid open with a loud yet comforting clang. The *Pit* might not be much, but it was home. And you know what they say: home is where the shower is.

Thankfully the hot water generator was functional. Red let the water run off her body until even her earlobes started to prune up. Then, feeling mostly human again, she wrapped herself in the only towel she could find that would bend and headed to the kitchen. She made herself a makeshift snack and dripped into the bunkroom.

Bonk was on the hollowed-out mattress that used to be Red's bed. It blinked its eyes and started its gargling purr.

"You have no idea," she muttered, stuffing a fistful of Tootsie Froots into her mouth. She washed down the crumbs with a swig of the flavorless brown water that called itself instant coffee. She'd been saving the Tootsie Froots for a special occasion. If waking up next to a dead man and narrowly avoiding arrest for his murder didn't qualify as a special occasion, well, she didn't know what did.

Red dressed between bites. By the time the package was empty, she felt ready to think seriously about the events of the past . . . how long had she been gone? She punched up the time stamp on the bunkroom's info screen. It was late morning the day after her drunken binge at Chuck's. Okay, that was a start.

She took a few aspirin with the last gritty swallow of coffee and lay down on the floor where she'd been sleeping since Bonk's excavation project. She lit a half-smoked cigar she found under a sock and tried to pull new details out of her memory. There was that obnoxious group of sparkly people, the bottle of whiskey, Hunter's tongue in her ear, "Booty Glow" on seemingly endless repeat, that weird tasting beer.

The beer. She could remember more or less everything until that beer. It was probably drugged. Duh, of course it was drugged.

Next question: did Hunter drug the beer? Probably. But she couldn't be sure.

Okay, so. She was drugged, and Hunter was probably the guy who did it. But why? What happened next? Who killed Hunter? What couldn't she remember?

Red scratched her armpit and tossed away the butt of her cigar. Chuck. She had to talk to Chuck.

~ ~ ~

Red pounded on the door of Chuck's Tap. It was a few hours before his regular opening time and the place was dark, but she couldn't wait.

"CHUCK! I know you can hear me, dude. Open up!"

Red continued to hammer on the door until it suddenly opened, catching her mid-swing. She stumbled forward into Chuck's doughy body. She stepped back and rubbed her hand.

"Hey, Chuck, I gotta ask you some stuff."

He said nothing, just scowled at her from underneath his eyebrow.

"I wouldn't ask but it's important. Can I come in?"

Chuck didn't move.

"I really need your help. It's about last night, the guy I was with. He said his name was Exley. Hunter Exley. Did you see him?"

Chuck went dim, like he was on a vidscreen with a bad color converter. Red had seen this before; it happened when he was checking in with himself someplace else. Red waited patiently for several minutes.

When Chuck became fully solid again, he stepped away from the door. "Come on, then," he grunted.

Red stepped into the cool darkness of the closed bar, and Chuck locked the door behind them.

"You want a drink? On the house."

Red blinked. "Um. Yeah, sure." Chuck nodded and got a bottle of Tolmarine wine from behind the bar. Red grabbed two glasses and they sat together at a table. Chuck poured the emerald green wine into both glasses, and held his up. He looked Red in the eye.

"It's good to see ya, Red."

Red clinked her glass with his. "Um. Thanks. I mean, I was just here last night, though, right?"

Chuck shrugged and looked away. Something weird was going on. She took a swallow of the wine. It burned like ice in her throat.

"So. Chuck. Did you see the guy I was drinking with last night? Hunter Exley?"

"Yep. I seen him."

"And? Do you know him?"

Chuck played with his glass, swirling the wine. "No."

Red slammed her hand on the table. "Dammit, Chuck, I woke up this morning with no memory and a dead body. I need some answers here."

Chuck drained his glass and refilled it. He moved to top off Red's, but she pushed the bottle away.

"Okay, Red. Why don't you tell me what happened."

Red swallowed another mouthful of wine and cleared her throat. "I was pretty drunk last night—"

"You're telling me."

Red glared at him. "—and this Hunter guy comes in with that obnoxious group, yeah? We start drinking and, uh, stuff. Then he gets some beer, only it has this funny taste, like chalk or something. I figure it was drugged, because I don't remember anything after that until I woke up today in the back of a cargo ship with a screamer of a headache like I've never had before. Hunter was there too, only he was very dead. I got myself the hell out of there and found the *Pit* right here where I'd left her."

Chuck went dim again, but only for a few seconds. "Let me guess. This cargo ship was all rusted out, no markings. Chains on the floor. Am I close?"

"Yeah, but . . ." Red sputtered.

Chuck held up a hand. "You're one lucky bastard, Red. You escaped being the latest addition to the Zoldroni'i royal family's personal harem."

"And Hunter?"

"Their acquisitions agent."

Red's sympathy for the recently deceased Mr. Exley disappeared like a fresh yozzie in a fazzer cage.

"Chuck," she whispered. "Chuck, did I kill him?"

He shrugged. "Does it matter?"

"Yes, yes it does actually matter. I'd like to know if I've killed a man in a drugged-out haze."

He picked at an invisible speck on the table. "No. You did not kill Hunter Exley."

Red's breath came rushing out of her. She finished her wine and emptied the dregs from the bottle into her glass. She sat back in her chair and looked at Chuck. "So? Who did?"

Chuck stood up, gathered the empty bottle and his nearly empty glass, and took them over to the bar. "I have to get ready to open. Finish your drink and get out."

The glass struck him square in the back of the head. Emerald wine sprayed everywhere.

Red's holoknife pressed against Chuck's throat before the last drop hit the ground. "Chuck," she hissed through clenched teeth. "I love you, but you will tell me this."

Chuck smiled. "Cute. Completely useless, but cute." He pushed away the holoknife and looked at his stained shirt with disgust.

Red shifted her grip on the weapon. "I swear on my parents' grave, I will kill this and every other nasty-ass body you've got scattered around this galaxy if you don't tell me right now who killed Hunter Exley."

Chuck's smile fell away. "Red, we go back a long way. You know I have nothing but respect for you. But I can't tell you."

"Can't or won't?"

He was silent. Red was startled to notice that he looked like he might cry. She retracted the holoknife and touched his arm. "Please, Chuck."

He turned away. "I'm sorry, Red. All I can tell you is that you have someone looking out for you. And I'm gonna catch hell if he—"

"He?"

"If *anyone* finds out I've told you even that much. Now please, go." He picked up a bar towel and started cleaning up the spilled wine.

Red hesitated, another question on her lips, then turned and walked out of the bar without saying a word.

CHAPTER 18

Red and the *Pit* drifted about in space for several days. She spent her time staring blankly at the scopes, ignoring the scanner, and replaying the conversation with Chuck in her head. Sometimes she remembered to eat; mostly she fell asleep sitting up in the captain's chair. Once, she pinged Woodman, but regretted it immediately and was relieved when he didn't respond. What would she tell him, anyway? That she had some kind of mysterious fairy godfather watching her every move? Swooping in to save the day?

Her mind wandered back to her childhood on Sept Magossii, a place she didn't let it wander often. Where was her savior then? Why let her parents die, but save her from the Guild and the Zoldroni'i?

As usually happened when she thought about Sept Magossii, Red found herself orbiting Sept Magossii, planning her descent toward the suburbs of Magross. Toward Granny.

Granny had lived in the same tiny house as long as Red could remember, with the same flowers growing beside the door and the same smell of homona pie coming from the kitchen.

The greeting was always the same, too. "Mildred!" she cried, taking Red into her arms and squeezing harder than her frail frame should've be able to.

Red let the hug go longer than usual before pulling away. "Hi, Granny. Is it a bad time?"

Granny waved a hand and snorted. "It's never a bad time for you to drop by." She looked critically at Red and narrowed her eyes. "You look awful, dear. Have you been eating?"

"Not really. It's been a rough couple of days. Weeks. Uh, months."

"Well, you go on upstairs and take a nice hot shower, and I'll find something in the kitchen for you."

"Oh, Granny, that sounds great."

Granny gave her a little push toward the stairs. "Go on, then. Go!"

Red went.

When she emerged, she discovered Granny had laid out some faded but clean clothes from the closet in Red's old room. The t-shirt was for a band she hadn't listened to in years, Deltonic Implosion. Her favorite song of theirs, "HoloLove," ran through her head as she dressed.

The kitchen was warm, light, and smelled of roast darna and fried juta. Granny brushed her hands on her apron and put an overflowing plate of food on the table. "I was going to make this for dinner, but since you're here now, there's no reason to save it. And there's homona pie when you finish that. It's from yesterday, I'm afraid, but I can put some ice cream on it for you."

"Thanks," Red mumbled through a mouthful of darna. Granny busied herself with dishes while Red ate, occasionally refilling her glass of milk or putting more slak sauce on the juta.

When Red finally scraped up the last smear of ice cream from her pie, she felt better than she had in forever.

"So, Mildred, when are you going to tell me what's wrong?" Granny asked as she sat down at the table across from Red.

Red chased some pie crumbs around the table with her finger. "What? Why would something be wrong?"

Granny chuckled. "You only visit me when something's wrong, dear."

"Granny, no, I—"

Granny took her hand. "It's all right. You've always been a free spirit. That's one of the things I love best about you. And I'm happy to be the one you can always come to."

Red squeezed her hand and tried to pretend she wasn't crying.

"Tell me what's bothering you."

Red took a deep breath. "Well, I had a close call the other day. I—I don't want to tell you about it. I was stupid. Really stupid. Anyway, I only got through it because someone helped me."

"Someone helped you? That doesn't sound so bad. Who?"

Red shook her head. "That's what I can't figure out. I'm pretty sure it's the same someone who helped Woodman get me, us, away from the Guild." Red stood up and started pacing the room. "It has to be someone watching me all the time. Someone powerful, powerful and dangerous. I just can't figure it out. I can't figure it out and I hate it."

She looked up and stopped in her tracks. Granny's face had gone white. Her flour-speckled hands were shaking. Red rushed to her side.

"Granny, what is it?" Their eyes met, and Red went cold. She knew something.

"It's nothing, dear. It's—"

At that moment, the vidscreen in the living room lit up with a ping notice. Through the open kitchen door Red could see the caller: Chuck. The ping notice had the red border that meant it was urgent.

When she turned back, Granny had regained her composure. "You'd better see what that fellow wants," she said, patting Red's arm. "I have some laundry that needs folding." She went upstairs, leaning heavily on the handrail.

Red cursed, kicked a chair, and stomped into the living room to see what Chuck wanted that was so goddamned important.

CHAPtER 19

"Chuck, what do you want that's so goddamned important?"

He had called from a room that sure wasn't a bar. It looked like an office, the kind with black grumskin furniture and older secretaries named Dolores who wanted to be called administrative assistants. Red had never seen him anyplace but a bar. It was weird.

"Get your ass to the bar at the Modern Mandrake Hotel in Andulia City on Gambora. You know where that is?"

"How do you know this vidcode? And how did you know I was even here?"

"Do you know that hotel?"

"I can find it. Chuck—"

"Get over there. I got something for you." The screen went dark.

That sneaky, greasy, fazzer-biting son of a bitch, ordering her around. She'd get him. Next time she got her hands on a case of blood rum she'd find some other schlub to sell it to. That would probably mean losing her drinking privileges at Chuck's bars, but . . .

Yeah, never mind.

Plus she'd never been to Andulia City. Mostly because she wasn't a celebrity, galactic politician, thousand-credit hooker, or any combination of those.

Good thing she'd showered.

Red went upstairs and found Granny sitting on her bed, gazing out the window, a photo album open in her lap. The photos were obviously old. The people grinning at the camera wore clothes and hairstyles that had gone out of fashion decades earlier. In one, Red recognized Granny as a young woman, her husband and children gathered around her. Red saw her father as a young boy, and his older sister Susan with her crazy curly hair. Huh. Who was the baby in Granny's arms?

As Red leaned closer to get a better look, Granny suddenly noticed she was there and snapped the book shut.

"Oh! You startled me. I was . . . remembering things." She shook her head slightly and put the album on the nightstand. "Are you planning to stay the night? I still have the bed made up in your old room."

"Um, I wish I could, but, ah, I've got to go, there's this thing . . ." Red stuffed her hands in her pants pockets.

"That's all right, dear. Did you want to take some leftovers with you? I'll go pack you a few things. I'll never eat it all myself. Do you have a freezer for the ice cream? Marge Blattz brought it last week when I had the girls over for bridge, but I didn't care for this brand. That's Marge for you! She can't even get ice cream right."

Red followed Granny and her monologue back downstairs and into the kitchen, trying to remember how much fuel she had left, and figuring whether it would be enough to get her to Andulia City.

~ ~ ~

Half an hour later Red stumbled back to the *Pit*, loaded down with plastic tubs of food, a coldpack filled with ice cream and heat-and-eat casseroles, and a stack of mail Granny had neatly tied together with green yarn. Red dumped the mail on a half-empty FlinkBar crate to look at later, when she didn't have Chuck breathing down her exhaust port.

She cleared a ton of crusty, putrid-smelling cans out the fridge to make room for all Granny's leftovers. The tiny freezer fit everything except one container of ice cream. Red took this as a sign that she deserved a second dessert. She couldn't find a spoon, so she found a wrench with a flatish handle and wiped off the engine grease on her Deltonic Implosion shirt.

Bonk was on her captain's chair, so she pushed it to the ground and plopped herself down. The cat made a metallic coughing sound and walked toward the wall. Red gave it a shove with her foot and it managed to find the door on the first try.

Red shoveled ice cream into her mouth with one hand while tapping in a search for the Modern Mandrake Hotel with the other. Pictures, pricing info, and ads starring Ephrasia Pfeff filled the vidscreen. Red whistled at the prices, spraying ice cream all over the control panel. Maybe one day she could afford to step foot in the lobby, if she saved up her credits for the next twenty years and robbed a bank or two.

She sent the coordinates for the hotel directly from the ad to the *Pit*'s nav. She felt the thrusters spit to life, and sat back. She used the non-ice cream end of the wrench-spoon to select the hotel's official photo gallery. Image after image showed a marble-encased lobby with lush, blood-red carpet; cavernous guest bathrooms with towels so thick you could use them to prop up the broken support leg of an air skiff; and a semi-grav racquetball court the size of a parking lot.

Toward the end of the gallery, Red found what she was looking for: photos of the bar. It was called the Mandrake Room (of course it was), and Red didn't think they'd have Old Wo'hall'a on tap. It reeked of money. A giant curved window gave people in the dark, intimate booths a panoramic view of the city. Bottles lined up behind the gleaming bar were artfully lit from below, turning the expensive booze into a glittering rainbow. There wasn't a crumpled napkin or puddle of beer or even a fingerprint in the whole place.

Red tried to imagine Chuck working in a place like the Mandrake Room, and laughed so hard she choked on her mouthful of ice cream.

She checked the navcomp for the travel time: only four hours.

She'd just close her eyes for a few minutes, then clean up the kitchen a little and maybe do a little laundry.

Chapter 20

The nav beeped and Red woke with a snort. The wrench-spoon clattered out of her lap to the floor, followed by the tub of melted ice cream. So much for the laundry. She winced at the thick splat and sticky puddle, kicked some papers over it, then turned her attention to the viewport.

The planet Gambora, home to the galactic government, filled the viewport. The *Pit* started its descent toward Andulia City, then beeped again for Red to take over. She cracked her neck and her knuckles before taking the manual controls. She guided the ship through the lower atmosphere and into the city. The nav led her along a series of air routes that took her to the business district. She spotted the Modern Mandrake Hotel long before she arrived, which wasn't surprising since it was the tallest building in the area and featured the double-M logo in letters three stories tall.

As she approached the hotel, its system sent her a welcome video.

"Welcome to the Modern Mandrake Hotel," Ephrasia Pfeff purred from the vidscreen. "If you have a reservation, please enter your confirmation code now. Jade Club members, you may proceed directly to your suite. All others please continue to the landing pad to the rear of the building. Enjoy your stay at the Modern Mandrake Hotel!"

Red, being an other, set the *Pit* down at the back of the building. While still elegant, this entrance was obviously for people not good enough to enter through the front. Red climbed out of her ship and walked toward the entrance. She looked back at the *Pit*, squatting between an Uberlux cruiser and a flashy Phoenix XT. A hot flash of shame shot through her. She shook it off and stepped through the enormous gilded doors of the hotel.

A man dressed in a tuxedo approached her the moment she entered the lobby. "Excuse me, ma'am," he said, raising an eyebrow. "Can I . . . help you?"

Red put her hands on her hips. "Yeah, how do I get to the bar?"

The man gave her a thin smile. "There are several bars in the neighborhood. If you would like, I can direct you to—"

"No no, *your* bar, the Mandrake Room. Which elevator?"

"Ma'am, to ensure our guests have an enjoyable experience, our dining establishments have a dress code. Perhaps you would like to freshen up?"

Red looked down at herself. Her Deltonic Implosion shirt was stained with wrench-spoon engine grease, her pants with ice cream.

"No, I think I'm okay."

"Ma'am, I really think you would be more comfortable at the Bearded Orl down the street."

"Look, buddy, I'm—"

"My name isn't 'buddy,'" the man sniffed. "My name is Spencer."

"Of course it is. Spencer, I'm not going to crash any VIP parties. I'm just here to pick something up from Chuck."

"Chuck," Spencer said, a finger to his thin lips. "I am afraid no one by that name works in the Mandrake Room."

Red poked him in the chest. He backed up half a step. "Chuck. He's a bartender. He told me to meet him in the Mandrake Room. Now, the sooner you help me find him, the sooner I can leave, and the sooner we'll both be happy. Okay?"

Spencer's smug smile wavered. "Perhaps you mean Charles. He is the one who runs the Mandrake Room. Take the express to the 56th floor." He gestured to an elevator in the corner.

"Thanks, man!" Red punched his arm lightly and headed toward the elevator. He hurried off, brushing at his jacket sleeve and muttering to himself.

In the elevator, Red stared at her reflection in the polished doors and frowned. Aside from the clothes, she didn't look that bad, really, except that her hair was sticking out from one side of her head. She spit in her hands and ran them over her hair to flatten it down. Good enough.

The doors slid open noiselessly and Red stepped out into the Mandrake Room. The suns were setting over the cityscape outside, casting the room in a spectacular array of red and orange light. It was still early, so only a few booths were occupied, mostly with couples. On her way to the bar, Red passed Sept Magossii's galactic rep sharing a bottle of champagne with a woman at least twenty years away from being mistaken for his wife.

Red pulled a chair out from the bar. The legs scraped against the floor, shattering the hushed atmosphere and drawing looks from the other patrons. Red gave them a toothy smile and a double thumbs-up as she sat down.

The bartender had his back to Red, talking to a man in the corner who was smoking a cigarette. "Hey!" she called, waving her hand. "I'm looking for Chuck."

He turned around, and Red almost fell out of her chair. It was Chuck, all right, but she'd never seen him like this. His greasy hair was combed back from his face instead of hanging into his eyes, and it looked like he had washed his face as recently as that morning. He even had two distinct eyebrows.

"Holy shit, Chuck, look at you." She whistled.

"My name is Charles," he said, "and I must ask you to keep your voice down."

"Hey, you invited me here, remember?"

"Yes. I have been asked to deliver something to you. I shall retrieve it from my office. Please excuse me, I will return shortly."

Red had to bite her lip to hold back a flood of laughter at his voice, which had picked up a pinched Luforian accent. Chuck narrowed his eyes at her as he left through a nondescript door.

Red drummed her fingers on the bar. They left satisfying smudges. She wrote a filthy saying for Chuck to clean up, got bored, and looked around for something else to do.

The smoking man was staring at her. He was an older man, thin, with blonde hair that was greying in an attractive, natural way other men paid hundreds of credits for. He had cold blue eyes and was pale. Red figured he'd spent far too many hours in dark hotel bars, leering at women.

Red scratched her eyebrow with her middle finger. The man smiled faintly and raised his glass at her. He exhaled a mouthful of smoke. It swirled up toward the ceiling like calligraphy. It made Red's fingers itch for a cigarette. She was about to ask if she could bum one when Chuck returned.

"Our business here is now complete," he said, putting an envelope down in front of her.

Red picked it up. It was thin and blank. She went to open it.

"Not here," Chuck said with a touch of anger. "I expect you have many things to do, and will be on your way now."

Red shrugged and crammed the envelope into the back pocket of her pants. "Whatever you say, *Charles*. See ya at the Crud & Bucket." She glanced at the smoking man again, but he was looking out the window at the darkness creeping over the city.

On her way back through the lobby, Red saw Spencer behind a desk, shuffling papers. She strode over, grabbed his face between her hands, and planted a noisy kiss right on his mouth.

"That was from Chuck," she said over her shoulder as she walked out the door, leaving him red-faced and spluttering.

~ ~ ~

Red waited until she got out of the city and set the *Pit*'s nav to return to orbit before she pulled out the envelope. Apart from being a bit grungy from its stay in her pocket, it was completely nondescript. Red tore it open and pulled out the single sheet of paper inside.

The few lines of text were written in a familiar narrow script that had haunted Red for months.

Reckless. You are better than this.

Chapter 21

Red couldn't take it. She opened a second container of Marge Blattz's subpar ice cream and ate it while pacing the ship, kicking anything that got in her way. Beer cans clattered happily. Tools, boots, dirty clothes, and boxes flew around like orls in a storm.

When the ice cream was gone and her kicking leg was sore, she suddenly felt exhausted. She slid down the wall and sat among the newly rearranged mess. She landed on something bulky that turned out to be the stack of mail from Granny's place.

Red didn't have much use for mail. One of the perks of being a free agent was the lack of paperwork. Still, there were times when she needed deliveries and living in your ship made it hard for mail to find you. So she used Granny's address.

She flipped through the stack, tossing the junk aside. That was almost everything: parts catalogs, "final notice" bills, notices for failing to appear in court on various petty charges, even an admag for a dating service. She paged through the admag for a minute, then wadded it up in disgust and threw it across the room.

The last piece of mail was a smallish package that wouldn't have been more battered if it had traveled across the entire galaxy on a buntling's back. The return address was obliterated by a sticky brown stain. Red pulled out her holoknife and slit open the tape. The box fell apart, revealing a couple of electronic components wrapped in plastic and a thin photostatted booklet that said INSTALLATION INSTRUCTIONS. Below the words was a cartoon of a cat looking at a map.

Holy shit. The tracking device! She'd ordered it so long ago, she'd completely forgotten about it. Damn Andarians, you'd think they could fill a simple order in less than a year.

She eagerly opened the booklet.

THANK YOU for your recent purchase of a VALU-KAT® Programmable Long-Distance Tracking System! We are confident that our SensoTrak* technology will bring you HOURS of treasure-hunting FUN!

Simply follow these easy-to-read instructions to install the SensoTrak* device in your cat IN MINUTES.

It's THAT EASY!

Included with this booket:

- one (1) SensoTrak* circuit board
- one (1) SensoTrak* pad (DELUXE KITS ONLY)
- one (1) set insulated wires

You will also need:

- two (2) anodized weldbolts
- fifteen (15) nonanodized weldbolts
- a size D5 sonic wrench
- electroputty

*Patent pending

"Bonk!" Red called, scanning the surprisingly brief installation directions. "Bonk, we've got some work to do!"

~ ~ ~

Hours later, Red was still tits-deep in the project. Bonk, powered down for the installation, lay on its back between her legs. A tangled nest of wires stuck out of its open belly panel. Weldbolts in a dozen different sizes were scattered on the floor around them. Red had one good-sized blob of electroputty in her hair and another on the side of her nose.

"It's that easy, my ass," she muttered, giving the sonic wrench (size D5) a violent yank. There was a snap as the jammed timing plate finally came loose. Red shoved the circuit board into place and sifted through the weldbolts for one that would fit the socket. After three or four tries, she found the right size and spun it tight. She picked through the loose wires for the one that should run to the cerebral processor.

It was too short.

She glanced at the installation instructions to make sure she had the right one. They were no help at all.

"Attaching to panel glorious with weldbolt the same," she read aloud. What did that even mean? The whole booklet sounded like it was written in Glorreen by a mentally unstable fazzer after a sixer of beer. Her favorite part was Step 21, which didn't exist at all. The list went straight from Step 20 to Step 22.

She needed a break.

Red threw down the sonic wrench and got to her feet. She'd been bent over that damn cat for so long her back was cramped, and her eyes stung from squinting at wires and weldbolts. She put on some music—Deltonic Implosion, she was feeling nostalgic—lay down next to her bed, and closed her eyes. As the familiar guitar licks throbbed in her head, her thoughts returned to the latest anonymous note.

Reckless? She'd never exactly been a careful person, not even as a kid. Rule-breaking and risk-taking were her favorite hobbies. She wasn't stupid, and she could handle herself just fine. She'd gotten herself *and* Woodman away from that baega, after all. No help from anyone. No reason to think she wouldn't have gotten away from the Guild. That Exley guy too. Who knows, maybe she would have even liked being a Zoldroni'i sex slave. Probably have a better wardrobe. A bed without a giant hole, at least.

She must have drifted off to sleep because the vidscreen pingback woke her up. She dragged herself to the cockpit, glaring at the partially disemboweled Bonk as she passed by.

It was Woodman. Red slapped the vidchat button and yawned. "About time you pinged me back."

"Did I wake you up, darlin?" he drawled. "Lemme guess: you were dreaming of me again."

Red snorted. "You still on Orgulla 5 with that chick?"

"If you mean Natashka, then no. She, well, there was a disagreement over finances."

"She asked you to chip in for rent, didn't she?"

"No!" Woodman coughed. "The, ah, water bill. She's got this amazing shower, it's like a waterfall. I'm going to get one for the *Chopper*. If you're nice to me, I'll let you try it." He leaned toward her in the vidscreen. "Looks like you need it. What's that stuff on your nose?"

Red touched the dried blob of electroputty. "Nothing. Look, while you've been shacked up with whats-her-name, I've had all kinds of news. Where are you now?"

"Mom and dad's place."

Ha. Where else would he be? "Can I swing by? There's too much for vidchat."

Woodman shrugged. "Sure. I'll be here a couple days at least. When can you get here?"

"I'm over Andulia City now, so . . ." Red did some quick math. "Tomorrow? Later in the day?"

"Andulia City, eh?" Woodman whistled. "What are you up to out there? A job, or—wait, did you find some rich old dude who's into engine grease and cigars?"

"Cute. No, look, I promise I'll tell you everything when I get there."

"Sure. But shower first, huh?" Woodman's eyebrows scrunched together. "Everything okay?"

Red tapped the coordinates for the Woodmans' place into the nav. "Dunno. Maybe."

"Could you be more vague, please? I'm not thoroughly confused yet." It was Woodman's turn to roll his eyes.

Red entered the final number and sat back. "I think I have a way to find out who's been killing people for me."

CHAPTER 22

During the trip to Sept Magossii, Red got back to work on Bonk. Sleep had energized her. Plus, there was no way Woodman could know she couldn't install a simple tracker in a cat. She had a rep to think about. Work was hard enough to come by without him laughing about this all over the galaxy. That dude had a mouth bigger than Ulatu.

Cigar clenched between her teeth, she sat down on the floor next to the cat. She tugged thoughtfully at the too-short blue wire, then picked up the installation booklet and examined the diagram on page 2 for the hundred and fiftieth time. She squinted, turned the booklet around. The diagram had been printed upside down. Of course it had.

Red grumbled a string of creative obscenities about Andarians and their female relatives as she removed the weldbolts that held the backwards circuit board. Once it was turned the right way, it snapped right into place, no wrestling or banging necessary. The shiny ValuKat logo stood out among the dusty diodes and peeling wires that filled the rest of Bonk's belly cavity. Red felt a little stab of emotion. Poor Bonk.

She pushed that aside. It was just a cat, a tool. A glitchy tool. An annoying glitchy tool that just might be able to lead her to Mr. Mystery.

With the circuit board in the right place, the blue wire was plenty long enough to reach the cerebral processor. Red weldbolted it tight, then found the SensoTrak (patent pending) pad. It was triangular, pink, and rubbery to the touch. Even without a proper diagram, Red knew exactly where it would connect: to Bonk's nasal input sensor.

A few more weldbolts, a fresh layer of electroputty to complete the connections, and she was done. Red tucked the hanging wires back into the belly cavity and popped the panel back on. She hauled the cat upright and took a deep breath.

"All right, Bonk," she said, tossing her cigar butt away. "Let's see how we did." She pressed the power button at the base of its tail and watched its mismatched eyes blink on. There was a whirring sound and Bonk's tail twitched a few times. Then it was still.

"Welcome back," she said. "Now how do we get you tracking?" She grabbed the installation booklet but the final instructions were to "Rubbing to be the done with much sample success!"

Oh well. She'd figure it out later. She picked at the electroputty on her nose. Woodman was right, she needed a shower. And more music. The Poly Torrents. Good stuff.

~ ~ ~

It was late afternoon when the *Pit* landed at the Woodmans' estate. Red knocked on the back door, bouncing a little as she waited.

Mrs. Woodman answered the door. "Red! It's so nice to see you again. Mark mentioned you would be stopping by. Oh!" She put a hand to her cheek. "Where are my manners? Come in, come in!"

"Thanks." Red stepped into hallway. Like the rest of the house, it was expensively, but tastefully, decorated. The original Andres Mandorak watercolors lining the walls reflected in the polished tile floors. Red checked her boots for grunge, winced, then pulled them off and left them on a small Luxorian rug next to the door.

"Something smells great, Mrs. Woodman," she said. "I hope I'm not interrupting dinner."

Mrs. Woodman waved a hand as she closed the door. "Oh no, you're just in time to join us. I had Mark set you a place. Do you like bepaia?"

Red grinned. "Only if there's quusberries on the side."

"Of course! Is there any other way to eat bepaia?" Mrs. Woodman gestured toward the back of the house. "Mark is in the kitchen. I've got to run upstairs and change." She put a hand on Red's arm. "Would you please remind him to stir the quusberries? He never remembers to stir them."

"I sure will."

Red could have found her way to the kitchen blindfolded. She had spent so much of her childhood with Woodman that his house was as familiar as her own. She never quite got used to seeing him here, though. She always called him a mama's boy, but that wasn't quite right. It was like he was a different person entirely when he was with his parents. Like now: he was wearing an apron, for Gravnar's sake. He took a taste from a pot on the stove, sprinkled something powdery into it, and stirred. He didn't see Red watching from the kitchen doorway until he bent over to look in the stove and she grunted at the view.

"Hey, babe, how long you been standing there?" He grinned and wiggled his ass.

"Long enough." Red threw an oven mitt at him and sat on the counter, swinging her sock feet. "Your mom says to stir the quusberries."

"Yeah, yeah. I'm stirring." He made a show of stirring the pot again with exaggerated strokes, twitching his hips and making the apron swing. He took another taste and waggled his eyebrows at her. "You wanna try my spicy sauce?"

It was too much. Red laughed so hard, deep from her gut, that she fell off the counter. Woodman rushed over to help her up.

"I haven't heard you laugh like that in ages," he said as she tried to catch her breath.

Red's laughter turned to hiccups. She wiped her eyes on her sleeve. "I feel really good for the first time in ages. Like things are finally going my way. You know?"

"This must be some news."

"How much time do we have before dinner is ready?"

He glanced at the oven. "Fifteen minutes?"

"That should be enough." She filled him in on everything that had happened since they split the *Gumdrop*'s take: how she'd lost it all, the drunken night with Hunter, waking up in the sex slave cargo ship, the talk with Chuck (Woodman didn't know about Chuck's cross-dimensional tax status, so she had to fudge some details), the Modern Mandrake, and the second anonymous note.

Woodman listened patiently, asking a question here and there, occasionally stirring the quusberry sauce. When she was done, he set the spoon down and wiped his hands on the apron.

"Shit, Red. That's . . . I don't see how this puts you in a good mood. What am I missing?"

"I finally got that tracking system I ordered for Bonk. Remember? I can use it to find the person who wrote the note."

Woodman looked at her skeptically. "Does it even work?"

Red scratched her neck. "I mean, I'll have to test it. You can help me. Tonight, after dinner. Yeah?"

Mrs. Woodman stuck her head into the kitchen. "Mark, is the bepaia done? Your father is hungry and you know how he gets."

"Yeah, Mom, I was just taking it out now."

"Wonderful. Put it on this platter. Red, if you would please get the bowl of salad from the refrigerator? I'll get these quusberries into a dish and meet you in the dining room."

Red grabbed the bowl of chopped vegetables and brought it to the dining room. Woodman's father, Joe, was already sitting at the table, sipping a glass of pale red wine and reading a newspaper. He stood up when he saw Red.

"Look who it is! How have you been, stranger?" He pulled Red into a hug.

Red blushed and clutched the salad bowl awkwardly. Joe Woodman was an older, handsomer version of his son, only without the annoying macho personality. Ever since she was old enough to notice, she'd had a confusing attraction to him. Some psychologist could probably retire to a beach on Plest from analyzing that one. Troubled youth, daddy issues, need for discipline . . . she could practically write the report herself. Luckily, Mr. Woodman was away on business a lot.

"I'm fine, Mr. Woodman," she said when he finally let go. "How's work?"

"Oh, you know," he said, pulling out a chair for her. "Stressful. Why can't work be more like jatball?" He picked up a bottle. "You like Ophesan red? Picked it up last month when I was there doing some consulting for an outfit that makes raycron shielding for gas mining ships."

Red nodded and he filled her glass. "Granny's always saying you should retire."

"I will someday. Say, how is your granny? Does she still play bingo with that group from the senior center?"

"Oh yeah, she wins all the time. She says it keeps her in knitting needles."

"Ha! I bet it does." He stood up again as his wife and son came into the room carrying steaming dishes of food. "Here, let me." He took the dish from Mrs. Woodman and kissed her on the cheek.

"Thank you, Joe. Mark, put the bepaia there, near Red. You've got your wine? Wonderful." She settled into the chair Woodman pulled out for her at the head of the table. She continued to direct them all until every glass and plate was full.

The meal passed slowly but pleasantly. Red devoured two huge helpings of the flaky bepaia, which she learned was Woodman's own recipe, and drank too much wine. Mostly they talked about Mr. Woodman's business travels and Mrs. Woodman's charitable work with homeless children.

Red noticed that Woodman avoided talking about his own life, apart from his opinion on the Crolinian Psycats' chances at a championship. If his parents knew he had just spent several months living with an Orgullan woman with an amazing shower, there was no sign of it. Red found this hilarious.

Of course, that could have been the wine.

After dessert (triple chocolate cake), Mrs. Woodman dabbed her mouth with a napkin. "Red, will you be staying the night? I've got the Shell Room made up."

Red shot a glance at Woodman, who seemed far too busy straightening his silverware than could be considered normal. Sigh. A real bed would be nice.

"Sure, that would be great," she said. "Thanks!"

"Wonderful!" Mrs. Woodman clapped her hands together. "Now, do you two have plans for the rest of the evening, or will you be joining us for a few games of jester's scrap?"

Woodman cleared his throat. "Uh, Red's got some stuff she needs my help with, Mom. Can we do the jester's scrap thing another time?"

"Oh, that's all right. I figured it was a long shot anyway." She laughed. "Your dad can lose to me just as easily as he could to you."

"Hey!"

Woodman stood and picked up his dirty dishes. His mother tutted. "No no, I'll take care of those. You two go. Good luck with your project, Red."

"Thank you both for dinner," she said, putting her napkin next to her plate. Mr. Woodman gave her a smile she felt in her knees. She mumbled something about her ship and dragged Woodman out of the room.

They went outside to the *Pit*. Bonk was sitting on the floor of the bunkroom, performing a regular cleaning of its exterior components. When it saw Red and Woodman, its hydraulics pulled the limb casings back into position, snug to the torso, and the polyfiber scrub pad retracted back into the head cavity.

Red dragged the cat into the main living area—best to keep Woodman out of the bunkroom. At least for now.

"See?" she said, tapping the SensoTrak pad. "I think you have to do something with this to get the tracking to work."

Woodman squatted down and looked at the pad. "Didn't this thing come with instructions?"

"Yeah, good luck with that," she said, tossing him the booklet.

He flipped to the back. "'Rubbing to be the done with much sample success,'" he read. "What does that mean?"

"You tell me," Red said. "The whole thing is like that. I'm lucky I got the thing installed at all."

"Rubbing."

Red kicked him. "Hey. Stay focused."

"I am! I'm thinking that . . . hang on." He pulled off his shirt.

"Dammit, Woodman, not now!"

"Calm down, babe. I have an idea. Take this." He handed her the shirt. "Give me maybe five minutes, then rub this on Bonk's nose pad thing. Got it?"

"Oh, I think I know what you're doing."

"Okay, good. See you in a few minutes." He left the *Pit*, leaving the hatch open.

Red waited a bit, then rubbed the shirt on the SensoTrak pad. A whirring sound came from Bonk's guts, and its green eye blinked twice. It started walking and managed to find the open hatch on its own. Holy shit, maybe that SensoTrak thing actually fixed it.

Bonk walked out and headed across the huge lawn. Red closed the *Pit*'s hatch and followed. It led her through the aggrippinia grove, past the pool house, and ended up at the *Chopper*. It tried to walk through the hull. So much for the Great SensoTrak Miracle of Sept Magossii.

"You glitchy cat," Red groaned. "The door's right there." She gave it a shove with her foot and it walked through the open hatch.

Inside, Red expected to see Woodman, but the main room was empty. Bonk headed toward the bunkroom and she groaned. That dude just couldn't keep his mind out of his pants. Red made herself stop thinking about his pants and followed Bonk into the bunkroom.

It was empty too. Huh. Bonk walked to one corner of the room and started going in circles. Red moved closer and noticed one of the floor panels was sticking up a little on one side. She grinned and knocked on the panel.

"Come on out, Woodman. We found you."

The panel lifted and Woodman stuck his head out of the hidden compartment. "About time, too. It's cramped in here."

"Maybe a little less triple chocolate cake, and it wouldn't be so cramped."

"Ha ha. So? It worked."

Red's eyes sparkled. "It worked. It *so* worked."

Woodman pulled himself out of the floor and sat on the edge of the hole, looking at Bonk. "And now you're going to try it with that note."

"Hell yes, I am."

"Are you sure that's a good idea? I mean, you don't know who this guy is, and he seems to want to keep it that way."

Red grabbed his bare arm and squeezed. "Woodman, I have to know."

"I know," he sighed. "Just promise me you won't do anything too stupid. Do it right, do it careful, do it smart."

"Don't be a drama queen. What could go wrong? The guy obviously wants me alive, right?" She tossed Woodman's shirt in his face and stood up.

"But if you're that worried, you can come with me."

Chapter 23

Red woke up in the Shell Room. Alone. She was still mad about that part. She and Woodman had stayed up arguing over details of their plan—what little plan they had, anyway. He stormed out around midnight, leaving Red frustrated in more ways than one.

It was a cloudy morning, with rain threatening to start at any time. Breakfast was awkward. Woodman pushed his eggs around his plate and didn't say much, while his mother struggled to keep up a steady stream of light conversation. To Red's relief, Mr. Woodman had left early. If she'd had to watch him eat a fat, ripe zuranfruit, she wouldn't have been responsible for her actions.

Also to Red's relief, the rain held off until they had broken through the clouds over Sept Magossii. She hadn't had a chance to waterproof the *Pit*'s hull in a few years, and the last thing she needed right now was an iced-up grav plate.

Woodman didn't say a word from the copilot's chair until they hit orbit. "For the record, this is probably the stupidest thing you've ever done."

"Probably."

"Fine. As long as we agree on that, let's get it over with." He stood up. "Where are the crates?"

"Kind of everywhere. Just grab what you find. Make sure they're sturdy, though. Bonk's pretty heavy."

It didn't take long to find more than a dozen crates that might work. Red gave them each a firm kick, either grunting her approval or replacing it. When they were done, the crates made a rough circle in the main room of the ship. Bonk sat in the middle.

"Okay," Red said, pulling the note from the Mandrake Room out of its envelope. "Let's see what kind of range this thing has."

She rubbed the paper on Bonk's SensoTrak pad. There was the whirring sound again, only this time nothing else happened. Red was about to give up when Bonk's green eye blinked twice and it walked toward the kitchen. It hit the crate but kept trying.

"Looks like we have our course," Red said.

~ ~ ~

They spent the rest of the day flying manually, adjusting course when necessary to keep Bonk walking toward the front of the ship. It was clumsy and annoying, what with the fiddly adjustments to go around planets and constant bonking, but Red had booze and loud music. She even put on some Vulvato for Woodman—his favorite—as a peace offering, and let him have the last beer. He didn't stop pouting, but at least he was speaking to her again. Or he had been, before he fell asleep in the copilot's chair. Red didn't consider snoring to be speaking.

She was tired too, dammit. It was after midnight, and the Shell Room was a long time ago. The nav charts on the vidscreen were starting to swim in front of her eyes. She even had a weird sense of déjà vu, like she'd done this before somehow. She needed to sleep, to be ready for whatever, whoever Bonk was leading them to.

On top of all that, she was still frustrated from being shut out cold the night before. Stupid Woodman. She glanced over at him. He was, as usual, wearing a shirt that was too small on purpose. And the pants. Who did he think he was, Indar Skjov? He did have the same kind of jawline, sort of chiseled, with just enough beard to chafe a girl raw, in a good way. And it had, many times. Just not lately.

Red shifted a bit, her own pants suddenly feeling uncomfortably tight. She felt the familiar tingling and figured what the hell. She sure wasn't going to get any satisfaction from anyone else. She'd just take care of business, then wake up the asthmatic grum so she could get some sleep. Let him stare at the viewport and listen to Bonk's bonking for a few hours.

She got up quietly and tiptoed out of the cockpit, past Bonk's crate circle, and into the bunkroom. She undid her pants, laid back on a pile of clothes, and thought about Woodman's tight pants as her hand wandered southward.

It didn't take long.

Afterward, she lit a cigar. She was too relaxed to get up and wake Woodman. Even the bonking sound had become soothing and hypnotic. She watched the smoke from the end of the cigar curl and twist toward the ceiling. Through her half-closed eyes, it looked almost like writing, like calligraphy . . .

Calligraphy! Red bolted upright, suddenly wide awake. The déjà vu she'd felt earlier made sense now. It felt like she'd done this before because she *had* done it before, only in reverse.

She dashed to the cockpit and gave Woodman a shake. "Wake up, I think I know where we're going."

He grunted. "Huh?"

Red pulled up some charts on the vidscreen. "Look: we're here." She pointed at a flashing blip on the chart. Woodman sat up and rubbed his eyes. "And Bonk's been leading us this way." She dragged her finger on the screen in a straight line toward a hazy blob. "This is the Gambulon nebula. We're almost there now. And on the other side . . ." She ran her finger through the blob and tapped a dot. "That's Gambora."

Woodman yawned and stretched. "Red, why are your pants undone?"

"Never mind. It's Gambora! As in, Andulia City. As in, the Modern Mandrake Hotel." Red stared at the dot. "Hope the bar's open for brunch. We should be there by ten."

"Wait, wait, wait," Woodman said, running his hands through his shaggy hair. "Why would Bonk be taking us there? It doesn't make sense."

"Dunno. You'd have to ask Bonk. But that's where we're headed. I'd bet a case of Finebock on it."

Woodman was silent for a minute. "Do you think maybe it's tracking to the bartender?"

Red shook her head. They'd passed half a dozen of Chuck's places by now. If it were tracking Chuck, it would have taken them to the closest one. But Woodman didn't know about Chuck and Red wasn't about to get into that now. "No," she said. "We're tracking the note, not the envelope. And the bartender only touched the envelope."

"That you saw, anyway."

"And if it *is* tracking to the bartender, then he's got some explaining to do."

Woodman shrugged. "I guess we'll find out."

"Yep," Red said. "I'm going to get some sleep. You good to drive for a while?"

"Sure. Unless you need help with those pants?"

Red smirked. "No thanks," she said, buttoning them up. "I helped myself already."

CHAPTER 24

Back on Sept Magossii. She climbed up the homona tree and through her bedroom window. Granny was there with a bowl of ice cream, but wouldn't let Red have any. Granny kept pulling it away while Red chased her around the room. Then Chuck was there, tossing the ice cream back and forth with Granny while Red got hungrier and hungrier. There was a blinding flash and Granny was gone, another flash and Chuck was gone. The bowl of ice cream was on the floor, and Red was reaching for it, about to pick it up—

"Hey. Hey. Hey. Hey." Woodman poked her face. "Hey, we're here."

She swatted his hand and sat up, yawning. "Gambora?"

"Yep."

"You sure it's the place?"

"Oh yeah. I flew past it and Bonk spun like a navcomp dial. It's the place."

Red stood up and stretched. "Told you so."

"Whatever. We're about half an hour from Andulia City. Figured you'd probably want a shower."

Red sniffed herself and shrugged. "I'd rather have some breakfast."

They reheated one of Granny's tubs of leftovers and ate in the cockpit. The final approach to Andulia City needed manual control because of all the traffic. You'd think rich people could afford chauffeurs who actually knew how to fly. The *Pit* had dugger mites that were better pilots than these guys.

As they dodged limousine cruisers, Red pulled up the hotel info for Woodman. Ephrasia Pfeff splashed across the vidscreen and Red was glad she'd already had coffee. There's only so much cleavage she could take without caffeine.

"D'you think we'll run into her?" Woodman asked, his eyes glued to the vidscreen.

Red tossed her empty plate at him. "We're not here to play around. We'll go straight up to the bar and see what we find."

"I bet we find nothing."

"Don't be a grumstain."

Woodman put up his hands. "You're the boss. I'm just tagging along to pick up the pieces."

Ephrasia switched to her welcome spiel. Red ignored it and flew the *Pit* around to the back entrance to her regular spot. If someone last week told her she'd have a regular parking spot at the Modern Mandrake Hotel in Andulia City, she'd have blasted them before she got infected with their space rabies. Weird old thing, life.

Once landed, she shut Bonk down and geared up. She didn't anticipate any trouble, but Woodman insisted she take her holoknife. He wore his multi-pocketed jacket, and while Red didn't ask, she assumed it was loaded.

It was a hot, sunny morning in Andulia City, but the lobby of the Modern Mandrake was cool and dark. Red's tuxedoed friend Spencer rushed over from behind the desk. Woodman tensed and reached into one of his pockets.

Red elbowed him. "Don't be stupid," she hissed. "Leave him to me. We go way back." Woodman grumbled but stepped back as the man approached.

"I am sorry, ma'am—"

"Ma'am!" Red put a hand to her chest in mock indignation. "Why, Spencer, I thought we were friends."

"I'm sorry, *ma'am*, but you and your friend will have to leave." His chin was set defiantly. It was adorable. The sweat on his brow, not so much.

"Oh, Spence, let's not do this again." She put her arm around his shoulders and nodded at Woodman. "You see this guy? The one with the ridiculously tight shirt and bad attitude? He's kind of over-protective of me. It's embarrassing, really, but what can you do, right?"

Woodman cracked his knuckles, and Spencer's eyes got wide. "I am going to have to call security."

"Completely understandable," Red said, slapping him on the back. "Tell 'em to meet us up in the Mandrake Room. No hurry." She pushed Woodman toward the elevator.

When the doors slid closed, Woodman turned to Red. "Okay, no matter what happens, we do this right, we do it careful, we do it smart."

"Don't worry, it'll be fine. These kinds of places don't like scenes. You'll see. No one's even going to raise their voice."

The doors slid open on an empty bar. "Okay," Red said, glancing around. "I figure we have five minutes to get this party started before security arrives. Let me do the talking. You just stand there and look intimidating."

Woodman scowled at her.

"Yes! Just like that. Come on."

No one was behind the bar. Red went around and helped herself to a beer, some fancy microbrew she'd never heard of called Teraius. She offered one to Woodman, but he just shook his head and looked around nervously, like he expected armed guards to jump out from under the tables or something.

Red took a swig from her bottle and crept over to the nondescript door she'd seen Chuck use on her last visit. She leaned over to listen, but heard nothing. She looked at Woodman, who shrugged and glanced back at the elevator. Red took another drink, then pushed open the door.

Just as she thought, it was an empty office. The place was a disaster: papers everywhere, cobwebs decorating the grungy coffeepot, dead plant on a dented filing cabinet. An Orgullan pinup calendar hung crookedly on one wall. Red grinned. He could call himself Charles and talk like a Luforian, but this was a Chuck office.

Red poked around in the papers, but found nothing interesting.

"What the hell are you doing?"

She dropped her beer and jumped back. Chuck was sitting behind the desk. He had the Charles hair and clothes, but the rest of him was still Chuck: voice, pimples, charm.

"Dude, you need a minute to get yourself together? I can turn around."

"Red, why are you here?"

"That note? I tracked it back here."

"So?"

"So I figure, either the author is here or was here. I want to meet him."

Chuck shook his head. "You have no idea what you're getting into."

"That's the whole point, Chuck."

There was a pounding on the office door. "Red, we've got company," Woodman hissed.

Red leaned over the desk and locked eyes with Chuck. "Look. We can do this the easy way, or we can do it the hard way."

Something thumped against the door. Red pulled out her holoknife and started using it to trim her fingernails. "Personally, I like the hard way," she said. "It's good exercise. How about you? Looks like you could use a little cardio yourself, pudgy."

From behind the closed door came a muffled scuffling and the whine of a mini faze cannon warming up. Red examined her fingernails and gave one a final swipe with the holoknife.

"You want to meet this guy? Fine." Chuck spat on sticky floor. "But this is it between you and me. We're through. You got that? No more business, no more free drinks. We're finished."

Red blinked. "Chuck, I—"

"Someone will be in touch. Now get out of here and take that meatwad with you." And he disappeared, as if he'd never been there.

Red opened the office door to find Woodman pinned to the wall by four no-necked thugs with "security" tastefully embroidered on their jackets. The two partially crushed halves of his mini faze cannon buzzed on the floor between his feet.

She smiled sweetly at them. "Woodman, aren't you going to introduce me to your handsome friends?"

"Eh, you're not their type."

"Quiet, you." One of the thugs yanked Woodman's arm up his back.

He grimaced. "Geez, try to do a guy a favor and you get a dislocated shoulder for your trouble."

"Well," Red said, "You gentlemen probably have flowers to arrange or tea cozies to knit. Don't let us keep you. We can find our own way out."

"Oh no, you don't." One of the security thugs detached himself from Woodman and put a thick hand on Red's arm. "We're walking you out."

Red batted her eyelashes. "And they say chivalry is dead."

"Let's go." He jerked her toward the elevator while the other thugs dragged Woodman by the jacket.

In the lobby, Spencer stood with a whispering group of guests, looking smug. "Don't worry, Spence," she called. "There's plenty of me to go around. I'll have these guys save you a juicy slice of this." She grabbed her ass and squeezed.

His angry flush was worth the rough yank she got from her escort.

The light outside was blinding after the dark interior of the hotel. The security thugs pushed Red and Woodman so they stumbled into the lot.

"Neither one of you is welcome at the Modern Mandrake Hotel," one growled, pointing a stubby finger at them.

Red saluted him with two fingers.

On their way back to the *Pit*, Woodman rolled his neck and stretched his shoulders. "Hey Red, you were right," he said.

"Oh yeah?"

"Yeah. No one raised their voice."

Chapter 25

Andulia City fell away as Red piloted the *Pit* into orbit. In the copilot's chair, Woodman rubbed his face.

"We're getting too old for this shit, Red."

"Speak for yourself, grandpa."

Woodman leaned back, his hands behind his head. "So what, exactly, did we get out of all that?"

"Chuck is going to set up a meeting with our mystery man."

"Who the hell is Chuck?"

"The bartender."

"Wait, back up. You're on a first-name basis with the bartender at the Mandrake Room?"

"It's a long story." Red set the *Pit* to maintain its orbit. "You got anywhere you need to be? I could use the backup when this meeting goes down."

"Don't be stupid. This Chuck guy isn't going to set up any meeting. He doesn't even know you. He just wanted you out of his office. He'd've told you Archie Noligg wanted to hook up with you if he thought it would make you go away."

Red shifted uncomfortably. Chuck was a cross-dimensional being of his word, and she trusted him. She didn't like keeping secrets from Woodman, and even if Chuck really had written her off this time, a promise was still a promise. Plus, it didn't hurt to have a card to play if Chuck ever decided to be difficult. "I guess we'll just have to wait and see."

"We? We nothing. I'm done with this detective shit. You can drop me off at my parents' place. If you were smart, you'd—"

The overhead display flashed an incoming message.

<<<YOU ARE BECOMING TIRESOME. BE AT THE STATUE OF VLADMIR IV IN THE LHAORN MARKET ON GLOR ON THURSDAY AFTERNOON. WE HAVE MANY THINGS TO DISCUSS.

Red hooted and pointed at the display. "Ha! Take that, Woodman! Good old Chuck." She tapped at the controls and brought up info on the Lhaorn Market. "I've never been to Glor, have you? Granny's friend Marge has a cottage there. Bought it with her first husband's life insurance policy, the cheeky thing. Today is, what, Tuesday? Glor is about a day and a half from here, so it's perfect. I'll just . . . Woodman, are you even listening?"

He was staring at the screen, his face blank but his jaw tight. "Are you really going to go?"

"Why not?"

He slammed his hands on the control panel and stood up. "I'll tell you why not," he shouted, grabbing Red by the shoulders. "He thinks you're tiresome. A *murderer* thinks you're *tiresome*. You know what murderers do with people who are tiresome?" He gave her a shake. "They kill them, Red. They kill them. Because they're murderers."

Red pushed his hands away and stood up, her nose inches from his. "You think you can scare me into letting this go?" she growled. "You know me better than that."

"I thought I did," he said, shaking his head. "But what do we always say? Do it right, do it careful, do it smart. Which part of this is right, Red? Which part is careful? Cuz it sure ain't smart."

Her fist flew before she had time to think. He reeled back, his nose gushing blood.

"Oh my god, Woodman, I'm—"

The profound sadness on his face stole her words. "Take me home, Red," he said. Then he left the cockpit, nose pinched between his fingers.

Red dropped into the captain's chair. She rubbed her knuckles and stared blankly at the Skysweeper Resort ads that still flashed across the display. She heard noises from the back of the ship—a slamming door, a crash, cursing, water running.

Red sighed. She started tapping in coordinates, then paused. She bit her lip, deleted what she'd entered, and started again with a different string of numbers. The thrusters hummed and the gravity modulator groaned as the *Pit* left orbit over Gambora. She found a half-smoked cigar on the floor, brushed off some unidentifiable crud, and lit it. It was stale, but it helped calm her down enough that she could think.

He had it coming. Right? He was so grumheaded. He still thought of her as the little kid back on Sept Magossii, eating stolen yozzies at the market and joyriding in her neighbors' ships. But she wasn't a kid anymore. She was a grown-ass woman who took care of herself just fine. Except for that Exley thing. And the run-in with the Guild. And she could have gotten out of those herself too, only there was this new asshole trying to play the white knight and rescue the damsel. Well, he can just go to hell, thanks very much. She was no damsel, and she'd be beat ten ways to Gravnar if she was going to let some guy she didn't even know treat her like one.

She spat on the floor. That was what Woodman didn't understand about this whole thing. She knew the risks of this meeting. Hell, she was scared—not that she'd ever tell him that. She barely admitted it to herself. But there was someone out there with the power to take her out at any time, and there was nothing she could do about it. As scared as she was to meet that person, being under their control was outright terrifying.

She didn't need Woodman to come along, but she wanted him to. She'd never tell him that either. She flexed her fingers, grimacing at the bruises that were starting to darken on the knuckles. She'd never punched him before, not a real punch. Guilt swelled up inside her like a hot balloon. He was a good guy, underneath all the macho swagger and ridiculous chivalry. Besides Granny, he was the only one she trusted with her life, the only one she could count on.

Red was surprised to wonder if she might actually love the big doofus.

The cigar had burned down to a nub, so she crushed it out on the navbox and brushed off her hands. Time to break the news to Woodman that he wasn't going home, not yet.

She found him taking a shower. Steam rose over the curtain and fogged up the mirror. His blood-stained shirt was crumpled on the floor. Red picked it up and twisted it in her hands.

"Woodman? Can we talk?"

He didn't say anything, so she continued. "I'm sorry. About the punch, I mean. I didn't mean to. I was just . . . Is it broken?"

"No."

"Oh, good. Good. I'll rinse your shirt. The blood should come out since it's not dry yet. I've had some experience with rinsing out bloody clothes. You know? Usually it's my own, though." She put the shirt in the sink, plugged the drain, and turned on the cold water.

Woodman yelped. "Dammit, Red, you're scalding me!"

"Shit, sorry." She turned off the faucet and poked the shirt down into the water.

The shower shut off. Woodman stuck one hand out from behind the curtain. "Would you please hand me a towel?"

Red grabbed one from the hook on the back of the door and stuck it in his hand. "Look, I know you're worried about this. But I know what I'm doing."

More silence from the shower.

"And I get that you're mad. I would be too." Red put the lid down on the toilet and sat. "But please, can you just try to understand how this is for me? There's this guy out there. He's been watching me, saving me." She looked at her hands. "Why? Why me? I'm nobody."

Woodman pushed back the curtain. "Red—"

"No, let me finish." She looked at him. His swollen but unbroken nose made her chest hurt. He had the towel wrapped around his waist, and water glistened on the bare skin of his chest. But for once, she didn't want him to jump her bones. She wanted him to hold her and tell her everything would be all right. "My life sucks, we both know that. But someone thinks it's worth killing for. I've got to know who that is. I've got to know why."

"Oh, babe." Woodman stepped out of the shower and took her in his arms. Her face pressed against his shoulder. He smelled like soap.

"It's going to be okay, Red. It's going to be okay," he whispered, stroking her hair. I'm a dirty space weevil with a defective cat and busted-up ship. I've got no family except for Granny. I've got no friends. My job is to be a petty criminal, and I'm not even very good at it. Half the time I don't even have the credits to buy enough booze to forget how much I suck at life.

"I'm sorry," she mumbled, trying to hold back tears.

"Don't be," he said. "You act a tough game, Red Darkling. You always have. And you've fooled a lot of people with that game." He pulled back a bit, put a hand under her chin, and met her eyes. "But you can't fool me. I've seen you naked." He grinned. "And I don't mean that fine body you've got."

Red sniffled. "Don't make me punch you again."

"Hey, I'm trying here, but your shirt is all wet now and I'm only human." His grin faded and he took her hands in his. "Red, I want you to know something. I . . . you mean a lot to me, and . . . well, if anything happened to you . . ."

"What are you trying to say?"

"I want to come with you. To meet the guy. If you still want me to."

"You don't have to. I'll be fine."

"Oh, I know you will," he said. "But I'd rather die in a blaster fight next to you than have to face Granny if this thing goes south."

A small laugh escaped Red. "I don't blame you. Her knitting needles are really sharp."

Woodman clapped his hands together. "All right! Let's get this baby turned around and on course to Glor."

"Yeah, um, about that? Funny thing." Red turned to busy herself with his shirt in the sink. "There wasn't enough time to take you back to Magross and still make it to Glor by Thursday."

"What! You weren't going to take me home?"

Red went up on her toes and kissed the tip of his bruised nose. "You forgot that I've seen you naked, too. And I don't mean that ridiculous ass of yours." She pulled the towel off his hips and grabbed one cheek with a smack.

Woodman pulled off Red's wet shirt. "How long before we get to Glor?"

"About thirty hours," she said, biting his earlobe. "However shall we pass the time?"

He answered by lifting her onto the counter, sending clutter crashing to the floor, and burying his face in her neck.

CHAPTER 26

By Thursday, Woodman had returned to his normal grumheaded self. It was a relief, really. Red knew how to deal with the old macho-asshole Woodman, but the new you-mean-a-lot-to-me Woodman threw her off balance. It might be fun to be off balance once in a while, but being hours away from a potentially deadly encounter was clearly not one of those times. Red was glad to fall back into the familiar rhythms.

Like now, for example.

"This? Really?" Woodman dangled Red's tattered old swimsuit on his finger, his nose wrinkled. "I've seen Fardic nuns with sexier swimsuits than this."

"Dude, this isn't a pleasure cruise." Red tried to snatch it out of his hand, but he yanked it away.

"Not with a rag like this, it's not. Remind me to buy you a proper suit. Preferably one without dugger mites."

Oh, for Gravnar's sake. "Save it for your Orgullan chicks. We've got to get kitted out, it's only half an hour until we get to Glor."

Woodman shrugged, but tossed the suit aside and followed Red to the main storage compartment. She pushed Bonk off the large strongbox where she kept her weapons. The cat blinked its mismatched eyes and emitted a burst of squealing static.

"Oh, shut up. Why don't you go do something about the weevils in the kitchen?"

The cat stalked out of the compartment, only to bump into Woodman's legs. He gave it an absentminded shove with one foot and opened his bag of goodies. Most of his personal arsenal bulged from the bag. He took his time distributing the blasters, mini faze cannons, dibromide grenades, and plasma rods into various pockets and holsters. Red had much of the same in her strongbox, plus a handful of spring-loaded caltrops. A girl never knew when she'd have to slow a pursuit.

"Okay, you ready?" she asked, slipping a holoknife into her boot.

"Ready as I'll ever be, darlin," Woodman replied. He adjusted his grumskin jacket to cover the blaster strapped to his side. "How do I look?"

Red gave him a critical once-over. "No grenades hanging out, if that's what you mean."

"I thought you liked my grenades hanging out," he smirked.

Red glared at him. From the cockpit, she heard the nav beep their arrival over Glor. "Well," she said, slamming the strongbox shut. "Time to get this party started."

The planet of Glor spread out below the *Pit*. Red had seen pictures, of course, but pictures left her completely unprepared for the real thing. Much of the planet was heavily forested, which wasn't unusual as far as planets go. But unlike every other known planet, Glor's oceans were pink. The color was deep and rich at the equator, like a quusberry, and faded to a powdery pale pink at the poles. Red had done a school report on Glor's waters back in third year. It seemed like a hundred years ago and she didn't remember much, just that some kind of peculiar combination of rare salts and bacterial life caused the color.

Whatever it was, it was weirdly beautiful and Glor didn't hesitate to exploit it. Tourism was the main industry in most of the planet's nations, though the wealth was concentrated in a thin strip along the coasts. The vast majority of the population was landlocked and impoverished.

Red double-checked the coordinates of the Lhaorn Market as the *Pit* began its descent through the atmosphere. "So, this market is enormous," she said, pulling up a map on the display. She pointed to a blip in the middle of a plaza that covered a square mile. "That's Vladmir. I say we land . . . here." She put her finger on a landing deck wedged into the jumble of walkways just north of the plaza. "What do you think?"

Woodman leaned forward and frowned. "What's in this plaza besides the statue? Any photos?"

"Probably." Red tapped a few keys and pulled up a digital tourist brochure. "Here, this looks like it." She selected one of the pictures and it filled the display. It was an aerial shot, showing crowds of people shopping at the hundreds of temporary booths, tables, and food carts that filled the plaza. The hundred and fifty foot bronze statue of Vladmir IV astride a snarling clomis loomed over it all from a pedestal in the center.

"Lots of cover, good and bad," Woodman muttered under his breath. "Crowds, witnesses, good. Exit strategy a problem, awful lot of distance back to the ship."

"Yeah, but it's all tourists," Red said. "Easier to blend in if we have to. We don't exactly look like native Glorreen. Unless you have a bunch of green makeup I don't know about."

"Not with me, no," he said absently. He pointed at the base of the statue. "There's no vendors around the base, not for a good thirty yards or so. We'll be exposed." He sat back. "Well, nothing for it but to do it. How close are we?"

Red flipped the display to navigation. "We're coming in right over the market, so just a few minutes."

As they watched through the viewport, the ship broke below the clouds and the Lhaorn Market appeared.

"Holy shit, Red, you weren't kidding. This thing is huge!"

It was. From their height, they could just make out the edges of the market on the horizon. The western side bordered the pink ocean. Vladmir's plaza was somewhere in that direction, just one of dozens of similar squares—many much larger—scattered throughout the market.

"Kinda makes the market back home look like a vidbooth," Red said. She took over manual control and followed the nav's prompts toward their destination.

"Any way we can take this map with us? Not real excited about getting lost in that."

Red flew with one hand and fished in her pants pocket with the other. She pulled out a small tube-shaped device and tossed it to Woodman. "Plug this into the output port. No no, *that* one." Woodman grunted as the device clicked into place. "It's a holographic data display. You should be able to figure out how to get the map on there. I gotta watch out for—SHIT!"

Red swerved to avoid crashing into a ship that had suddenly appeared in the viewport. Grum-biting tourists. They never knew how to fly properly, always cutting randomly in and out of altitude and making last-minute turns. Red's flying was more than adequate, but tourists always made her clutch the controls a little tighter.

Ships crowded together on the landing deck. Red squeezed into a spot that would have been tight for a smaller ship. Luckily, the *Pit* was so battered that any dents or dings from her neighbors could only improve its appearance.

As the engines powered down and the ship settled onto its belly, Red closed her eyes and took a few deep breaths. When she opened them, Woodman was pocketing the data card.

"You ready?" he asked.

"Guess so. You?"

"Always. Remember: we do this right—"

"Careful, smart." Red smiled. "I'm really glad you're here."

"Me too. Let's go."

They exited the ship, locked the hatch, and made their way down to street level. Immediately, the sights, sounds, and smells of market swallowed them up. People of all sorts—more species than Red could identify—jostled to browse merchandise filling the shop windows or make purchases from vendors shouting from their doorways. Shops several stories tall loomed on either side of the road. Suspended sidewalks connected their upper floors, obscuring what little sky was visible between the rooftops. The street was primarily pedestrian, though hired autorickshaws still buzzed through at ridiculous speed. The whole scene was cramped, dark, hot, and busy.

A huge C'longi bumped into Red, its fleshy tentacles knocking her into group of Blixic hippies passing out leaflets. As she stepped back, apologizing, she felt an autorickshaw fly past just inches from her. She spun around, disoriented. She almost cried in relief when she saw Woodman a few yards away, ogling a display of Orgullan novelties. She pushed through the crowd and grabbed his hand. He looked down, surprised, and raised an eyebrow.

"Why, Red, I had no idea!"

"Don't get excited. I just don't want to get separated."

"Uh huh."

"Look, do something useful and pull up that map. I'm all turned around."

Woodman pulled out the data display device. He fumbled with the keypad until the hologram flickered to life above the device.

"Okay, it looks like . . ." He squinted at the map, twisting the device and cocking his head. Then he looked up at the street around them and nodded to the left. "We go this way."

"I'll take your word for it," Red said as they picked their way through the throngs of people.

While Woodman navigated, Red kept an eye out for trouble. No one followed their every turn, no shadowy figures peered at them from alleyways, no blaster scopes reflected the sun from the roofs. Red was suspicious of how unsuspicious it was. She shook her head. There's careful, and then there's paranoid.

Finally, Woodman made a turn and the sky opened up before them. Red shaded her eyes against the sudden glare and examined the plaza. From the ground, its size was lost in a sea of booths and tables. Many had set up umbrellas or draped sheets over posts, to shade the vendors from the sun. Ahead of them, Vladmir IV's bronze head and shoulders glinted above the chaos.

Red squeezed Woodman's hand before dropping it. She discreetly loosened the clasp on her hip holster. He snapped off the map and returned the data card to his pocket, and they headed toward the statue.

It was a longer walk than Red expected. The sun was hot overhead, and she wished she had a few credits for a bottle of Breme soda or an ice pop from the food carts they passed.

She wiped a trickle of sweat off her forehead. "Are we there yet?"

"Heh. Cute." He glanced at her. "I take that back. You know, you're ugly when you're sweaty."

"At least I don't smell like a grum with a hygiene problem."

"I don't smell—"

"Shut up, look." Red pointed at the ground in front of them.

Sunk into the pavement was a glowing red line that went in either direction, encircling the empty space that surrounded Vladmir's statue. A small plaque next to the line read NO VENDORS PAST THIS LINE: ORD 4018F. VIOLATORS WILL BE SUBJECT TO EXPULSION AND FINES UP TO Č50,000. A few dozen people milled about taking pictures, but there wasn't a single booth, cart, or stand. The openness was refreshing.

"I wondered about that," Woodman said. "Any idea who or what we're looking for, here?"

Red shook her head. She scanned the scene for anything that looked out of place, but again, saw nothing suspicious.

Woodman shrugged. "Well, I assume they'll find *us*. Where should we wait?"

"Let's get into some shade. I'm dying."

The only shade was in Vladmir's shadow. Red sank down onto the pavement and fanned herself with one hand while searching her pockets for a cigar with the other. No luck. So much for being prepared.

"You got a smoke?"

Woodman ignored her. He was trying, and failing, to look like he was engrossed in sign describing Vladmir's military victories. His eyes flitted around the plaza, and he kept shifting his weight from foot to foot.

"You gotta take a piss? I think we passed a Port-O-Go back there."

His jaw tightened but he said nothing.

Red sighed. "You look ridiculous. Just—"

"Ms. Darkling? Mr. Woodman?"

CHapter 27

Red jumped to her feet and Woodman spun around. A short, fat, balding man stepped out of an autorickshaw. He wore a flowered shirt, swim trunks, and sandals, and had a camera around his neck. He looked like a hundred other tourists they had passed in the market. *This* was the guy? It couldn't be the guy. He was so . . . dorky.

"You *are* Red Darkling and Mark Woodman, right?" the man asked, timidly.

Red nodded.

"Oh, thank the Fourteen," the man gushed, flapping his hands. "I was starting to think you'd gotten lost. Or that *I'd* gotten lost. Oh my, that would have been a problem, wouldn't it?" He smiled broadly at them.

If this was the mastermind behind the Guild incident and the Exley fiasco, Red would eat her own head.

"You know who we are," Woodman growled. "So who are you?"

"Me?" the man squeaked. "I'm nobody. Just Charlie, at your service, here to pick you up." He gestured at the autorickshaw. "It's already programmed to take you where you need to go. Though I do recommend you take care of any, um, personal needs first. You'll be travelling a while and it can be somewhat bumpy. Oh! I hope neither one of you is prone to motion sickness."

"Wait, back up. Go? We're not going anywhere." Woodman dropped his hand heavily on Charlie's shoulder. "We're here to meet someone. If you're not that someone, then we'll just keep waiting." He grinned, showing lots of teeth. "You can wait with us."

Charlie's eyes got round and his mouth fell open. He was clearly terrified of Woodman, and Woodman wasn't even being particularly terrifying. "Mr. Woodman—may I call you Mark? Oh. Well. Mr. Woodman, you must understand that I was asked—told—to come here and meet you. I'm just the pick-up guy, you know. Just the pick-up guy."

"Who told you to pick us up?" Red demanded.

His jumped a little and his eyes flicked over to her. "My employer, Ms. Darkling. He's waiting for you at his beach villa."

Woodman let go of Charlie and leaned over to whisper in Red's ear. "We're supposed to get in that thing and go off to who knows where? On the say-so of that guy?" He jerked a thumb at Charlie, who blinked and started sweating more, if that were possible.

"Well, I mean . . ."

Woodman shook his head. "Red, you can't possibly think this is a good idea."

Red looked at Charlie. He pulled a paisley handkerchief out of his pocket and was mopping his balding head and face. "You say he's at the beach?"

"Oh, yes, yes indeed. By the ocean. The beach villa. It's very pretty. Pink, you know. The ocean. Not the villa. The villa's brown, mostly. You know, wooden. But also pretty."

She looked at Woodman and shrugged. "I want to see the ocean." She pushed past him and climbed into the autorickshaw.

Charlie clapped his hands together like a kid whose parents were taking him to Thraxian Park for vacation. "Oh, Ms. Darkling, you will absolutely love the ocean. Brought my wife here on our honeymoon, rest her soul."

Red settled into her seat and patted the one next to her. "Are you coming, Woodman?"

Woodman shot her a look that could kill a clomis at fifty paces, but he climbed into the autorickshaw anyway.

"What about you, Charlie?" she asked. "There's not much room, but I'm sure Woodman can shove over for you." This earned her another death glare.

"Oh, my, no, I'm not coming with you. I have other business to attend to, ha ha. You two go on, and enjoy yourselves. It's much cooler at the beach. Breezes, you know." He reached into the autorickshaw past a glowering Woodman, pressed a button, and the vehicle took off across the plaza.

"Toodles!" he shouted after them, waving his handkerchief.

Within seconds the autorickshaw plowed its way into the vendor zone. It moved through the crowds faster than Red thought possible, dodging between shoppers and around tables without hitting a single one. It made for a bone-shaking, teeth-clattering ride. Red had to hang on to the edge of the seat to keep from being thrown out.

The autorickshaw took them west out of Vladmir's plaza. Red thought about asking Woodman to pull up the map so she could follow their journey, but one look at his face and she decided the autorickshaw knew where it was going and that was enough for her. They left the paved plaza and entered the narrow streets. Uneven cobblestones made for a bone-rattling ride. Red bit her tongue several times before she learned to keep her jaw clenched tight.

Woodman's grim expression never changed.

Eventually the crowd thinned, the streets widened, and the shops appeared better kept. The cobbles gave way to smooth, glossy stones, much to the relief of Red's spine. A breeze sprung up. It smelled of salt and sand and exotic fruits—which was also a relief after what seemed like hours of alien body odor and greasy food. She stretched her back as the autorickshaw passed large storefronts glittering with plate glass and expensive wares. Red recognized every high-end retailer she knew: Barbazon Hill, Marborn and Sons, Slook's, Correth & Co., Mission, and more. Between these grand shrines to wealth, Red caught glimpses of the pink ocean crashing over rocks or rolling up on white sand.

She elbowed Woodman as the shops finally fell away completely, revealing a sweeping bay that curled into the distance. Sunlight played off the gentle waves, making the whole ocean look like it was encrusted with diamonds.

The autorickshaw followed the coastline for several miles. To the right, opposite the water, enormous houses perched on rolling hilltops to get the best view of the water. The road eventually turned away from the shore and into a tropical forest of banban trees draped with creeping ponta vines and fire orchids. Houses peeked through the greenery at larger and larger intervals until the road itself was the only sign of civilization. Red wondered if Woodman was right about this being a bad idea.

The autorickshaw finally made a left turn onto a winding gravel driveway. "I think this is it." Red nudged Woodman with her elbow.

He stretched. "I'm starved. Hope our mystery man has snacks. I really don't want to die hungry."

"They could have killed us a dozen times already," Red pointed out. "Why drag us all the way out here to do it?"

"Maybe this is where they have the torture dungeon already set up." He shrugged. "I'm still starved."

The forest ended startlingly close to the beach. Red had expected the villa to look like the monstrosities they'd passed earlier, and was surprised to see a small wooden structure with a pointed roof that looked like it was made of actual banban leaves. A canoe-type boat was tied to the rustic pier that jutted out into the water. A discreet antenna poking up from the roof was the only sign of technology from the last thousand years. Smoke rose from somewhere on the other side of the villa, and Red could smell roasting meat.

"Looks like you're in luck. They're having a barbecue," she said as the autorickshaw came to a stop. Her own stomach grumbled. "I could eat a mammoch myself."

"From the looks of this place, you might get that chance." Woodman climbed out of the vehicle and cracked his neck. "You ready?"

Red hopped to the ground and stretched her back. Her stomach complained loudly. "Ready. Should we knock?"

"Let's just go around back," Woodman said. "Hell, at this point, what difference does it really make? Besides, that barbecue is calling my name."

They made their way around the house to a stone patio that ran down to the sand. The roof sloped over the patio to block the sun but still allow breathtaking views of the ocean. A fire blazed from a pit on the beach itself, the flames licking at a large chunk of meat rotating slowly on a spit.

A thin, pale man sat in a wicker chair on the patio. He was older, with silver-streaked blonde hair. He wore casual but immaculate shirt and pants, dark sunglasses, and was smoking a cigarette. On the table next to him was a cut-glass tumbler full of some deep red liquid that looked like blood rum. He did not seem surprised to see them. He took his time stubbing out his cigarette, took a drink from his glass, and only then brushed off his hands and stood up.

"Red, Mr. Woodman, so glad you could come," he said, taking off his sunglasses and tucking them into his shirt pocket. Red recognized his cold blue eyes instantly.

"You!"

Chapter 28

Woodman's jaw dropped. "You know him?"

"He was at the Modern Mandrake. In the bar!" Red sputtered.

"I don't remember him," Woodman said. "I tend to remember a man who tries to pull my arms off."

"No no, not that time. When I got the letter. He was staring at me."

The man smiled thinly. "Yes. As I recall, you gave me the finger."

"Damn right I did," Red spat. "You should learn some manners. Didn't your mommy teach you not to stare at strange women in bars?"

A strange look flickered across his face, almost like surprise, then vanished. "You are quite right," he said apologetically. "I forgot myself. It will never happen again." He glanced toward the house and nodded slightly. A nondescript man in a cheap suit, who had been standing motionless near the doorway, disappeared inside the house.

"Please forgive my attire," he said, turning back to his guests. "I'm on vacation at the moment. I don't often mix business with pleasure, but I thought I could make an exception in your case." He studied Red a moment, his eyes sliding over her. She shivered in the warm air. "Of course," he continued, "this meeting may be more pleasure than business after all."

Woodman cleared his throat. "Look, you invited us, remember?"

"I did, indeed. I am not being a good host. May I offer you a drink?"

"No!" Red shouted, startling a flock of birds from a nearby tree. "I don't want a goddamn drink. I want to know who the hell you are, and why you've been helping me."

The thin smile returned to the man's face. "Introductions, yes. Thank you, Red, for cutting straight to the point. My name is John Smith." He extended his hand. Neither Red nor Woodman made any move to shake it, so after a moment he shrugged and withdrew it.

"John *Smith*?" Red snorted. "You can't possibly expect us to believe that."

"And why not? Please, sit." Smith gestured to some chairs, then settled back into his own. Red shot Woodman a look, and they both sat. Red tried not to get comfortable, but it was hard not to. The chair didn't look like much, but damn, it did feel good.

"If you're going to have a fake name, it should at least sound real," she said. "Like, what's wrong with, I dunno, Jason York? William Applegate? Diego della Herrera? Hell, you could get away with Ephrasia Pfeff better than John Smith."

"I have found John Smith more than suitable for my purposes," Smith said, taking a sip of his drink. "It reminds me of what the poet Etienne Krysia once wrote: 'The true test of a person is who they are when they are nobody.' Have you read Krysia? His early work has a devastating emotional depth, but I find his later pieces somewhat tainted by maudlin sentiment."

Red shook her head. "Enough with the chitchat. Who are you really? How do you know me? Are you following me? Why have you been messing around in my life? And for how long? Since the Guild thing? Before that? I want answers, dammit!" She pounded her fist on the arm of her chair.

Smith raised an eyebrow. "You have a lot of questions."

Red crossed her arms and sat back. "Are you going to bother answering any of them? Or are you just wasting everyone's time here?"

Smith chuckled. "Fair enough. But let's postpone our discussion of such weighty topics until after dinner. You both must be famished."

Red glanced at the meat dripping over the fire, and her stomach growled again.

"It's Ulatuan grum loin," he said. "Some consider this method of cooking primitive, but I think the banban wood balances the natural umami of the meat. Simplicity is often its own reward. Wouldn't you agree?"

Red didn't know what to say. Her hunger was distracting, and besides, this guy was talking in circles. Umami? What the hell was that? This was not going at all the way she had expected.

"Fine. We'll eat. But we'll talk *while* we eat. And I don't want any of that umami crap. I'm allergic."

Smith's mouth twitched at the corners. "Wonderful. I'll get the carving knife. Oh no, Mr. Woodman," he said, as Woodman's hand drifted to his holster. "You will not need any of your weapons. I assure you, I have no interest in shedding blood here at the villa. I am on vacation, after all."

He rose. "Please, you must have a drink. Help yourself." He gestured at a small bar in the corner of the patio. "The blood rum is excellent, but there is a bottle of hundred-year-old Scothian whiskey if you prefer something a little more . . . industrial." He flashed his thin smile and disappeared into the house, leaving Red and Woodman alone on the patio.

Woodman leaned over to Red. "We're going to stay for dinner? Have you gone completely insane?"

"Dude. I'm starving. You're starving. We've got at least a two hour ride back to the *Pit*. Did you pack some duoofish sandwiches? Homona tartlets, maybe? No? Neither did I."

"Red, this guy isn't going to tell us anything. We barely know his *fake* name. Which is ridiculous, by the way. You think a little conversation over grum loin is going to get him to open up?" He shook his head. "Every minute we spend here, we're in danger."

"Give me a break, Woodman."

"I know you don't see it, but it's true. We're all alone out here, babe. Who knows where we are? We could disappear and no one would never know where to even begin looking."

"You're being paranoid. I'm not saying we should have a pajama party and do each other's hair. But he's done nothing remotely threatening. Sometimes a carving knife is just a carving knife."

"I don't trust him."

"I don't trust him either, ya grumstain." Red ran her hands through her hair. "Let's just have some dinner and see what happens. Okay? Now, I'm getting some of that blood rum. That shit's hard to find. Want any?"

Woodman sighed. "One of us has to be the adult and stay sober. Might as well be me."

"Your loss." Red went to the bar and poured some of the blood rum into a tumbler. She took a sip. The flavor was metallic, coppery. For the first time, Red wondered if blood rum was more than a name. The thought didn't kill her hunger, but it did maim it a little. She emptied the glass into a pot of fire orchids and replaced it with several fingers of Scothian whiskey. Much better, smoky and creamy.

"You oughta try this Scothian stuff. I think I could get spoiled for the Finebock."

Woodman grumbled something about drinking from random bottles.

Smith returned then, carrying a large knife with a curved blade. Woodman jumped to his feet at the sight of the knife, but Smith ignored him. The man in the cheap suit trotted behind him. He pushed a large wheeled table covered in plates, flatware, and a bowl of greens.

"It's been a while since I've carved an Ulatuan grum loin," Smith said. "It is a delicate skill, you see, best kept through regular practice. I apologize if my technique is a bit rusty."

Smith pointed the knife at Woodman, who froze in place. After a moment, he smiled and spun the knife around in his hand, offering Woodman the handle.

"Mr. Woodman, perhaps you would be so kind as to hold the carving knife while George and I remove the meat from the spit."

Woodman squinted at the ornately carved handle, but did not take it.

"Oh, for Gravnar's sake, I'll hold it." Red stalked over and snatched the blade from Smith's hand. She waggled it at Woodman. "See? Now I've got his big, bad knife."

"Wonderful. Now, Mark—may I call you Mark? No? Fine. Mr. Woodman, would you please fetch the serving platter from the table? Or are you afraid I'll stab you with that, too?"

Woodman cursed under his breath and spat in the sand. But, he did grab the platter while Smith and George, the Cheap Suit Guy, donned protective gloves and lifted the spit off the dying fire.

Smith's back was turned, his hands both gripping his end of the spit. It occurred to Red this was the moment when she could end the whole charade. The knife grew heavy in her hand. One well-placed thrust and she could be free of him and whatever he was. A second thrust for George and they could leave the beach villa and never look back. Time stood still. Red tightened her grip on the handle. She could feel its carvings digging into her skin. Now, dammit, before—

Chapter 29

With one fluid motion, Smith twisted the spit and somehow the grum loin slid onto the platter. Woodman almost dropped it under the sudden weight, but managed to get the platter to the table without incident.

The moment was gone.

Smith turned to Red, taking off his protective gloves. He glanced at the knife, clenched beneath white knuckles, then met her eyes. He gave her the oddest look, almost like pride. Red flushed and thrust the knife handle in his direction. A ghost of a smile appeared on his thin lips. She took a hasty swig of her whiskey and glanced at Woodman, who was giving her his own odd look. What the hell was going on with everybody? The whiskey going to her head, maybe. She lifted a finger at Woodman and sat in the chair that George pulled out for her at the table.

"Please help yourselves to the salad while I carve," Smith said, pointing at the bowl of greens with the knife. Red dumped some on her plate. She looked expectantly at Woodman. He was still standing there with that stupid look on his face. She pointed at the chair next to hers.

"What the hell." He sat and grabbed the bowl from Red. They watched together as Smith cut portions from the roast, the blade flashing in an intricate series of swoops and swirls. He slid several thin slices onto each of their plates, then his own. He nodded at George and settled into his chair. George refilled Red's glass, then disappeared into the villa.

Red's hunger got the best of her and she attacked the food. It was like nothing she had ever tasted. The meat was rich and juicy, the greens refreshingly crisp. It was gone in minutes.

"It is truly satisfying to see one's work so much appreciated," Smith said drily as Red helped herself to a few more slices of the roast and another pile of salad.

"I don't suppose you've got any slak sauce."

Smith chuckled. "No, sadly, I do not."

"Eh, it doesn't really need it anyway." Red smothered a burp and elbowed Woodman. "You gonna eat that?" she asked, pointing at his half-eaten meal. He pushed the plate toward her, and she added his food to her own.

"So," she said to Smith, around a mouthful of greens. "Talk."

"What do you want to know?"

Red swallowed. "Let's start with how you know so much about me."

"I've been following your activities with great interest for many years," Smith said.

"What the hell does that mean?" Woodman demanded.

Smith shifted his eyes to Woodman. "It means that Red interests me."

"Why, though?" Red asked. "I'm nobody special."

"Ah," Smith said, folding his napkin and placing it on the table. "That is where you are wrong."

Red flushed again, and immediately felt disgusted with herself. This was ridiculous. "And what, exactly, is supposed to be so special about me?"

"The Fardic monks have a saying: ask not what you dread to know."

Red slammed her fork on the table. "Do you ever just answer a question?"

"That depends on the question."

"Fine. Try this one: who are you really?"

"I am a businessman."

"Uh huh," Woodman grunted. This earned him another look from Smith.

"What kind of business?" Red asked.

"I have many diverse ventures. Mostly I deal in construction, but I also dabble in retail development, pharmaceuticals, and the arts. Are you familiar with *Dreams of Godaro*?"

Red nodded. "You did that one?"

"My production company financed it. I had no direct control over the project, though I did suggest Indar for the role."

Red's jaw dropped. "You know Indar Skjov?"

"Of course. He operated a semi-grav forklift on a few of my construction projects on Sept Magossii. I suppose you could say that I discovered him. 'Pluck'd from the dust,' as Krysia might say. Perhaps you would like to meet Indar sometime?"

"Well, sure, I mean—Ow!" Woodman pinched her leg under the table. "What the hell, man?"

"You can drool over Indar Skjov later," he said through gritted teeth. "Let's stick to the subject."

"Mr. Woodman is right," Smith said smoothly. "Our time here is short, and I suspect you have not yet asked all your questions."

Red shot Woodman a dark look, then turned back to Smith. "Right. So. Why have you been helping me?"

Smith raised an eyebrow. "Are you complaining?"

"Maybe. I can take care of myself just fine."

"Is that so?"

"Yeah, that's so."

"I see." He paused long enough to light a cigarette. "Your plan for escaping the Zoldroni'i flesh merchants must have been too subtle for me to comprehend. Perhaps you would be so kind as to explain it to me. I am always eager to learn."

Red flushed again, this time with shame. "Look, I didn't ask for your help."

"You should not put yourself into a position where help is needed."

"Why do you care? Who do you think you are, my father?"

Smith tapped some ash off his cigarette and sighed. "You are right. I knew this day would come. I was a fool to think you would react any other way." His smile was sad. "I have never known anyone so fiercely independent as you, Red Darkling. It serves you well. It did with the baega you were unfortunate enough to encounter."

"Hey, how the hell do you know about that?"

Smith ignored her. "It serves you well, but if not harnessed, it may lead to your undoing."

"Yeah, well, that's my problem. Not yours."

Smith held up his hands. "That is more than fair. Perhaps, though, we can come to an arrangement."

"What kind of arrangement?"

"You're not actually going to listen to this . . . this guy, are you?" Woodman waved his hand at Smith, who simply smiled his thin smile.

Red turned to Woodman, anger burning in her eyes. "Dude, this is *my* life. You have zero say in what I do. Quit trying to protect me." She waved a hand at Smith. "You're as bad as he is."

Woodman looked like she had punched him in the gut. He pushed away from the table and stormed off toward the water. Red watched him uneasily, silhouetted against the setting sun, then quickly squashed her guilt. Dammit, Woodman. This was no time for his stupid white knight act. She'd deal with him later. Right now . . .

"You were saying something about an arrangement?"

Smith continued as if nothing had happened. "On one hand, you have made your desire to be self-reliant quite clear. On the other, I have resources at my disposal that you would be foolish to refuse. Does that seem accurate to you?"

"I suppose so," Red said, hesitantly.

"Good. Then what I propose is this." He leaned forward. "Get to know me."

Red blinked. "What?"

"Spend time with me. In exchange, I will not provide any assistance to you that you do not specifically request."

"I don't get it. What do you mean, spend time?"

"Go places with me. Meet my friends. Be my companion at ribbon-cutting ceremonies."

Ah, so that's it. Figures. "I'm not a hooker, asshole."

"You misunderstand my intentions." He looked her square in the eye. She flinched under his icy gaze, but didn't look away. "I understand that you cannot accept help from a stranger," he said. "But you might accept help from a friend. I could be that friend."

Maybe it was a trick of the light, the way the sunset reflected off the pink waves. But Red thought she saw a flicker of warmth in John Smith's eyes.

Chapter 30

A shadow fell across Smith's face. Woodman stood at the end of the table, his hands crammed in his pockets. He looked old. "Red, we should go."

"Yeah. That's a good idea." She drained the last drops of whiskey from her glass and stood up.

Smith stood as well. Whatever warmth Red saw in his face was gone. He gestured to George, who hustled over from the deepening shadows near the bar.

Smith reached into his shirt pocket and pulled out a card. He handed it to Red. "You can reach me at this number, if you decide to take me up on my offer."

"Yeah. Sure. Whatever." Red felt Woodman's eyes burning into her. She shoved the card into her pocket. "Um. Thanks for dinner and everything."

"It was a pleasure, and long overdue. Now, George will take you back to your ship. I hope—" He hesitated, then abruptly strode inside.

George motioned for them to follow, and they did. He led them around the side of the villa to a landing pad hidden behind a drapery of vines. He opened the hatch on one of the small but expensive-looking ships.

"You ever ridden in a Zed Alpha?" Red whispered to Woodman as they buckled into the plush passenger seats.

He said nothing. Didn't even look at her.

"Gee, Red, I haven't," she chirped to herself. "Yeah, me neither."

In the cockpit, George must have started the engines because the ground fell away outside the windows. Red had never heard—or, not heard, really—such quiet engines. Even when they cleared the forest canopy and accelerated through the dusk toward the Lhaorn Market, she couldn't detect any noise. Unlike the *Pit*, which threatened to deafen small children and animals even on its best days.

Red tried a few times to make conversation, but Woodman just stared out the window. He was being a real fazzer. It's not like someone died or anything. Smith had been perfectly pleasant. Hell, the guy quoted poetry half the time. In fact, the only one who had been nasty at all was Woodman himself. All that macho crap.

She thought back to their conversation in the shower on the way to Glor. He'd been so sweet, with the puppy dog eyes and that "I've seen you naked" stuff. It was all bullshit, and like an idiot she'd fallen for it. He didn't really know her at all. He still thought of her as a kid picking pockets for pizza money. She'd worked hard to leave that kid behind and she'd be damned if some asshole with a savior complex was going to get in her way now. She couldn't believe she'd actually thought she could be in love with him. He didn't love her, that was for sure. Maybe he did once, but not now.

She thanked the Fourteen that it was full dark now. It hid the stupid tears in her stupid eyes.

~ ~ ~

Red expected the market to be empty when they finally got back to the *Pit*, but it was even more crowded after dark. There was no place to land on the deck. Luckily, the Zed Alpha had the only high-end hover stability servos on the market. It floated over the *Pit* without a breath of downgust. George lowered a stepladder and Woodman climbed out without a word. As Red was about to follow, George grabbed her arm.

"Be careful," he said in a low voice.

He probably meant the stepladder.

On the ground, Red wrestled open the *Pit*'s hatch, pounding the panel to unstick the faulty mechanism. Damn piece of junk. Maybe it was time to start thinking about upgrading to a ship that had more functioning parts.

"All right, let's get out of—" She turned around but Woodman wasn't there. She raced around the front of the ship but he was nowhere in sight. Her mind immediately flew to George's cryptic comment. Did Smith—

Then she saw the back of Woodman's head disappear down the stairs toward the boisterous throngs. She cursed under her breath and took off after him. "Woodman? Woodman! Wait!"

Red fought her way through a wall of people until she was close enough to grab Woodman's sleeve. "Dude, what the hell are you doing?"

He spun around. Anger flared in his face, then just as quickly dissolved into sadness. "I'm going to find somewhere to stay for the night. Tomorrow I'll ping some people and catch a ride back to my parents' place."

"What? Don't be stupid. Come on—hey, watch it, asshole!" She shoved a punk kid who helped himself to a squeeze. "Come on, Woodman, let's get out of here."

"No, Red. You go without me."

"Look, we need to talk. I get that. I do. Let's just go back to the ship and—"

"No!" he shouted. He closed his eyes for moment, then continued in a soft voice that Red had to strain to hear over the market noise. "No. I'm sorry, Red. I can't be part of this anymore. I can't watch you—I just can't. Besides, you can take care of yourself. Right?" He turned and melted away, leaving Red standing alone in the crowd.

She made her way back to the *Pit*, numb. She and Woodman had gotten into plenty of fights before, but this was different somehow. She felt his absence in the clutter she kicked away from the cockpit door. The copilot's chair was full of no one as she slammed some coordinates into the navcomp and shot out of Glor's atmosphere. And space, well, that was the ultimate emptiness, wasn't it?

This was ridiculous. It was just Woodman. She needed to take her mind off the whole thing. Maybe take a shower, get rid of that smell. She sniffed herself, then decided that the smell was probably coming from the drifts of garbage that had accumulated in every corner and under every piece of furniture. She swept a pile of FlinkBar wrappers and cigar butts off the control panel with her arm. The bare patch looked nice. Red licked her finger and rubbed a blob of unidentifiable goo off the panel.

Four hours later, she fell asleep on the floor of the main storage compartment, a wet sponge in her hand. She dreamed about pink waves and a dark shadow.

Red woke with a stiff back and aching muscles. The sponge had dried to a crusty brick that stuck to her hand. She peeled it off, stretched, cracked her neck, and got up to make some coffee. She admired her work as she sipped. The cockpit practically sparkled. The trash had been picked up and bagged. She'd scrubbed the control panel, the navcomp, the override box, and the various screens and displays. She could see the floor.

The main room was just as clean. Bags piled up near the hatch, ready to be dropped off at the next available disintegrator facility. She'd sorted the tools, clothes, utensils, and other useful stuff into piles for later cleaning and storage. Red made a mental note to swing by Granny's to do the laundry. It would probably take a couple days, but at least it would be free and she could stock up on leftovers.

The thought of leftovers made Red's stomach request a trip to the kitchen. Compared to the rooms she'd already tackled, it looked awful. Why had she let it get so bad? Dugger mites wouldn't even live in such filth. She opened the fridge to find breakfast and realized that dugger mites had lower standards than she thought. Red made another mental note: set Bonk loose in the kitchen before attempting to clean the fridge.

Red popped open the last container of Granny's leftovers and examined the contents. Looked like a casserole, maybe darna with nintha? It wasn't Ulatan grum loin roasted over an open fire on the beach, but she wasn't in a position to be picky. A quick sniff confirmed that it had turned. Eh. Nintha never really went bad, it just lost its crunch. Red stuck the container in the micro (mental note: scrub out the micro). While it heated up, she made another cup of coffee and wiped off a fork from one of the piles.

She ate cross-legged on the floor of the main room and planned her attack. Finish the storage compartment, then move on to the kitchen. Then she could do the bathroom and take a shower. That would leave just the bunkroom and a few minor storage areas. Then she could deal with the trash and laundry and finally have a chance to . . . well, she had plenty of time to worry about that later.

Red could only choke down half the casserole. She scraped the rest into a garbage bag. Then she carefully washed the container and the fork, without realizing until it was too late that there was no clean place to put them down. Oh well. She dropped them back in the sink and figured she'd do them again later, with the rest of the dishes.

The ship was too quiet, even with the engines grinding away and the grav plate squealing at random intervals. Red decided she needed music. She tapped the panel on the bunkroom wall and the pounding guitars of Vulvato flooded the ship. Damn, Woodman must have been the last one to pick music.

Woodman . . .

Red quickly flipped to some Fog Machine. Much better. She wiped her nose on her sleeve, found the sponge, and picked up scrubbing where she'd left off the night before.

Chapter 31

Somewhere around the time she finished cleaning the kitchen, Red adjusted her course for Granny's and pinged her to let her know she was coming. Hopefully she'd recently stocked up on laundry detergent and the good brand of ice cream. After all this scrubbing and washing, Red would need both.

Physical labor, combined with constant non-Vulvato music blaring at full volume, almost managed to keep Red from thinking about both the Woodman problem and the Smith situation. They kept trying to creep into her thoughts, though. Like when she found one of Woodman's t-shirts stuffed under her bed, and the time Smith's card fell out of her pocket when she changed clothes. The t-shirt went into the laundry pile after a fifteen-minute debate with Bonk over whether she should just throw it out. The card she actually did throw out. That lasted an hour before she dug it out of the bag, shook off the grit, and taped it to the navbox. She probably would never ping the number, but you never knew when something like that could come in handy. That's what she told herself, anyway.

She finished the heavy work, but wasn't due to arrive at Granny's until the following day. Red was down to organizing and reorganizing her tools (first alphabetically, then by brand, then by size, then back to alphabetically) when Sept Magossii finally appeared through the viewport. She immediately took over manual control and piloted the *Pit* through the familiar landscape toward Granny's.

Red always felt a weird kind of nostalgia when she flew through the old neighborhood. These streets, these buildings, these people made up her childhood, but she'd called the *Pit* home for so long that the memories were always at a distance, like seeing them in a movie. This time was different. The nostalgia was still there, but there was something else too. Red couldn't quite figure out what it was. Uneasy, she tucked it into the back of her brain with the rest of the stuff she didn't want to deal with right now.

It was late fall in Magross and the flowers growing beside Granny's door had faded for the season, their dead parts neatly clipped away. Fresh mulch heaped up under the trees, and the lawn looked tired but neatly trimmed. Had the shutters been painted? Maybe just cleaned. Red never noticed before how much the whole place stood out among the other houses on the block, which were slowly sinking under peeling paint and patchy grass. For the first time, she wondered how Granny kept up with it all.

"Mildred!" she exclaimed when she opened the door. She had her purse and sweater tossed over one arm. "What rotten timing. I was just on my way out to bingo. I thought you were Hubert—that's Marge's husband. It's his turn to drive us girls."

Red gave her a gentle hug. "It's okay, Granny. I can get my laundry going while you're out. Hey, is that garbage disintegration place still over there by the market? I've been, um, cleaning."

"You don't need to go there," Granny said, waving a hand. "I have the service that comes to the house, you know. They can take it for you."

"I dunno. I mean, thanks, but I have kind of a lot."

"Nonsense! I'm sure they can handle it. Why don't you show me what you've got." She walked past Red and out to the *Pit*, which was parked at the curb.

"Granny, you don't understand—"

Granny poked her head through the hatch. "Oh. I see. Well, I suppose you'd better take this straight down to the disintegration facility in the morning. I don't think those nice young men who collect my trash will quite be able to fit this in their truck."

A double beep came from the street. "That'll be Hubert," Granny said, pulling on her sweater and patting her hair. "There's food in the fridge, dear, so help yourself. Don't forget to use fabric softener, the static has been horrible lately. I won't be back late."

"Thanks, Granny. I'll see you later. Good luck!"

Granny winked and patted her cheek. "I don't need luck, dear. I have you."

Hubert's ancient air skimmer idled at the curb behind the Pit. Granny accepted his hand to climb in beside Marge and a few other women. Hubert gave the *Pit*, then Red, a dirty look. Red waved cheerfully and mumbled a few choice words under her breath as they puttered off.

Red spent half an hour moving the mountain of dirty clothes into the house. She crammed as much in the washer as she could, dumped in a bunch of soap, and hoped the machine could handle it. It didn't immediately start smoking or rocking, which she thought was a good sign. She wandered into the kitchen and made herself a plate of odds and ends. Granny didn't have any beer or whiskey, which was disappointing, but Red did find a dusty bottle of cooking wine that hadn't yet turned to vinegar.

She dropped onto the couch with her meal and zoned out in front of the vidbox. Red watched the second half of a comedy about a female Orgullan spy who had to go undercover in a Fardic monastery. She was half asleep when the program switched to local news. Same old stuff: skirmishes over mining rights, a controversial tax referendum, new regulations on trade guilds, blah blah blah. The wine made it all seem fuzzy. Like her head. Warm and fuzzy . . .

The washing machine's harsh buzzing woke her with a snort. The news had devolved into some good, old-fashioned celebrity gossip. Red yawned and swapped out the laundry and started a new load. She went back into the living room for the dishes and froze when she saw John Smith's face plastered on the screen. Red scrambled for the remote and cranked up the sound.

"—a star-studded concert that has everyone talking. Smith, the billionaire industrialist who has the eye of single women across the galaxy, announced the event in a press conference earlier today."

The picture was replaced by a video of Smith behind a podium bristling with microphones. "Childhood hunger is simply unforgiveable," he said. "We must all do what we can to bring nourishment to those who are in the most desperate need. The FoodAngels program has made great strides in this endeavor over its two hundred years of dedicated service, but there is always more work to be done. For this reason, I have organized the Angels Among Us charitable concert event, the entire proceeds of which will benefit the FoodAngels program."

The camera switched back to the news anchor in the studio. "The lineup for next month's concert promises to be a blast from the past, featuring a dozen classic alt-rock favorites like Fog Machine, Deltonic Implosion, and the Poly Torrents. This will be the Poly Torrents' first performance since lead singer Arien Spar quit the band more than ten years ago. Sources close to Spar say the band is working on a new album. Could this mean that concertgoers will be the first to hear new music from the band?

"Music isn't the only exciting thing about this concert," the anchor continued. "Sept Magossii's own homegrown hottie, Indar Skjov, will be taking a break from filming his latest steamy flick, *Unsheathed*, to host the event. Sorry, ladies, we have no details about what Skjov plans to wear—if anything, ha ha.

"The concert will be held at the Septimal Center Arena in Septimal City. Tickets are on sale now . . ." The anchor touched his ear and frowned. "I'm sorry, I'm being told that the concert has already sold out." He gave a little smile. "John Smith, if you're watching, I sure would like a backstage pass, ha ha." He shuffled some papers. "Finally this evening, a heartwarming story about a little boy who—"

Red shut off the vidbox and sank onto the couch. All her favorite bands. The Poly freaking Torrents! Back on stage, with new music! And Indar Skjov, like a juicy sex cherry on top of the cake. It was like someone had read her mind and put all her favorite things in one place.

Maybe someone had.

That thought squashed her mood like an overripe zuranfruit. It was so obvious. He was baiting her. Pathetic, to think she wouldn't know exactly what he was doing. Well. She'd be beat ten ways to Gravnar before she'd give him the satisfaction of begging for a ticket. No way.

She picked up her dishes and took them to the kitchen, where she refilled her wine glass to the brim.

Chapter 32

Red awoke to the smell of pancakes. Staying with Granny certainly did have its perks. She rolled out of bed, scratching her head and yawning, and wondered if there was also coffee.

There was. Red poured some into a mug and kissed Granny on the cheek.

"Good morning!" Granny chirped, placing a stack of steaming golden pancakes on the table. "What are your plans for today?"

Red poured half a bottle of syrup on her pancakes. "Not much. I need to do more laundry. Take the trash over to the disintegration place. How was bingo?"

"I lost a few credits, but it was still a lovely time. Marge was the big winner. She'll be impossible to live with now." She sat down across from Red and smiled.

"Granny, I was thinking. How do you manage to keep up this place? I mean, the flowers, the lawn, all of it. I get tired just washing dishes, I can't imagine having to do all that stuff too."

"Oh, you know." Granny stirred her coffee. "It's not so bad. The flowers are no trouble, and I have a service take care of the rest."

"That's got to be expensive."

"You shouldn't talk about money, Mildred," Granny scolded. "It's *common*."

"I just—"

"And please, dear, don't talk with your mouth full."

Red swallowed a huge wad of half-chewed pancakes. "I'm sorry. It's not my business. I just want to make sure you're okay. I mean, I dunno, maybe I could help out, or—"

"Oh, don't you worry about me," Granny said, topping off Red's coffee. "Now. You finish your breakfast. I'm going to work on that laundry of yours. Heavens, I didn't know one person could own so many clothes!" She shook her head and tutted to herself as she left the kitchen.

Something was odd there. Growing up with Granny after her parents . . . well, they had lived comfortably enough. But Red had no memory of Granny ever working. Maybe she inherited a lot of money from her husband? Red had never met her grandfather—he had died when his children were young. Granny never really talked about him. Red wasn't sure what he'd done for a living, but it must have been something big to have sustained Granny for so long.

Red made a mental note to follow up on Granny's caretaking service. You know, after she did the laundry and got rid of the trash and found some work and figured out what to do about Woodman and Smith and maybe fixed Bonk and got a new bed in the *Pit* so she didn't have to sleep in a damn hole anymore. When did life become so exhausting?

Eventually she reached her limit of pancakes and stabilized her caffeine levels enough to get moving.

Since Granny was still puttering in the laundry room, Red decided to hit the disintegration facility first. She dressed, brushed her teeth, and ran her fingers through her hair before setting out.

The disintegration facility squatted in a small industrial lot on the edge of the market, just a short hop from Granny's neighborhood. The place was deserted, despite the OPEN sign blinking on the office door. Red landed the *Pit* near the drop off platform and went to find the guy in charge.

She recognized the tech immediately. "Buck! Holy shit, man, it's been what, ten years?"

Buck's wide, dopey face lit up like fireworks on Galactic Liberation Day. "Red? Is that really you?"

"Of course it's me! I thought you were still in the lockup."

Buck twisted an oily rag in his hands. "I got out about a month ago. Good behavior, I guess. Parole officer got me this job here." He gestured at the building behind him. "It's okay, for a straight job. Better than mining. I mean, look what happened to Frankie."

"Yeah, but that's Frankie, right? They should never have let a klutz like him anywhere near a laser drill. Remember that time he managed to fall out of my 'hopper?"

He chuckled. "We had some good times, didn't we? Buncha dumb kids. You still keep up with any of the old gang? Zanda? She's married now, kids and all. Schnozz?" Red shook her head. "Well, what about Woodman? I heard you guys were a thing there for a while."

"Nah." Red kicked at some stones. "I haven't seen him in a while, is all."

"Jeez, sorry Red. I didn't mean nothing. It was just something I heard, is all."

"No worries, man. Hey, I got a lot of trash here. You think we could, you know?"

Buck nodded vigorously. "Oh yeah, sure, of course." He tucked the rag into the pocket of his overalls and pulled on a pair of work gloves.

Red showed him the pile of bags that took up almost the entire main room of her ship. He whistled. "Jeez, Red, what have you been up to?"

She shrugged. "I cleaned."

"This is gonna cost ya," he said, apologetically.

"No problem, Buck. How much?"

"Three credits a bag?"

"Yikes." Red did a little mental math. "No way you can get me a discount?"

"No, I mean, I would if I could, you know I would. But I gotta stay straight now, and the boss—"

"Okay, okay, I'll help ya drag it all out."

"Cool. Put em on that platform."

Red took the job of slinging the bags out of the ship, while Buck dragged them onto the platform. It didn't make for easy conversation, but that didn't stop Buck from trying.

"D'you still like the Poly Torrents?" he puffed. "They've got a new album coming out."

Red rolled her eyes and tossed him another bag. "Yeah, they're pretty cool."

"They're going to be having a concert, too. Did you see the news? It's all sold out, though."

Red grunted.

"Boy, I bet you'd do just about anything to see that show. Right, Red?"

"Yeah, just about." She blew a strand of sweaty hair out of her face.

"I mean, you liked them all the way back when we were kids. I remember you played them all the time. Used to drive us all crazy. Especially Woodman. He hated the Poly Torrents. Remember that one time—"

Red tossed a particularly heavy bag a little harder than was strictly necessary. He stumbled back a step to avoid being knocked down. "Hey, watch it!"

"Heads up!" she chirped.

Buck rubbed his neck. "Sorry, Red. I just thought—well, never mind. How much more you got?"

"That's the last one." Red hopped down and wiped her hands on her pants.

Buck swung the final bag up onto the platform next to the rest. He flipped open the top of a metal box hung on the wall of the office.

"Okay, watch out, here goes," he said, and pressed a button. Nothing happened. "What the—oh, right, forgot the safety. Hang on." A second later there was a low hum and the trash disappeared.

"Thanks, man." Red handed him a stack of ragged credits.

"Hey, no problem." He crammed them into a pocket. "You here in town long? Maybe we could get some beers and a pizza over at

Shellchuckers. See if Schnozz and them wanna go. Think you could ping Woodman? It'll be like old times. What d'ya think?"

Red thought she'd need more than beer if she was going to spend more than a few minutes with Buck. She was already itching for a shot of something much stronger—something like Smith's fancy whiskey, though in this case she'd settle for Finebock or even Good Tymes.

"I'll let you know, okay? Look, I gotta go. Poor Granny's been doing my laundry."

"Hey, yeah, you know where to find me." He grinned. "Sure is good to see you again."

"You too, Buck." She turned toward the *Pit*.

"Don't forget to ping me about Shellchuckers."

She shot him a double thumbs-up over her shoulder and shut the hatch behind her. Damn, Buck hadn't changed at all. Still the same sweet, dopey, clueless guy. Shellchuckers? Schnozz? *Woodman*? Ugh. And if he could shut up about that stupid concert for five minutes. Red wondered if maybe this visit with Granny wasn't a huge mistake. You can't go back, and why would anyone want to?

Chapter 33

Red spent the next week sleeping, eating, and zoning out in front of the vidbox. That damned concert was everywhere: interviews with the bands on the news, constant ads for licensed merchandise and grey-market tickets, even a disappointing hour-long documentary on the Poly Torrents that was mostly old concert clips slapped together.

One afternoon, Red was slumped on the couch, drinking a Breme and watching a tabloid report on John Smith. Granny wandered in on her way to the kitchen and stopped to watch. The host speculated that Smith had amassed his fortune as the head of a massive criminal empire that seemed included everything from drugs and gambling to blackmailing politicians and buying elections.

"Can you believe this shit, Granny?" Red pointed at the screen.

Granny swatted her. "Watch your language, Mildred."

"Sorry. It just bugs me. The guy tries to do something nice, and they make him look shi—I mean, they make him look bad."

Granny's frowned, her brow wrinkling even more than usual. "A man who makes such a show of his charity must have quite a guilty conscience."

"What? You don't believe he's really a gangster, do you?"

Granny sighed. "Mildred, dear, no one is ever quite what they seem."

"So you *do* think he's a gangster?"

"I leave the gossip to Marge Blattz and the rest of them." Granny sat down next to Red. "Now, I wanted to talk to you, dear. You've been moping around the house for days now. You need to get out and do something. Go to the market, visit your friends. That Buck fellow has pinged you several times." Red rolled her eyes. "Well, what about Mark? I ran into his mother at the post office this morning. She says he's in town for a few days."

"Um, Woodman and I aren't exactly, well, we kind of had a fight."

"Oh, Mildred! What happened?"

Red didn't take her eyes off the vidbox. "It's a long story."

"That's such a shame, dear." Granny patted her arm. "He's such a nice young man. Is there no way you can make it up with him?"

Red shook her head.

"You two have been friends for so long. It would be a shame to let something come between you." Granny stared off into the distance. "You know, when I was a girl, I had a friend named Sally. She and I did everything together. She was the one who taught me to knit. Then, when we got older, we met a boy . . ."

Granny looked back at Red and smiled. "I don't even remember his name, isn't that silly? But Sally and I never spoke again. To this day, I regret losing her friendship. She was worth a thousand of him, whoever he was."

"Why don't you look her up?"

Granny shrugged. "She died of a heart attack about, oh, it must be forty years ago now. No one expected it because she was so young. You just never know. That's why it's so very important to grab the chances life throws our way. Grab them tight and never let go." She patted Red's arm again. "Why don't you go take a shower, dear, while I make lunch."

"Yeah, okay, I will." Red paused, then flipped off the vidbox and stood up, stretching. "I'm gonna go out to the *Pit* and ping a few people first, though."

"Oh, that's fine." Red helped Granny up from the couch. "Thank you, dear," she said, smiling. "Now go make your calls while I make some sandwiches."

Red hadn't been in the *Pit* since her trip to the disintegration facility. It was longest she'd been away from the ship since she'd gotten it years before. She almost didn't recognize the place. The air inside was slightly stale, and the lack of clutter made the place seem cold and empty. It made her feel sad.

She shook it off and headed for the cockpit. Bonk, sitting in the copilot's chair, blinked at her lazily. "You look bored," she said, sinking into her own chair. She fished a pack of Crolinian cigars out from under the control panel. "Don't tell Granny," she warned the cat. Granny didn't approve of smoking, so Red had to sneak one in whenever she could. And her extended stay on the couch meant she hadn't had a smoke in over a week. No wonder she felt so off-kilter.

She lit a cigar and pulled up Buck's number. Might as well get it over with. She could go for a pizza, and besides, it's not like she had anyone else pinging her to hang out. She messaged him that she'd be around town at least through the weekend and maybe they could meet up at Shellchuckers on Friday. Red conveniently forgot to tell him that Woodman was in town. No need to open *that* fazzer cage.

She smoked quietly, staring at nothing in particular. When the cigar got down to a nub, she gave Bonk a pat and headed back into the house for lunch.

~ ~ ~

Red had a few days to kill, and the impending meetup at Shellchuckers infected her with a severe case of nostalgia. She started taking long walks through Magross. She wandered around the neighborhoods, stopped in at the old hangouts, poked around the markets she used to haunt with the gang. It was a mistake. Half the places were gone, torn down to make room for new housing developments or simply closed, their broken windows like rotten teeth. Everything that was left looked like a drab, dirty version of itself. A raw, grey streak of weather didn't help; it somehow made the peeling paint, weedy lots, rusted ships, and trash-clogged gutters more vivid.

Late one afternoon, Red made her way to the crumbling aqueduct. She and Woodman used to come here to get away from the rest of them. One time Red found a battered blaster and they spent an entire day daring each other to try shooting it. Another, a cave mouse the size of a fazzer bit Woodman on the thumb. It swelled up twice its normal size, and Red had to pop the blister with a Poly Torrents pin. Mostly, though, they'd putter around the rubble, kicking stones and swapping insults and talking about how awesome it would be when they were old enough to get off that dumb planet.

Unlike everything else, the aqueduct hadn't changed much. The same grimy light fell on the same graffiti-splattered concrete walls. The place still attracted the same kind of people, too—kids looking for, or hiding from, trouble. Red's visit startled a few who had been lurking in a mess of sickly trees that were struggling to grow through the cracked asphalt. One of them, a girl maybe ten years old, pulled a holoknife out of her pocket and sneered in a way that was probably supposed to be threatening. Red pulled back her jacket to reveal the blaster strapped to her hip, and the girl and her companions slunk away. Red smiled grimly.

The girl would have something to brag about over pizza later, in the safety of a crowded restaurant, saying there was no way she was afraid of the gnar-biter with the blaster.

The graffiti had grown over the years, as new generations of young miscreants added their own brand of artistic delinquency. Red crouched down among the beer cans and cigarette butts, looking for the mark she had left when she was thirteen. The sun had nearly set by the time she found it: RED, caked in dirt and half obscured by a skull done in fresher paint. Her fingers traced the letters and a wave of memories washed over her.

It was a hot, sticky summer day. She had been tossing rotten zuranfruit at passing 'hoppers with Buck, Zanda, Frankie, and, of course, Woodman. One angry man called the police, and the group scattered. As usual, she and Woodman found each other here. Here, among the trash and the weeds, adrenaline coursing through their bodies, invigorated by their escape, sweaty and breathless, he kissed her. A thrill of something beyond adrenaline hit her hard and seemed to last forever. It was her first, and his. Later, the kiss an unspoken thing between them, she'd written her name, and Woodman . . . he had drawn . . .

Red scraped at a patch of moss that grew on the wall near her name, revealing a crooked heart. The MD+MW had faded almost completely away.

Chapter 34

The night of the reunion, Red took a long shower. She trimmed, plucked, polished, waxed, exfoliated—in short, all the girly things she rarely bothered with. She would have put on makeup, but all she had was some mummified mascara and a dried-out lipstick she'd found in the back of a drawer, behind the socks. What was the point, anyway? This was Shellchuckers, not the Mandrake Room. Who was she trying to impress? Buck? Ha, no. She compensated for the embarrassingly extreme hygiene by throwing on a t-shirt with the holes in the elbows and pants that looked like a baby weevil had used them for teething.

On her way out, she kissed Granny goodbye. "I won't be back late."

"Have fun," Granny said, "but don't get into any trouble."

"I'll try not to," Red replied, and she actually meant it.

Shellchuckers was busy, even for a Friday night. Sometime in the last twentyish years, it had overhauled its image from a seedy dive to a respectable restaurant offering kids meals and half-price ice cream sundaes on Tuesdays before five. Red pushed her way through a crowd of families, scanning the room for a familiar face, wondering if they even served beer anymore. With mounting panic she realized she should have stopped someplace else first, to get herself suitably buzzed to deal with this ridiculous reunion, which was looking like a worse idea all the time.

She was halfway out the door to find a real bar with real liquor when she felt a tap on her shoulder. The huge smile plastered across Buck's face made her cringe. She was stuck. "Hey, Red! I was starting to think you'd flaked out on us."

"Nah," she said. "I was looking for you, but the place is packed."

"I got us a table in the back. Just wait until you see who all is here."

Uh oh. What the hell did that mean? "Great, Buck. Hey, they do still have beer here, right?"

"Oh yeah, Red, they do. We've already got a couple pitchers of Ol Wo'hall'a going. Come on!" He grabbed her arm and dragged her through the restaurant.

They dodged tables and waitresses with trays piled high with food. In one corner, a TuneBot blasted out a fifty-year-old bubblegum-pop hit by Kiwi Club; in another, a hologrammatic snowturtle danced along.

Red groaned. Crappy beer, obnoxious pop music, screaming kids, *and* a nightmare-fuel mascot? This was hell. One hundred percent, grade A, nine-star hell. Nothing short of actual death could be worse than this, and even then, Red wasn't willing to put money on it.

They got to the table at last. "Red, look!" Buck pointed. "It's Zanda! That's her husband Brad, and their kids."

"Oh my god, Red! It's been—no no, Ritchie, don't do that with the crayon, honey." Red remembered Zanda as a wiry, tough-talking girl who was good with a sonic wrench. Now, buried under fifty extra pounds of doughy weight, that girl spit on her napkin to scrub away food that crusted around her son's mouth. Her husband was pale and thin, like bad yogurt. Both boys struggled against the straps of their high chairs. The bigger one seemed to be trying to put things in the smaller one's nose.

"Hey, Zanda. Been a long time." Red forced a smile. "You still working on old ships?"

"Oh, god no. I haven't even looked at an engine since before the kids were born. I think the last time I—Ritchie, stop it! Honestly." She rolled her eyes at Red. "Kids, am I right?"

"And look, Red." Buck tugged on her sleeve. "It's Schnozz!"

"I prefer Scott, actually." Unlike Zanda, Schnozz hadn't changed a bit. He still had the giant hook nose that he always swore he'd get fixed when he got his first real job. Maybe he never got a job? He stood up to shake her hand, and she saw the gold holowatch on his wrist. Yeah, he was doing just fine in the money department. Red ran a hand over her holey sleeves. Why the hell did she have to wear the shirt with the holes? Jeez.

"Dude, nice to see you again. What are you up to lately?"

"Not much. I'm a banker now. Well, bank manager. I oversee mortgage applications. My wife, Cara, sends her regrets. She's preparing for a big case that's going before the judge in the morning. What about you? What's your line of work?"

Red grimaced. "Uh, you know. This and that. Hey, pass me that pitcher, would ya? Did you guys order? I'm starved." She squeezed into the only available chair and reached for a glass.

"Okay, we're just waiting for . . ." Buck said, craning his neck to look around the room. "Where did he go, the bathroom? Oh! There he is." He waved at someone Red couldn't see.

Red leaned over to Schnozz. "Hey, Schnozz, who's he talking about?"

"Scott. It's Scott."

"Yeah, Scott. Sorry."

"That's all right. Anyway, I think he means Mark."

Great. Hell just got even hellier. Time to go. "Hey, you know, I'm such an asshole. I just remembered that I'd promised Granny I'd pick her up some, ah, milk. I gotta go." She stood up just to come face to face with Woodman.

"Surprise!" Buck grinned so wide Red thought his head would split. "Are you guys surprised? I wanted it to be a surprise cuz Red said you hadn't seen each other in a while and, well, here we all are!"

Woodman was so close Red could smell his cologne. Nakari. He always wore Nakari. "Hey," she said, weakly.

He ignored her completely and sat next to Schnozz. Buck's face scrunched up in confusion.

"Guys, come on! What's the matter? I thought this would be fun. You know, old times and everything. Red, we can get nintha on the pizza."

"Oh, my Charlie can't have nintha," Zanda piped up from the other end of the table. "He's allergic. Breaks out in hives something awful."

Red stared at the snot-crusted kids. Schnozz—no, *Scott*—adjusted his glasses, the holowatch glittering. The TuneBot launched into another bouncy pop song, lights flashing in time with the beat, rhythm pounding into her brain. Woodman just sat there, staring at the table, like she didn't even exist. Something thick and hot rose up in Red's chest, a nauseating mixture of anger and disgust and . . . was that jealousy? What the hell?

It was too much.

"For Gravnar's sake, Zanda, no one cares about your kid's goddamn allergies!" Red roared. Zanda's mouth dropped open and the smaller boy started to cry. Mr. Yogurt sputtered, a startled look on his bland face.

"Red, please," Buck pleaded. "Stop, you're—"

"And you!" She spun around and stuck her finger in his face. "What the hell did you think you were doing here? Screwed shit up, just like always. No one actually likes you. You know that, right? You're a loser. We were all losers, miserable losers. I mean, just look at Schnozz."

Schnozz cleared his throat. "Well, now, Red, that's hardly—and I've told you, it's Scott."

"Oh, I get it." Red flung up her hands. She was making a scene, but she didn't care. "You're some hot banker man now, huh? Ha! You always *were* Schnozz, and you'll always *be* Schnozz."

She turned to Woodman. His face was brick red, but he stubbornly refused to look up. "I have just one thing to say to you—"

She didn't get to finish, which was probably for the best. A hand fell on her shoulder. "What did I tell you would happen if I saw you again?" a familiar voice growled.

Dammit, Buck. Of all the places he could pick, he picked a Chuck place.

She pushed Chuck's hand away. "Hey, man, I was just leaving anyway."

Chuck crossed his flabby arms. "You're lucky this is a family establishment. Get. Out."

"Fine! This place is a dump anyway. Just like the rest of this freaking town." Red knocked over a chair and stormed out of the restaurant.

Cold night air stung her flushed face. She hunched her shoulders against the bitter rain and hurried out to the *Pit*. She slammed the engines into gear and blasted out of the parking area, leaving scorch marks on the pavement and setting off a couple security alarms.

Dammit, Buck. Only an idiot like him could create such a disaster. Those gnar-biters could pretend all they wanted that they were somehow better now, better than her. Fat-ass Zanda and her bratty crotchfruit. Schnozz—I prefer *Scott* actually—flashing his thousand-credit watch around and oh, his lawyer wife with her big case tomorrow. But Red remembered when they were pimple-faced kids with juvie rap sheets a mile long. She remembered when they jacked ships and raised hell and actually *lived*. They were real people back then. Now?

Screw it. She didn't need any of them.

She blasted away from central Magross and headed for the sprawling industrial zone. As the city gave way to warehouses and loading docks, Red's anger burned itself out and turned to bitter frustration. Zanda and Schnozz, they had moved on, left their shitty lives behind. They didn't wake up in yesterday's clothes, smelling like stale beer. They didn't have to pick weevils out of their coffee, or worry about finding a gig that paid a couple hundred credits so they could make it to the next gig.

The jealousy she'd felt at the restaurant haunted her. Was that what she wanted? Tied down with kids, married to a yogurt? No thank you. Same for pushing papers around every day, like Schnozz did. None of that was part of the plans she'd made back at the aqueduct with Woodman. She'd wanted freedom, adventure. She'd wanted everything she had as a kid, only more.

Buck, though. *He* hadn't changed. *He* hadn't moved on. He was still the same guy he was back in the day. He'd never even left Sept Magossii, as far as Red knew.

Yeah. And Buck was the one who ended up serving time and was lucky to have a job zapping trash all day.

So that was it? Those were her choices? She could move on, start pumping out kids or pushing papers ten hours a day. Or, she could stay the same and end up grateful for the chance to zap other people's garbage. Hell no. There was no way in the seven hells she'd let herself end up like any of them.

Her eyes flicked over to the business card taped to the navbox. She knew what she had to do. It had been staring her in the face for weeks.

CHaptER 35

Red landed on a random access road near the docks. She lit a cigar and took a long, steady drag to calm down. She pulled Smith's card off the navbox and entered his number, fast, before she thought too much and changed her mind.

Business hours ended hours earlier, so the immediate pingback took her by surprise. An older woman in a business suit appeared on the vidscreen. "SmithCo executive office. How can I help you?"

Red sat up. "Yeah, lemme talk to John Smith."

"Mr. Smith is not taking calls at the moment. I'm Claudia, his personal assistant. Would you care to leave a message?"

"Nah, I'll talk to him now."

Claudia frowned. "I'm sorry, but as I said, he's not taking calls now."

"He'll take my call." Red blew smoke at the screen.

"Miss, I'm very busy. Do you have a message for Mr. Smith?"

"Tell him Red is on the line. I'll wait."

"Red . . ."

"Darkling? Red Darkling? Pretty sure he's expecting me."

"Oh!" She blinked. "Yes, Ms. Darkling, I'll put you through."

Red took a long drag on her cigar as the call went to a hold screen with a corporate logo. Maybe this was another bad idea. Not too late to disconnect—

The logo disappeared and there was Smith, wearing a tuxedo in a room that definitely more bedroom than office. "Red! What a pleasant surprise." He raised his chin to adjust his bow tie. "In the future, I expect you to speak to Claudia with more respect."

"Eh, sorry about that." Red stuck her cigar between her teeth.

"So what can I do for you?"

"I think you know."

He raised an eyebrow. Red raised one back.

"This charade does not become us, Red. Shall I assume this is about the upcoming FoodAngels concert?"

"Yeah. What's your game?"

"Game?" Smith tugged the sleeves of his jacket. "I often host charitable events. I believe it was the philosopher Exaius who described philanthropy as the only sane pursuit in an insane world. Why do you ask?"

Red narrowed her eyes. "I'm not an idiot, Smith. I know that concert is for me, like some kind of bait."

"My my, that does take a special kind of narcissism. Do you truly believe that feeding children is all about you?"

"Don't give me that crap. As you said, this charade does not become us."

"Indeed. In the interest of establishing a bond of trust between us, and for the sake of brevity, I will confess to arranging this particular event with your tastes in mind."

"I knew it. And you figured I'd be down on my knees like an Orgullan whore, begging for tickets."

"That was what I had hoped, though perhaps not in such graphic terms."

Red hesitated, playing with the cigar. "I've been thinking. About life. It's short."

"An astute observation."

"Shut up. I figure, I'd be pretty stupid to let this slide by just because of you."

"I would agree, but you would only tell me to shut up again."

"An astute observation. Look." She leaned forward onto the control panel. "If I do this, it doesn't mean anything. It's not a promise, it's not a payment, and it's *not* a date. Got it?"

He nodded. A smirk flashed across his face, subtle and quick, and was gone before Red could be sure she'd seen it.

"So. Pretty please. Can I have tickets?"

"That is all you ever had to say. I have a VIP box reserved for my personal use. Would you mind if a few of my close friends joined us?"

Red wondered what type of person John Smith would call a close friend. "Hey, it's your party."

"Wonderful. I will make the arrangements. Now, if you will please excuse me, I do have to go. The opera waits for no man, not even me."

"Sure, yeah, whatever." Red reached for the disconnect button, then hesitated. "Hey, Smith?"

"Yes?"

"Thanks." She hit the button and the screen went blank.

Red put her feet up on the control panel and smoked, watching the ships over the lake through the viewport. She didn't head back to Granny's until dawn.

~ ~ ~

She awoke when Granny opened the curtains. The rain had ended, leaving the world bright and sparkly. Red looked at the clock, groaned, and pulled the pillow over her head.

"Good morning!" Granny put a cup of coffee on the nightstand and sat on the bed. "I wouldn't have woken you, but there was a delivery for you."

Red poked her head out. "Who's it from?"

"I don't know, dear. Maybe there's a card inside the box."

Red swung her legs off the bed and stretched. "Thanks for the coffee."

"You're welcome." Granny smiled. "I put the package in the kitchen. Hurry up, I'm dying of curiosity."

Red stumbled downstairs, sipping coffee and rubbing sleep crusts from her eyes. She blinked at the large, flat package on the kitchen table. She tore open the brown paper wrapping to reveal a white box with a silver logo embossed on the front.

Granny gasped. "Slook's! I've seen their ads in the magazines at the hairdresser's. Who do you know who shops at Slook's?"

Red shook her head and lifted the lid off the box. Inside, a card sat on top of something wrapped in tissue paper. She opened the envelope and read the note aloud: "Be ready at five o'clock on the fifteenth. J."

She pulled a black dress from under the tissue. "Holy shit," she breathed. The fabric was a shimmering liquid in her hands, rich and flowing. She had never owned anything like it.

"Mildred," Granny snapped. "Language." She put on her glasses and squinted at the note. "Who is this J. person? And where are you going on the fifteenth?"

"Remember I told you about the person who was always helping me?" She held the dress up in front of herself. "Well, that's him. We're going to a concert."

"What kind of concert?"

"That big charity one that's been all over the news."

"I thought that was sold out! Mildred, who exactly are you going with?"

"Um. Well, funny thing actually. It's, ah, John Smith."

The note fell from Granny's hands and fluttered to the floor. "John Smith? But—" She sank into a chair one hand on her forehead. "Don't you know who he is?"

Red bristled. "Yeah, he's a guy with too much money who wants to throw a little my way."

"I don't understand. I thought this man was dangerous!"

Red put the dress back in its box. "Well, maybe he is, maybe he isn't. He's never been anything but pleasant to me. Anyway, it's just a concert. It's not like I'm marrying the guy."

"That's not funny."

Red grabbed a zuranfruit from the bowl on the counter and peeled it. "I don't know what the big deal is," she said, popping a chunk into her mouth.

"Surely you're old enough by now to know that a man who sends you a dress from Slook's is up to no good."

"Gimme a break. I'm not stupid. But this isn't anything to worry about. I swear."

Granny clasped her hands together in front of her chest, as if praying. "Mildred, don't go to this concert with this man. Tell him you changed your mind. Tell him anything you want. But please, don't go."

"Jeez, Granny. Something good is finally happening in my life. Can't you just be happy for me?"

"I want you to be happy, dear. But this isn't the way."

"And how would you know what would make me happy?"

Granny took Red's hands in her own. "Think about your parents. Would your mother say? Your father?"

Red pulled her hands away. "They're both dead."

"I'm sorry, dear." Granny wrung her hands. "That was an unfair thing to ask you. I'm just so worried. I wish you could trust me."

"I know. But you need to trust me too. I know what I'm doing."

"But that's what I'm trying to tell you, dear. You don't know what you're doing."

Red grabbed the dress box. "I love you, Granny, but I'm not a kid you need to protect anymore." She stalked out of the room. Granny called after her, but she didn't look back.

Red took the dress out to the *Pit* to try it on in the tiny bathroom. It slid over her head like a waterfall. Thin straps exposed her shoulders, which was weird. Red couldn't remember the last time she'd worn anything without sleeves. The neckline was scooped but nothing was hanging out. She twisted around, trying to see the back in the mirror. Damn, her ass looked amazing. The fabric clung to her just right.

She wanted to wear it everywhere.

She made herself take it off, hung it up neatly in the closet, and put back on the ragged clothes she'd slept in after the fiasco at Shellchuckers the night before. Buck's confused face flashed in her mind. She fingered the holes in her shirt, then tore it off and pulled on a fresh one.

That part of her life was over. Moving on.

Chapter 36

Red avoided Granny as much as possible over the next few weeks, even sneaking food from the fridge to eat in the *Pit*. If nothing else, she could smoke out there without getting scolded. She picked up a case of beer and a couple bottles of whiskey, too.

She also got herself some makeup and a bottle of perfume called Solara Nights. Red thought it smelled like quusberries and cinnamon. She practiced with the makeup, imitating different designs she saw in the magazines she picked up at the market. Her hair was hopeless, though. She trimmed it over the bathroom sink, trying hard to keep it even, but it still ended up looking lopsided. In the end, she cut the short side even shorter, hoping it would look edgy instead of ridiculous.

By the time the fifteenth came around, Red was practically crawling out of her own skin from boredom. There was only so many times she could draw on her eyelids before she cracked. That afternoon, she took a shower so long the Pit's hot water ran out. She waxed everything that could be waxed, polished her nails, painted her face, rubbed some goop in her hair, doused herself in Solara Nights.

The dress looked and felt as amazing as it did the first time. She did a little twirl. The woman in the mirror, the New Red, did the same. Her makeup job was passable, and her hair probably looked like it was that way on purpose. The dress more than made up for all that, though. Red felt beautiful.

She headed to the cockpit to check the time: ten minutes until five. She didn't notice the cat sitting in the middle of the floor until her big toe connected with it. "Bonk!" she yelled, hopping on one foot. "Ugh, that'll teach me not to wear . . ."

Shoes. She'd completely forgotten about shoes.

She limped into the bunkroom and dug through her recently cleaned and organized closet. The choices were underwhelming: boots, more boots, different boots, a pair of sneakers crusted with orange mud. Red pulled them all out and arranged them in a row for inspection. The sneakers were obviously no good, so that left—

Three sharp knocks on the hull of the ship made her jump. "Ms. Darkling, I'm here to pick you up," said a muffled voice.

"I'll be right there!" She picked the least cruddy black boots of the bunch and shoved her feet into them. Another series of knocks rang out as she pulled the second boot's laces taut.

"I'm coming, jeez," she muttered. She spat on a corner of a towel and scrubbed the dust and grit off the boots, which made them cleaner if not polished. She stood and examined her feet. Oh well. It was the best she could do. If Smith didn't like it, too bad. He should have sent shoes too. Maybe he would next time, if there was a next time.

Outside, Red broke out in goosebumps from the cold. As long as she was talking next times, Smith could spring for something more weather-appropriate, like a parka or thermal jumpsuit. The Zed Alpha idled on the lawn. Neighbors poked their heads out of windows and leaned over the fence to gawk. Red hunched up her shoulders and hugged her elbows with her hands. She saw Granny at the back door. She gave a little wave, but Granny turned back into the house, closing the door behind her.

A uniformed man waited nearby. He glanced down at her boots, but didn't comment. Smart. He offered his arm, which she took gratefully. He escorted her into the Zed Alpha.

"My name's Patrick. Would you care for a drink?"

"You got any whiskey?" Red settled into the plush seat, crossing her legs and smoothing the dress over her knees.

"Of course," Patrick said, closing the hatch. "Mr. Smith said you prefer a well-aged Scothian. Ice?"

"Are you crazy? No!"

Patrick busied himself at the little bar. "Mr. Smith wanted to be here himself, but there was a problem at the concert venue that required his personal attention. He asked me to send his regrets, and tell you that he will meet you in the VIP box." He handed her a glass.

"Okay by me." She took a sip, trying to look like she was served expensive whiskey by a servant in the back of a Zed Alpha every day.

"If you're ready, I'll give the pilot the go-ahead."

"I'm good whenever."

He knocked on the closed door of the cockpit, and the ship immediately lifted. Red watched Granny's neighborhood grow small outside the windows, then disappear into the distance. She caught Patrick staring at her neckline, so downed the rest of her whiskey in a single gulp, held up the empty glass, and burped to get his attention. He turned an adorable shade of pink from his collar to the tips of his ears. He hurried to refill her glass, and Red didn't catch him staring again.

Septimal City, where Smith had arranged the concert, was halfway across the planet. Red wondered how long it would take for the Zed Alpha to make a trip like that.

As it turned out, not long at all. Once they got clear of the Magross traffic lanes, the pilot opened her up to speeds Red could only guess at for a surface-restricted ship.

When they arrived at the giant Septimal Center Arena, Patrick collected Red's glass and opened the Zed Alpha's hatch. Her eyes dazzled at flashing lights from every direction. He took her arm and gently steered her past the photographers, down the red carpet—an actual, honest to Gravnar red freaking carpet.

They ducked through a doorway into the relative quiet and dark of the lobby. Patrick led her to another door, this one labeled VIP ONLY—MUST SHOW PASS. He flashed a card at the guard, who nodded and stepped aside. The door slid open on an elevator. Patrick pressed the single unlabeled button and they ascended smoothly.

Red shifted her weight from foot to foot. She fiddled with her dress straps, straightened the skirt, fluffed her hair. She longed for a mirror.

The elevator opened on a large room. One side was open to the arena, where the growing crowd watched roadies running around the stage with wires. The room itself was filled with grumskin couches, tables overflowing with food and drinks, and people chatting and laughing.

"Holy shit, Patrick, is that Indar Skjov?"

Patrick grinned at her. "I'm sure you'll know most people here." His smile faded. "Here comes Mr. Smith."

"Red! It truly does my heart good to see you again. Please accept my apology for not retrieving you myself. Business, you understand." Smith kissed both her cheeks. "You look beautiful." He took her hands in his and slid his eyes over her. He saw the boots and raised an eyebrow. "Interesting. May I inquire why you chose this footwear to complete the ensemble?"

"What's wrong, Smith? They're from Slook's spring line. All the fanciest people will be wearing them next season."

His smile froze on his face. "Thank you, Patrick, for delivering this young lady with her wit intact."

Patrick shifted uncomfortably, then ducked his head and escaped back into the elevator.

Smith put his hand on the small of Red's back. She flinched, but allowed herself to be guided through the crowd. Patrick was right—she knew everyone in the room. Archie Noligg drank a beer and listened to racing pilot Dutch Dayton tell a dirty joke about an Orgullan man and a shiq. The primetime news anchor from Channel 98 stuffed her face with smoked olive croquettes. Andres Mandorak, the painter, leaned against one wall, frowning into a glass of Tolmarine wine and muttering to himself. A clump of galactic representatives whispered to each other in a corner.

And, of course, Indar Skjov himself. Smith shook his hand. "Indar, my good friend. I cannot thank you enough for your participation in this event."

"I am glad to do it, John. What do you think of my beard?" Skjov stroked it thoughtfully. "I grew it out for my latest film, but I am not sure if I should keep it."

"Ah, I am the wrong person to consult about men's fashion. Perhaps we should ask my companion? Only a few moments ago, she was kind enough to enlighten me on upcoming trends in footwear."

Skjov turned his intense green eyes to Red. "John, where have you been hiding this gorgeous creature?" His husky, honeyed voice turned Red's knees to pudding.

Red's mouth flapped, but no sound came out.

"Indar, I would like you to meet Red Darkling. Red, this is Indar Skjov."

Skjov raised her hand to his lips, never taking his eyes off hers. "I hope she is not your lover, John. You will think me very naughty if she is."

"No!" Red blurted. "I mean, I'm not his lover or anything."

Skjov laughed. "Then I insist on getting you a drink so you can tell me how much you like my beard."

"Now, Indar," Smith interrupted. "Don't you need to be preparing for tonight's duties?"

"John, you always know best." Skjov sighed. "Red, don't go anywhere. We'll continue this when I get back." He kissed her hand again, then left for the elevator.

"Do not be fooled by his charms," Smith said, handing her a glass of wine. "He is like that with all women. A character flaw that has served him well over the years, but a flaw all the same."

Red flushed. Of course he was like that with everyone. He was Indar Skjov, and she was, well, herself. The fanciest dress in the galaxy wouldn't change that. She wished she'd brought a jacket.

Smith stopped a passing waiter and plucked a drink off his tray. "Here," he said, offering the glass to Red. "No need to await Indar's return."

"What is it?" Red sniffed the brilliant purple liquid. She knew her liquor, and this was like nothing she'd ever seen.

"Rootwine. I am told it is the latest craze among artists of a certain, ah, vintage, if you'll forgive the pun. I thought it appropriate for this particular event."

"Hey, a drink's a drink." She took a sip. It tasted like water. She took a mouthful and swished it around before swallowing. No, not water. More like water that had all of its flavor removed. It didn't even have the bite of alcohol. She waggled the glass at Smith. "I don't get it."

He laughed. "We are in agreement on that one. Rootwine enthusiasts claim its emptiness provides a blank canvas for the tongue to paint its own flavor landscape. At least, that was the sales pitch from my caterer."

"My tongue isn't painting anything," Red said. "I guess I'm more of a whiskey-and-beer girl."

"Of course." A man in a suit approached Smith and whispered something in his ear. Smith nodded. "My work is never done. Please forgive me, there is a situation which requires my immediate attention. I will return shortly. The concert will start in a few moments, so make yourself comfortable. Should you require anything in my absence, my colleague here will see to your every need."

"Colleague?"

"Yes, I believe you know him." A glowering man popped out of thin air next to Smith.

Red almost dropped her rootwine. "Chuck!"

Chuck grumbled something but refused to look at Red.

"I understand that there has been some unpleasantness between you. Justified, no doubt, on both sides. However, I must insist that you repair your relationship. I simply cannot tolerate friction among my friends. Now, you must excuse me." He left, the man in the suit hurrying behind him.

"Look, Chuck, I—"

"Don't. Just don't." Chuck crossed his thick arms. "I'll make nice with you because Smith says so. But that's it."

"You work for him?"

"No, Miss Fancybritches. I don't 'work for him.'" Chuck dropped his bulk onto a couch. "I'm more of an independent contractor. I have certain skills that he finds valuable."

Red sat next to him. "What does that mean?"

"Come on, Red, you're not this stupid. You know, um, what I am. I'm in the information racket. I keep an eye on things."

"Things like me?" Her face darkened.

"Yeah. Things like you."

"He must have been pissed when you cut me out, then."

Chuck shrugged. "A little, but it's not like I'm his only source, you know?"

CHAPtER 37

Red didn't get a chance to squeeze Chuck's throat until he explained exactly what he meant by "not his only source." The audience below erupted in a thundering cheer that drowned out all conversation in the box. Everyone crowded up to see what was happening on the stage below (except Mandorak, who just stared silently at his now empty glass). Red elbowed her way to the window and leaned out.

Indar Skjov tapped on a microphone, his holographic image projected behind him, twenty times life size. Even the people in the cheap seats, a quarter mile away, could see every hair in his beard.

"Ladies and gentlemen," he announced. The audience roared. Skjov grinned and waited for a moment before continuing. "It is my great honor to welcome you to the Angels Among Us charity concert event. When my dear friend John Smith asked me to be your host tonight, I knew I couldn't say no." The people in the box tittered uncomfortably.

"There's someone else here tonight I won't be able to say no to." Skjov pointed at the VIP box. "Red, my temptation, I still owe you that drink."

The spotlights swung around and suddenly her giant holographic image loomed behind Skjov. Red flushed furiously. She didn't know what to do, so she gave a little wave. The crowd whistled and hooted. It was a relief when the lights went back to Skjov and he started his canned speech about FoodAngels and the night's lineup.

Red tuned it out, too busy trying to ignore the whispers and stares from everyone else in the box. She pushed back from the window, bumped into Archie Noligg and spilled his beer. He scowled at her as he scrubbed at his shirt with a napkin.

"Sorry," she mumbled. Ugh, could this night get any more awkward?

She found Chuck near the elevator. "Dude, I need you to find me some whiskey."

"I ain't your bartender tonight."

Red lowered her voice. "Smith said you'd get me anything I needed. I need whiskey."

Chuck heaved a sigh, but he did disappear and reappear a few minutes later. "It ain't the fancy stuff you've gotten yourself used to, but it'll have to do." He thrust a bottle and glass at her.

"Gee, I guess babysitting duty is harder than you thought." Red filled the glass and raised it to him. "To independent contracting."

A rapid drumbeat flooded the room. Red recognized it immediately as the beginning of Fog Machine's hit single, "Biosculpted Boys." She fought her way back to the window, brandishing her whiskey bottle at a knot of politicians' wives and accidentally-on-purpose stepping on Dutch Dayton's foot to get him to move.

Halfway through Fog Machine's set, Smith reappeared and joined Red at the window. She threw her arms around his neck and planted a sloppy, whiskey-scented kiss on his cheek. She laughed at the shocked faces around them. What a bunch of prudes. This was a rock concert, not a Fardic monastery. She looked good, felt good, and she'd lick a fazzer before she'd let them get in the way of her good time. Maybe that was the whiskey talking but hell, who cares?

The next few hours blurred together in a drunken haze of guitars and drums.

Chapter 38

Red woke up in the captain's chair of the *Pit*, still wearing the dress and one boot. It took her booze-soaked brain a minute to remember losing the other one to Noah Proog, the bassist for Deltonic Implosion, in a game of jester's scrap. Her head throbbed, and her stomach couldn't decide between nausea and hunger. Opening her eyes made it worse. She figured she'd give her stomach some time to work itself out, closed her eyes, and replayed the night in her head.

It was unbelievable, like something out of a movie. Skjov never did get her that drink, but she didn't really mind. The music was, of course, amazing, especially the new stuff from the Poly Torrents. All the bands wound up in the VIP box after their sets, and Red had met them all—including Arien Spar. Red cringed to remember how she'd gushed at the singer. Spar was cool about it, though. She'd even given Red a data chip with a rough cut of the new album.

Damn, if not for the missing boot Red would think she'd dreamed the whole thing.

A rumble from her stomach meant it decided to go with hunger, at least for now. Red cracked an eye and stumbled into the kitchen. She found coffee, but no food that was remotely breakfasty. Time to raid Granny's pantry again. First, though, she needed to get out of this dress.

She slipped into her usual clothes—well, they were clean, but otherwise usual. She had a shirt that covered her shoulders, at least, and a jacket with pockets comfortingly full of potential weapons. She stuck the odd boot back in the closet, with the crazy thought that she'd find Proog and win back its mate.

The sun was well up when she climbed out of the *Pit*. She found Granny's door unlocked, and Granny knitting in her well-worn rocking chair.

"Good morning," Granny said, not looking up from her work.

"Hi, Granny. Um. I was wondering, could I, ah, borrow something for breakfast?"

Granny sniffed. "Yes, I figured that's why you were here."

Red's euphoric high from the concert crashed and burned like a dumpster full of guilt. "I'm sorry, Granny, I really am." She picked at the polish already peeling from her fingernails. "I'll pay you back for everything I've eaten."

"Oh, Mildred." She put down her knitting and shook her head. "It's not about the food. I'm just so worried about you. You've been pushing everyone away. First Mark, then your other friends, and now me. I feel like I don't even know who you are anymore."

Hot tears threatened to spill down Red's cheeks. "Maybe I don't know either. I just want . . . I don't know. It's like I have this good thing happen to me, and no one wants me to have it. Don't I deserve something good?"

Granny stood up and smoothed Red's hair. "Honey, you deserve everything good. But maybe, just maybe, this John Smith isn't the good thing you want him to be."

"But maybe he is."

"You know what I think?" Granny put a soft, cool hand on Red's cheek. "I think you need to stop moping around here and get back to your life. Your *real* life. Get some perspective." She smiled. "But first, some breakfast. Come on, I'll make you some scrambled eggs and toast."

Red wiped her nose on her jacket sleeve. "Thanks, Granny. That sounds amazing."

Three eggs and four pieces of toast later, Red felt almost human again. A bit grungy, but nothing a shower wouldn't fix. She insisted on rinsing the dishes, then kissed Granny and headed upstairs to take advantage of the house's superior hot water supply.

As she scrubbed the goop out of her hair and off her face, Red thought about what Granny had said about getting back to her real life. Granny was right. Who was she kidding? The chick in the ass-hugging dress—that wasn't her. Yeah, it had been a fun night, but it was over, and Red needed to get back to reality. No complications, no fancying herself up. Just simple, straightforward, honest to Gravnar reality, starring plain old Red Darkling.

Besides, she did kind of miss how things used to be. Not the giant killer bugs, of course, or almost being eaten by a baega, or waking up in a slave ship next to a dead body. She could totally do without those parts. Still, open space in her own ship, no one to tell her what to wear, owing nothing to no one but herself—that she missed.

And hey, it's not like she couldn't hit Smith up for a bottle of that Scothian whiskey every once in a while.

By the time she'd toweled off, she was resolved to get off this rock and get back to work.

CHaptER 39

Getting off the rock was easy; getting back to work, not so much. Most of her old contacts wouldn't return her pings, and those that did wouldn't talk business. She picked a few jobs off the scanner, but they all dropped her like fresh grumshit on a hot day before she even had a chance to change course. If Red was a paranoid person—which she wasn't, but if she was—she'd think something was up. But she wasn't.

She spent a full week floating around the galaxy, eating her way through another fridgeful of Granny's leftovers. At least she had plenty of time to keep the ship more or less clean. Bonk hadn't had any vermin to catch in ages. All it did was sit around and blink at her. Occasionally it would perform its regular maintenance routine, though Red doubted its exhaust port got dirty enough to warrant the amount of time spent cleaning it. And there was absolutely no reason it should have to do that right in front of her every time. Red was tempted to start piling up the garbage again just so she wouldn't have to see it anymore.

At one point, Red considered using Bonk's long-distance tracker to find something to sell (who she would sell it to, well, she'd worry about that later). Problem was, since her cleaning binge, she had nothing left on the ship worth tracking, not even a fragment of luxite or a liquor bottle with a few drops in the bottom. No one would pay for empty food tubs.

Would they?

Nah.

She down to her last container of leftovers when she got a ping from a blocked number. Normally she would never be stupid enough to respond to an anonymous ping, but boredom and an empty fridge got the best of her.

The vidscreen flickered to life. With only mild surprise, Red recognized Smith's personal assistant. "Hey, Carla! Good to see ya again."

"It's Claudia, actually." She forced a smile.

"Claudia, right. So what's your boss want with me now?"

"I couldn't say. I'll put you through."

"Great, th—" But Claudia had already been replaced by the SmithCo corporate logo. Geez, and Red had tried being nice this time.

"Thank you for returning my ping so quickly." Smith sat behind a mile of desk in some sort of office.

"I'm, ah, between jobs at the moment."

An amused smile flashed across Smith's face. "Is that so? Well, if it means I can talk to you, then I am grateful for the lull."

"Whatever. Did you need something?"

"No no, not at all. A purely social call, I assure you. I had hoped that you would contact me after the concert. I trust you enjoyed the experience?"

Red sat back in her captain's chair and folded her arms. "It was great. Did I thank you?"

"I don't believe you did, no."

"Then thank you."

"You are most welcome, Red."

Awkward pause.

"So, was that the reason you pinged me? I didn't send a thank you note?"

"Partially. 'Gratitude, like love, is best when given freely.' That's another quote from Exaius, his Fourth Discourse on Virtue. Have you read any Exaius?"

"Oh sure, every day. Right after I practice my calculus."

"I was unaware of your interest in advanced mathematics."

Red rolled her eyes. "Dude, I was kidding."

"Ah. Well, you should read Exaius. Perhaps I might recommend a few titles."

"Uh huh. Look, did you have anything else to say, or are we just going to throw quotes at each other? Just so you know, all I got is song lyrics and lines from Ephrasia Pfeff movies."

Smith laughed. "Art and truth can be found in many forms. However, you are right. There is another topic I would like to discuss with you."

Here it comes. "Oh yeah? Like what?"

"If you are not currently engaged in any . . . employment, perhaps you would like to join me for a weekend in Crysallia."

That got Red's attention. "I don't ski."

"I assure you, that is not a requirement. The area has many other attractions as well. I have a piece of business to attend to there, so you would have some time on your own to explore, if you wished to do so."

"Wait, it would be just you and me?"

"I will have some associates with me, of course, and staff." He paused. "Mr. Skjov has returned to the movie set, I'm afraid."

Red flushed. "That's not what I meant."

"I know. I apologize for my poor joke."

"So, you want me to come with you to Crysallia for your business trip?"

"Had I not made that plain?"

"You probably won't answer this, but why?"

"I thought you would enjoy the experience. Have you been to Crysallia?"

"No, but I'm pretty sure you already knew that."

"If you are not interested—"

"I didn't say I wasn't interested."

Smith looked annoyed. "Red, I am a busy man with limited patience. I do not appreciate this type of meaningless banter. Will you be joining me in Crysallia this weekend, or not?"

Red hesitated, then remembered her empty fridge and the eviscerated mattress she had not yet replaced. "Okay, fine. Are we doing the whole secret agent thing again, or can I just get there myself?"

"It would be acceptable for you to meet me at my home on Crysallia. I will send you the coordinates."

"I could use some credits for fuel. I'm all the way out here by Andulia right now."

"Of course. I will have Claudia arrange an account for you and send you the access details. Should you encounter any problems, please inform me at once so I can take care of it."

"Thanks again, Smith."

"You are very welcome. Look for my message within the hour."

The vidscreen went black.

Crysallia. Red did a quick search and scanned the results that appeared on the display. It was known as a tourist destination for its cloud skiing resorts—one of only a few places in the galaxy where the atmospheric conditions produced the right density of cloud. Smith didn't mess around. Glor, Crysallia, the Modern Mandrake . . . Red wondered if there was any fancy place Smith *didn't* set up shop. Probably not. She'd have to ask him.

She quickly got bored reading about Crysallia's natural parks and city centers, and she didn't know yet where on the planet she'd end up. So, she closed everything out and cracked a beer to pass the time, waiting for Smith's promised message.

About twenty minutes later, it arrived. She opened it eagerly—it wasn't every day someone sent her credits. The message read:

> An account has been set up in your name.
> It contains Č10,000 to be used at your
> discretion.
>   Number: GXWR24C-MM@56
>   Sec Code: MDARKLING1

```
Arrive at Cloudtop: Thursday, 26 Nov,
between 47642.85 and 47642.95 GalStd Time
(1600 and 1700 local time).
    Coordinates (base Crysallia):
    54-29-59.99/158-56-59.99
```

Ten thousand credits! That would buy her fuel to Crysallia with enough left over to keep her in food, cigars, and whiskey for a year. Less, if she bought a new mattress. She stretched her back and decided it was a tradeoff worth making.

She immediately transferred the credits from the Smith account to her own—just in case he changed his mind before she stocked up. Once she received the transfer confirmation message, she lit up the nav and tapped in the coordinates of the nearest market.

Maybe she'd find some shoes to go with the dress. Again, just in case.

CHAPTER 40

One mattress, a full fuel tank, three crates of foodstuffs, two bottles of whiskey (Finebock, sadly), one case of beer, two boxes of Crolinian cigars, and a pair of dressy black shoes later, Red directed the delivery guys where to put everything. It felt good to have stuff in the main storage compartment again, even if it only took up a fraction of the space. One cute guy with a tight ass gave her a weird look when he saw the hole in the old mattress. She winked at him and offered to show him how the hole could be used to expand his sexual horizons. He declined, though Red caught him biting his lip. Maybe another time.

She'd gotten a bit carried away in the market. It was her first spree in ages, after all. She'd managed to keep her spending down to a dull roar. Who knew when she'd stumble across another ten thousand-credit gift? She'd tried on about eleven million pairs of shoes. Haggling with the liquor vendor had taken forever, plus then she'd had to find someone to get it all back to the *Pit*.

Red snagged a FlinkBar and some real coffee from the kitchen, then plopped into the captain's chair to program the trip to Crysallia. She checked the travel time against the clock and winced. It would be tight. She stuffed half the bar in her mouth and kicked the sublight drive up a notch. Technically illegal, given the trajectory. Galactic cops frowned upon speeding that close to planets with heavy industrial traffic. Red almost hoped she'd get tagged. She was more than a little curious to find out if dropping Smith's name got her any privileges with law enforcement. She nudged the sublight up a bit more.

It turned out to be an uneventful trip, and Red arrived several hours early. She settled the ship into orbit and used the time to tidy up the empty cans and wrappers and take a shower. Then she spent far too much time worrying about whether she should throw on some makeup, what Smith would think if she did wear it, and why the hell she cared anyway. She ended up putting it on, then washing it off while muttering about stupid girly shit.

Red returned to the cockpit and pulled up the directions from Smith. She plugged the local coordinates into the nav and wondered what the hell "Cloudtop" was. It wasn't listed in the tourist info as a resort or hotel. Well, she'd know soon enough. She took manual control down through the upper atmosphere.

From above, Crysallia looked like dozens of other planets: green and blue with random swirls of white cloud cover. Red learned the difference, though, when she flew into one of the clouds. The *Pit* immediately slowed down, the engines strained, and the controls got sluggish. It was like flying under water. She dropped below it as quickly as possible, worried that the intake would gum up or she'd burn out a thruster.

The upper layers of clouds weren't the only ones to avoid, it seemed. Pockets of dense fog sat in the wrinkles of the mountains, puddled over lakes, and filled in canyons. Birds sat on cloud tufts as if they were cottony boulders. In a few places, people on skis slid along the cloud surface. Red carefully avoided flying through any of the foggy areas. She didn't want to know what it would do to the ship.

She followed the nav's directions to a hilltop poking out of the fog. A large house perched there, with a steeply sloped roof, dozens of windows, and several chimneys sending smoke drifting through the twilight. Red set down on the landing pad and shut down the engines, then headed to the bunkroom. She tossed a few things into a pack: clothes, toothbrush, cigars. At the last second, she tossed a handful of makeup in there too. What the hell.

Bonk stopped cleaning itself and blinked at her from the doorway, one leg detached from its torso and standing up at an alarming angle. "Be good, now. No wild parties while I'm gone." It gargled at her as she hefted the pack on her shoulder. She patted the cat's head. "Ya big weirdo."

Red crossed the lawn to the front door and rang the bell. She noticed the tiny glass bubble of a camera lens at eye level in the door. She crossed her eyes and stuck out her tongue. A few seconds later, the door opened.

"Patrick!" she cried, slapping him on the shoulder. "Didn't know you'd be here."

"Ms. Darkling, it's good to see you again. Mr. Smith brought me with for the weekend, since we've already met." He stepped aside so she could enter. "Can I take your bag?"

"Sure," she said, offering him the strap and stepping into the house. It was big but cozy, with lots of wood and stone that somehow managed to be rustic and elegant at the same time. A fireplace snapped cheerfully in a nearby room.

"Mr. Smith is waiting for you in the library." Patrick gestured to a door down the hall. "I'll take your things to the room you'll be using, if that's all right."

"That's fine. Thanks, Patrick."

"I'll see you after dinner." He smiled and ducked his head.

Red walked down to the library door, which was ajar. She pushed it open and gasped. The flickering light from the fireplace danced over walls covered in books of all sizes and colors. Most of the books looked old and well-worn. Several overstuffed chairs were scattered around the dark wood floor. Red was not normally much of a reader, but this room made her want to sink into a chair with a stack of books.

"Do you like it?" Smith stood near the fireplace, a glass in his hand.

"Hell yes, I like it." Red wandered to a shelf and ran her fingers over the spines of the books. "Have you read all of these?"

"Of course. Most of them, several times."

She picked one up at random. "*Songs of the Delphine Soul*? You've read this?"

Smith smiled. "'Ah, to be loved, to be loved, as a babe held close in the night.' That is Delphine's cry to her child, upon the occasion of her lover's departure. It is a heartbreaking story, yet lovely even so."

Red stuck it back on the shelf and stuffed her hands into her pockets. "So? I'm here. Uh, thanks for the invitation."

"I am so very glad you were able to accept it," he said, putting his glass down on a table. "Please, sit." She did, in a chair so comfortable she could easily imagine spending the entire weekend in that spot.

Smith poured her a glass of something from a decanter on the mantle. She took it and he sat across from her, crossing his legs. "My business here on Crysallia will be rather dull, I'm afraid. I will appreciate the opportunity to spend my evenings in the company of someone other than Patrick and my housekeeper."

"I haven't met your housekeeper, but what's wrong with Patrick?"

"Not a thing. But he is not you."

Red didn't know what to say to that. She sipped her drink, some kind of fiery wine. "So . . . what kind of business do you have here, of all places? You planning to open a ski resort?"

"I would rather not talk business here at Cloudtop. I prefer to keep my professional life separate from my personal one."

"Cloudtop? You named your house?"

"Of course." He smiled dryly. "When one has many houses, one must distinguish between them somehow."

Red rolled her eyes.

"Now, Red. Your ship has a name, does it not?"

"That's different."

He raised an eyebrow. "Is it?" Red opened her mouth to argue, but he raised a hand. "Let us not debate the nuances of nomenclature. Oh, and speaking of debate, I have a gift for you."

Red frowned. "Oh yeah? It's not another dress, is it? I only just got shoes to go with the last one."

"No no, this gift is to adorn your mind, not your body." He handed her a book from the table next to him.

"*The Seven Discourses of Exaius*?" Red read.

"I think you will find his work to be both enlightening and inspiring."

Red flipped through the book. It was bound in black grumskin, the cream-colored pages heavy and smooth to the touch. Handwritten notes decorated the margins of several pages.

"That particular copy was owned by Vladmir V, son of the great Vladmir IV," Smith said. "He had that book with him at Ehlar when he thrust himself onto his father's throne. His thoughts on the text are a fascinating insight into his psyche during that troubling time." He shook his head. "The poor man never managed to escape the influence of his father, even after his death. So it is, so it ever shall be, when sons aspire to fathers' dominion. Is it the same for daughters, do you think?"

"I dunno. I suppose so." Red wasn't entirely sure she understood what the hell Smith was rambling about. The book had value, she got that much. "Well, thanks. Maybe I'll read a bit this weekend while you're busy with work."

"I confess, that was my exact hope."

Red stretched her legs toward the fire. "Hell, in this room, I'd read anything."

"Good. Now, though, let us move into the dining room. My chef has prepared an exquisite roast darna with a white pepper gravy that I think you will enjoy."

"Sounds great." Her stomach rumbled in agreement.

CHapteR 41

The darna was, in fact, exquisite. Red sniffed suspiciously at the gravy, but one taste (at Smith's urging) and she almost licked the plate clean.

Throughout the meal, Red probed for details about Smith's business. He ignored or deflected every question, no matter how vague, about his work in general and what he was doing on Crysallia. His smooth refusal to discuss it only piqued Red's curiosity. If he had nothing to hide, why not just talk about it? She'd figure this out, dammit, if it took all weekend.

After Red finished the final crumbs of quusberry tart and a servant cleared away the dish, Smith invited her for a walk around the grounds. She didn't feel much like walking—after all that gravy, sleep sounded far better—but she loosened her proverbial belt and followed him outside. Patrick joined them, though he walked behind them and never spoke.

Red's eyes popped at the spectacular views. Cloudtop glimmered like a jewel. Several of Crysallia's moons had risen, highlighting the fog peaks and turning the world beyond the hilltop into a frothy meringue.

"Have you ever walked on a cloud?" Smith asked as they approached the fogbank. Up close, she could see wisps trailing up into the night air, like smoke.

"Not, you know, literally."

"Then it is long past time you did."

She looked at the clouds skeptically. "You're sure it'll hold us?"

"Of course. It is almost like snow: packed underneath, but soft on top. See?" He stepped onto the cloud. His feet sank a little, but he didn't plummet to his death or anything. He stretched out his hand to Red. "If you are afraid . . ."

"I'm not afraid," Red protested, waving his hand away. "Just cautious." She lifted one foot over the fog, closed her eyes, and set it down. Her ankle felt cool and slightly damp. When she peeked, she saw her foot obscured by a thin layer of cloud. She put some weight on it, and it held. "Hey!" She brought her other foot out and watched the cloud swirl over it.

Smith started walking out over the fog, and Red followed. Patrick stayed back, glancing around.

"Caution is always advisable, particularly in cloudwalking," Smith said. "Even at the large resorts, there can be pockets with lesser density that can trap an unsuspecting person. Many of those pockets are indistinguishable to the naked eye. Every year people disappear into the clouds, never to be found."

Red stopped, alarmed. She looked back over her shoulder at the green solidity of land.

"Oh no, Red, please do not worry," Smith said. "I hire scientists to study the fogbanks here on a yearly basis, looking for any problematic areas. I can assure you that there are no dangerous pockets here at Cloudtop. You are perfectly safe."

She wiped her sweaty hands on her pants. "All the same, I'd rather go back."

His cold eyes cut into her. "Do you not trust me?"

"I'm here, aren't I?"

His eyes softened and a hint of smile touched his lips. "Indeed. Trust is a steep mountain to climb, and many are the corpses piled below its cliffs."

"Who said that, Exaius?"

"No, that is a lesson I have learned through experience. Tell me, Red, how many of those corpses are people who jumped, and how many did you push?"

She thought of Chuck, Buck and the gang, even Granny. But mostly she thought of Woodman. She shivered. The breeze must have picked up. Yeah, the breeze.

Smith put his hand on her arm. "Red, trust can only thrive when it is mutual. If it is not, then pushing someone off the mountain is the only way to be safe."

She pulled away and wrapped her arms around herself. "I'm ready to go back now," she said. "It's getting cold."

"Very well." They fell into step together, silently. Red felt better with solid ground under her feet.

Back inside Cloudtop, in the hallway outside the library, Smith kissed the back of Red's hand. "Forgive me, but I must retire for the evening. My business engagement requires me to depart early in the morning. I am sure you will find ways to occupy yourself until my return. I have instructed my staff to assist you with anything you may need."

"I could come with you."

"You would find it more tedious than I do."

"Don't you trust me? Maybe you're next off the mountain."

His face tightened. "Threats do not become you."

"Jeez, I was only joking."

"I see."

"Anyway, see you tomorrow, I guess."

"Indeed." He dipped his head, turned, and walked quickly away.

Red glanced around, unsure what to do in the big house by herself. Maybe Smith had an office she could snoop in? He was way too secretive about his business for it not to be something worth knowing.

"Ms. Darkling?" Red jumped. Patrick was so quiet she'd forgotten he was there. "Is there anything I can get for you?"

"No, Patrick, I—" Hang on a sec, maybe there was an opportunity here. "Actually, I could use a drink. And some company. Would you find a bottle of whiskey and maybe join me for one?"

He rubbed his neck. "I don't know. I can get you the liquor, of course, but technically I'm still on the clock."

"Oh, come on," Red purred. "Just one little drink. Besides, Smith said you're supposed to do whatever I want. And I want you to have a drink with me." She put her hand on his chest. "Please?"

Patrick swallowed hard. "Well, I suppose it would be all right. But just one."

Red laughed in a husky voice. "Just one. In the library?"

"Fine, I'll get a bottle and be right in." He hurried off toward the dining room.

Red let herself into the library and looked around. The fire had died down a bit, but that was perfect. She shrugged off her jacket and dropped it on a chair. She opened a button on her shirt, then one more.

After some thought, she arranged herself sideways on a chair, her legs draped over one arm.

Patrick entered with a tray holding a bottle and some glasses. "I didn't know if you wanted ice. I can get some if you do."

Red smiled. "No thanks, everything I want is right here already."

He laughed nervously and set the tray down on a table. He poured a meager amount in the glasses and held one out to Red. She peered at it, then tutted. "If you're going to have a drink, then have a drink." He splashed a little more in each glass. She took hers and tossed it back. "Mmm," she said, licking her lips. "Your turn."

He took a swallow. "Ms. Darkling—"

"Call me Red."

"Okay, um. Red. Look, I really should be getting back to work."

"What work could you possibly have to do at this time of night?" She patted the chair next to her. "Bring the bottle and sit with me."

His face twisted up, like he was arguing with himself. He did sit, though. "Just for a little while," he said, but he didn't sound very convinced.

"Handsome, I'll take what I can get from you." Red twirling a strand of her hair. "Drink up, or you'll never catch me. I mean, catch up to me."

Patrick flushed, then gulped the rest of the drink. Red gestured to the bottle and he refilled her glass.

"Aw, Patrick, come on. I don't want to drink alone." She put her hand on his thigh and smiled to herself when he flinched. She leaned over and took the bottle from his hand to pour him more whiskey. He looked straight down her gaping neckline.

Of course he did.

It had been a while since she'd seduced anyone (Exley didn't count). Good to know the old tricks still worked. He wasn't making it easy, but it sure was fun.

"You blush in the most adorable way," she said. He shifted under her hand, which was still firmly on his thigh. "Ooh, and you squirm too."

He didn't say anything, but he did take another swallow of his whiskey. Good.

"I don't get much chance to talk to anyone," she said, slowly stroking his leg. "It gets so lonely floating around in space. Just me and my cat."

"I'm sorry to hear that."

"So, Patrick," she said, "Do you get to travel everywhere Smith goes?"

"Not everywhere, but a lot of places."

"You must be pretty important for Smith to keep you around."

"I guess so."

"Oh, I bet you're more important than you think. And," she pointed to his empty glass, "you need a refill."

"I've already had more than I should."

Red laughed. "Why, do you have to get up in the morning?"

"Yes, actually. I'm supposed to go with Mr. Smith to his business meeting."

Aha. "But the night has barely started," she said, sticking her lower lip out in what she hoped was a sexy pout. "Surely this meeting isn't so early you can't stay with me just a little longer." She squeezed his leg.

"Ms. Darkling—Red, I mean—we shouldn't be doing this here."

"You're right," she said, putting down her glass and crawling into his lap. "I think you need to show me to my bedroom."

CHAPTER 42

Afterward, she curled a leg over his flushed body. Not bad, considering. Now to see if Patrick's tongue had loosened as much as his belt. "Can you stay?"

He sighed. "No, we're leaving so early."

"I can't even bring you breakfast in bed?"

"I wish you could," he said, kissing the top of her head. "But we've got to be in Vendantown by six and it's at least an hour's flight."

"And what's happening in Vendantown that's so special?" She stretched, arching her back. The sheet slipped down to her waist.

He stroked her bare breast idly. "Mr. Smith doesn't share those kinds of details with me. All I know is, we have to get him to a coffeehouse called Scarpio's by six."

"A coffeehouse in the morning? Poor baby, that sounds terrible." She poked his stomach and laughed. He poked her back, and they tickled each other for while, which predictably led to Round Two.

This time, there was no post-coital snuggling. Patrick dressed quickly while Red watched, propped up on one elbow.

"Mr. Smith can't know about this," he said, buckling his belt. "I'd be in a shitload of trouble."

"Don't worry," she said, handing him one of his socks. "I don't want him to know either."

"You don't understand. He's . . . it would be bad. Real bad."

Red sat up. "Dude, I get it. He won't find out from me."

"He can't know." He grabbed her by the arms and shook her. "You hear me? He. Can't. Know."

Red pushed him away, hard. "Back off, asshole. I said don't worry."

He sat on the bed and put his head in his hands. "I'm sorry, I didn't mean to be like that. It's just that you haven't seen what he can do when he gets angry."

The image of Exley's blood spilling from his mouth flashed in her mind. "I might, actually."

His eyes cut to her. "I guess maybe you might. Well, just remember that or we'll both be very sorry." He stood and slipped on his jacket. "You were great, you know. But this won't happen again."

Damn right, it won't. "So if I asked you to ping me?"

He gave her a wry smile. "I'll see you around, Red Darkling." And he left.

Red waited about ten minutes, then got herself dressed. She headed back downstairs and poked her head into the kitchen. Sure enough, the chef was still there, rolling out a sheet of dough.

"Hey, I'm out of cigars. You know where I can get some?" Red asked.

The chef scowled. "The nearest shops are over in Titen. But Mr. Smith does not allow smoking in Cloudtop."

"I'll do it in my ship, I just need the smokes."

The chef harrumphed and went back to her dough.

Cover story, check.

Red strolled out the front door of the house, crossed the lawn, and climbed into the *Pit*. While the engines warmed up, she did a quick search for both Titen and Vendantown. Titen was a tiny dot on the map about ten miles due east; Vendantown was larger, and to the southwest. Figures. She checked the clock. Eh, no problem, she had time. Red took the manual controls and took off over the fogbank to the east.

It didn't take long to get to Titen. Red bought a pack of cigars from an all-hours shop with security cameras crusted like barnacles on every possible surface. As if anyone would rob them of their expired FlinkBars and mushy zuranfruit.

Alibi, check.

Back on the *Pit*, she lit one of the cigars (stale, of course) and plotted a course to Vendantown that swung wide to the south of Cloudtop. She kept it on manual control, which forced her to stay focused. It was shaping up to be an all-nighter. Ugh. She wasn't seventeen anymore. This might be rough.

She arrived in Vendantown about 1:30 in the morning. She pulled up Scarpio's on the map and did a fly-by. The place was closed, obviously. It didn't look like much: flaking paint, torn awning, neon sign with half the letters burned out. Certainly not the kind of place Smith would be caught dead. Yet, this was where he was doing some super-extra-mega-secret business deal in a few hours. Intriguing.

Red found an abandoned lot a few blocks away from the coffee house and landed the *Pit* there. She made her way back to Scarpio's, keeping to the alleys and avoiding the main roads. Even at this hour, you couldn't be too careful.

The back of Scarpio's had an overflowing dumpster, a barred door, and a small window to one side. From behind the dumpster, Red scanned the building for security cameras, but saw none. She picked up a chunk of loose concrete, tossed it, and ducked back into the shadows. The rock clanged against the door. Red listened for an alarm, a barking dog, a nosy neighbor throwing open a window, but there was nothing.

After a few minutes, she eased her way out from her hiding spot and approached the building. The bars on the door were rusted but strong, and Red had never been able to master the fine art of lock picking. Woodman had tried to teach her a bunch of times, but it never stuck. Red figured that even if she tried, she'd only manage to make it more locked.

The window, then. She stood on tiptoe and peered in—a bathroom lit by a single dim bulb. Again, no security cameras that she could see, which made sense, since it was a bathroom. The window itself was a single pane of glass, and Red guessed she could fit through without difficulty. The hard part would be breaking it without attracting attention.

There was nothing for it but to try. She picked up the same chunk of concrete and threw it full force at the window. It shattered with a crash. Red ducked back behind the dumpster and waited. Still no response. She started to feel uneasy, like it was going too well.

She counted off a full fifteen minutes before sticking her head back out. Apart from the broken glass glittering in the moonlight, the scene hadn't changed.

Red crept out to examine her handiwork. There was broken glass poking out of the frame, but not much. She knocked the shards from the frame and they tinkled to the tile floor inside, where most of the glass was. More was scattered in the dirt outside the building, but it didn't look any different from the other broken glass on the busted pavement.

Right. She'd focus on the inside clean-up.

She held her breath and poked around in the dumpster. Luckily, she found what she was looking for right away: a canvas sack. It smelled strongly of duoofish, but it was in one piece and thick enough to do the trick. She folded it in half and draped it over the window frame to cover any remaining glass. It would be hard enough to clean up the broken glass; she didn't want to clean up blood too. Or, you know, be disemboweled.

With the sack in place, she pulled herself up and through the window. She hit the floor hard, and remembered that she wasn't twelve years old anymore. At least she'd missed cracking her skull on the toilet. Dying in the smelly bathroom of Scarpio's coffeehouse, covered in broken glass, within smelling distance of a dumpster, was not on her agenda.

She eased herself up, wincing at a shooting pain in her hip. It didn't seem permanent, so she yanked the sack inside and used it to brush off her clothes. She found a broom in one grimy corner and swept the glass behind the toilet, then tossed the sack out the window in the direction of the dumpster. Good enough. If anything, the place looked cleaner than when she'd gotten there.

Breaking and entering, check. Now the hard part: finding a place to hide.

She cracked open the door and peeked out. The bathroom was at the end of a cramped hallway. On one side was a door marked PRIVATE, on the other a door that said EMPLOYEES ONLY. Still no security cameras, though by now Red doubted there were any at all. The

PRIVATE door was locked. EMPLOYEES ONLY was the kitchen, with half a dozen coffee pots and a huge refrigerator humming in the darkness.

Past these doors, the hallway opened up on a small dining area. Enough light filtered through the filth on the front windows that Red felt exposed, even at this hour. She crouched down next to the wall and surveyed the room. Most of it was cluttered with shabby tables and mismatched chairs. To one side, though, was a booth tucked into a recess in the wall. It wasn't private, but it did seem to be the best seat in the house. Red guessed that whatever Smith had planned for this meeting, he'd do it right here in this booth. It's what she would do if she were him.

The question was, where could Red position herself to eavesdrop on that meeting? She slid into the booth and checked the sightlines. Just as she thought, she could see the entire room, from the front door to the back hallway and every table in between. There weren't even any tablecloths to hide under. Red leaned back against the wall of the booth in frustration.

That was when she heard a scraping sound coming from someplace near her feet.

She froze, her heart pounding in her ears. Something brushed against her ankle and she barely managed to smother a scream. Shaking, she leaned down and stuck her head under the table. A large gnar sat up, twitching its fuzzy antennae at her, a crust of bread clutched in its paws. She exhaled in relief. The creature startled and ran back toward the wall near Red's feet and disappeared.

Disappeared?

Red squatted down on the floor and saw a vent in the wall near the floor. There was a grate covering it, but it was broken, hanging by one hinge. Red could see the gnar behind it, silhouetted against a dim glow.

This was promising.

Red crept out of the booth and down the hall to the kitchen. This time she noticed a door on the wall to her left, which would back up to the dining area. Red pulled it open and found a pantry lit by a tiny emergency light over the door. A floor-to-ceiling shelving unit loaded with food boxes took up one whole wall. Crates stamped COFFEE were piled haphazardly in front of these. Red moved them aside and cleared off the bottom shelf. There was a vent near the floor, identical to the one in the booth. It even had the same broken grate.

She lay down on the bottom shelf, her head next to the vent. The gnar peered at her from the other side of the grate, a shadow in the pale light from the room beyond. This could work—*if* Smith used that booth, and *if* the restaurant wasn't too loud, and *if* she didn't get nabbed by a cook looking for a jug of spicy homona jam, then maybe. Maybe. It was a long shot, but it was the only shot she had.

Red spent a few minutes rearranging the coffee crates, then scooted as far back on the grimy shelf as she could go. She would probably have to trash these clothes when this was all over, but she'd worry about that later. From where she lay, she couldn't see anything but the bottom of the shelf above her and the backs of the crates. Chances were, if she couldn't see out, then no one could see in either.

In position, check.

Now all she had to do was wait. She yawned so hard her jaw popped. She wished she'd checked the time. Eh, it was still dark. Plenty of time to close her eyes. Just for a few minutes.

CHAPTER 43

Red ran up a cloudbank in the dark, chased by a faceless man. Her breath tore at her throat as she climbed ever higher. At every step, she sank deeper into the clouds. She looked over her shoulder at her pursuer. The man was closer now, his face obscured by shadow. His teeth snapped at her, like a psycat after its prey. She reached a ledge and jumped, fell, fell for miles, rushing toward a mountain of bones. Yet still the teeth snapped, and a hand grabbed at her hair . . .

She woke with a start, her heart pounding, disoriented in the tight, dark space. As reality crept back into her brain, she realized she could still hear the snapping noise of teeth, and felt a tug at her hair. She rolled over and found herself face to face with the gnar. Bits of her hair stuck out of its mouth.

"You little—" Red stopped abruptly. Voices drifted through the pantry door, nearly swallowed up by the grinding and whooshing of coffee being made. They must be getting ready to open. She had no idea what time it was, but the light coming through the vent was much stronger, so the sun must be up. Red stretched her stiff neck and as many other muscles as the cramped space would allow.

The pantry door swung open and a light clicked on. A warm gust of moist, coffee-scented air rushed in, accompanied by heavy footsteps.

The gnar scuttered off, but Red froze, holding her breath. Stuff shifted around on the shelves above her, creating a shower of dust and grit that stung her eyes. They must have found what they were looking for, because the light snapped off and the door slammed closed.

That went well. Terrifying, but well.

Through the vent came footsteps and chatter. She picked out different voices, but couldn't tell what they were saying. Red shifted to get her head as close as possible to the opening, trying to will herself to hear better. Maybe this wouldn't work after all, dammit. All that work and a gnar-bitten haircut for nothing.

Suddenly one voice slid into focus. "Everything checks out, sir." It was Patrick! Red pumped a mental fist.

"Excellent." That was Smith. "You look tired. Please, get yourself a cup of coffee while we wait for my colleagues. I recommend the Ophesan blend. Mild, yet powerful."

"Thank you, sir. I will. Can I get anything for you?"

Two black shoes appeared at the other end of the vent. "The usual, please. Chuck will know." This was a Chuck place too? Jeez, that dude really got around.

After a few minutes of staring at those shoes, Red heard Smith speak again. "Thank you, Patrick." A pause. "Ah. I see they have arrived. Would you please escort them over?"

"Of course."

A moment later, Red heard the distinctive broken-glass croaking of a Glorreen. Déjà vu tickled her brain, but she dismissed it.

Whatever the Glorreen said, it must have been funny because Smith chuckled. "Is that so? Well, it *is* early. Would you gentlemen like a beverage before we begin? Patrick here can fetch one for you."

The Glorreen said something else, then another voice said, "Nothing for me either." This must be the second colleague. His voice was familiar too, but Red couldn't immediately place it. Eh, either it would come to her or she'd worry about it later.

"Thank you, Patrick, that's all for now," Smith said. A pause. "Gentlemen, let's get to business."

"We're listening," said the familiar voice.

"There is an individual who has been asking too many questions. He has become a problem that requires your special kind of attention."

A rapid string of Glorreen.

"As far as I can tell, no. However, he may be closer than he realizes. The sooner he is neutralized, the better."

"What are we dealing with here? Military? Government intelligence?"

"Oh no, nothing like that. I suppose you might call him a free agent." Smith paused. "However, he does have a personal connection, and his emotional investment should not be underestimated. You may find him quite dangerous."

"He may find *us* quite dangerous." Laughter.

This was not your everyday business meeting about sales or a merger. The tabloids got this one right—John Smith was a criminal, and a big one. Red cursed herself for being so stupid. Of course he was a criminal. She knew he was responsible for killing at least three people: the two Guild guards and Exley. She'd let herself forget all that, dazzled by Smith's expensive cars and celebrity friends and fancy whiskey. What had she gotten herself into?

Red wondered about this free agent. Smith was obviously worried about the guy, or he wouldn't send hit men after him. Not military or government . . . could he be a reporter? They had plenty of questions. Whoever he was, he made Smith nervous, which made Red curious.

The Glorreen spoke again.

"Everything you need should be in the file," Smith said.

A minute passed in silence.

"These relatives on Sept Magossii," Familiar Voice said. "Parents?"

"Yes. I would prefer they were not involved. The father has . . . potential. However, I leave the matter up to your discretion. This is, as they say, your area of expertise."

"What about the girl?"

"Absolutely not. She must remain ignorant at all costs."

Parents? Girl? What the hell was going on here? They'd better drop this free agent's name or she'd go crazy. This half-knowing was worse than not knowing anything at all.

More Glorreen.

"I do not believe this job will warrant anything above the standard rate," Smith said. "Of course, should you encounter unusual difficulties, I will be happy to compensate you accordingly. We can discuss those details when the business is concluded."

Red couldn't hear the reply, if there was one.

"Excellent," Smith said. "Shall we adjourn this meeting, or did you have any further questions?"

Some scraping noises. "Don't worry," said Familiar Voice. "Your Mark Woodman problem is as good as solved."

Chapter 44

Time stood still. Woodman! They were talking about killing Woodman!

Red kicked away the coffee crates and scrambled out from her hiding place. Her legs cramped from spending a night on a metal shelf. She half ran, half fell through the pantry door. She ignored the startled shouts of the kitchen staff as she stumbled past the row of coffeemakers and into the hallway. Patrick stood at the opening to the dining area. He blinked and reached out to grab her, but she shoved his arm aside and ran to the booth.

Two men sat with Smith: the Glorreen with his brilliant green skin, and a heavyset man with enormous eye bags. Her breath caught in her chest. Someone grabbed her arm, probably Patrick, though it was far away, like it was happening to someone else.

Smith got to his feet and said something, but Red didn't hear, couldn't hear, because she was twelve years old again. Twelve years old, standing on a box in the basement, peering through a different grate, watching her father's lifeless body fall, seeing the light disappear from her mother's eyes, hearing Limey Jim and Joey Pockets laughing as the bodies of her parents cooled on the kitchen floor.

Limey Jim, the Glorreen, croaked something and gestured to her with his long hand. Joey Pockets shrugged and picked up a fat envelope from the table, slipping it into his jacket. Patrick had her by both arms now, trying to pull her away from the booth. Smith stood still, his face a mask, cold eyes locked on Red.

A woman wearing an apron hurried over, chattering and twisting her hands. Smith dismissed her by twitching a single finger in the direction of the kitchen.

"You . . . them?" Red found that she still had a voice, though it was thick and foreign to her ears.

"Patrick, it's all right, you can release her." Patrick let go and backed away warily.

Red's knees turned to water and she almost collapsed. Smith reached out to catch her, but she recoiled. "Don't you touch me," she growled.

"Red, please sit. We have much to discuss."

"No!" she shouted, drawing stares from the few other customers who were not already staring. "There's nothing to discuss. You need to tell these murderers to leave Woodman alone."

"Ah," Smith said. "It seems you have been eavesdropping." He paused, then took a sip of his coffee. "Very well. I will put this current project on hold, on one condition: you sit with me, calmly and rationally, and listen to what I have to say."

"Oh hold? No." Red jabbed her finger on the table. "You will call it off *now*."

Smith's mask slipped, revealing a dark, boiling anger. "I am not in the habit of rearranging my business at the whim of a silly girl who—" He closed his eyes and took several breaths. When he opened them again, the mask had returned to his face. "However, I cannot help but recognize my own culpability in the turn this has taken. So, in an effort to minimize further trauma, I will do as you ask."

He turned to the two men still seated in the booth. "Gentlemen, my apologies. Please consider this project terminated. I will, of course, compensate you for your time here today."

"If anything changes, let us know." They slid out of the booth and buttoned their jackets. Joey Pockets pulled the envelope from his pocket and handed it to Smith. He gave Red an amused look, then shook Smith's hand. "Always a pleasure."

"Indeed." Smith shook Limey Jim's hand, and the two hit men walked out the front door of the coffeehouse.

"Now," Smith continued, slipping the envelope into his own pocket and gesturing to the booth. "If you will please sit, we can talk." He nodded to Patrick, who rushed over.

"Please inform George that our departure will be delayed. Also, I need a second cup of Madame Scarpio's finest. Red, would you care for a beverage?"

Red sank into the booth but said nothing. She stared at the tabletop, refusing to even look at Smith. She struggled to keep her mind from spinning out of control. Smith settled himself into the booth across from her and watched her silently.

Patrick arrived with a fresh mug, then returned to his post by the hallway. Smith stirred his coffee and put the spoon on a napkin.

"This conversation is long overdue. I had hoped to arrange for a more private setting, but your unexpected appearance here has forced my hand. Still, perhaps this is best."

"Those men killed my parents," Red whispered. "Killed them, right in front of me."

"I know." He sipped from his mug.

Red's eyes bulged. "You know? That's all you can say? You sit there drinking coffee like nothing is wrong. My parents are dead. And all you can say is 'I know?'"

"I know this must be difficult for you—"

"Are you kidding me?"

"Please," he interrupted, putting up one hand. "I beg you, allow me to speak. This information is sensitive for me as well, as I think you'll come to understand in time."

Red crossed her arms. "Go on, then."

Smith took another sip of coffee and seemed to think. "I will begin by revisiting a question you asked back at the beach villa on Glor. 'Who are you, really?'" He smiled slightly. "At the time, I told you I am a businessman. While technically correct, clearly that was not the whole truth. I do own a large construction company. I also own several retail chains, a movie studio, and other traditional business ventures. However, those endeavors, while quite lucrative, are not the source of the bulk of my fortune and influence. I do not think it will surprise you to learn that I am the head of a powerful crime syndicate."

Red was not surprised, though it was odd to hear it spoken out loud, in public, over coffee. She shook her head.

"I would have been disappointed in you if you had not suspected something of this nature. Over the course of my life, I have built my empire from the bones of a dozen smaller, less effective organizations. I began at fourteen years old, when I infiltrated the Yahuzi Brotherhood and killed its leader, a man named Farzod, by piercing his arm with a poisoned dagger.

"As my power and wealth grew, so did the risk of ending up like Farzod: betrayed, abandoned, poisoned by my own hubris. I developed a moral code to guide and protect me. Oh, I realize the absurdity of a man like me discussing morality. All I can say is that has not yet failed me. I get what I want, and am still around to enjoy it."

Smith paused for another sip of coffee. "One of the underlying tenets of that code is intolerance of failure. If someone fails me, they face the consequence. If someone crosses me, well, that requires even stricter measures."

"What does any of this have to do with my parents? With me?"

"I was just getting to that point." He straightened the spoon on his napkin. "Crime, at least on the scale at which I operate, is extremely complex. I cannot do this alone. I have many employees and colleagues with whom I entrust various tasks related to my criminal dealings. For example, your friend Chuck is an extremely valuable resource for information, as you might imagine. I rely on Limey Jim and Joey Pockets, despite their ludicrous names, for tying up loose ends."

"That's an interesting way to say they kill people you want dead."

"It is not inaccurate."

Red looked away.

"They have failed me only once in twenty years. This was about sixteen years ago, now. Something was stolen from me, a data chip containing delicate information about my organization and its activities. I sent Joey Pockets and Limey Jim to retrieve it. They failed to do so. Rather, they succeeded, only to fail at the same task mere hours later."

"Quit talking in riddles."

"I apologize. It is painful for me to relive these memories, though I realize you do not believe me capable of such emotion."

Red said nothing.

"The data chip was stolen by a government agent named Xanther. My colleagues caught up with him, retrieved the chip before he could transmit the data to his superiors, and then killed him. While they were waiting for me to contact them regarding delivery of the chip, someone else managed to steal it from them."

A cold syrup of dread spread through Red's veins.

"The chip contained a tracking device," Smith continued. "This is what led Joey Pockets and Limey Jim to Xanther, and it is what led them to the home of the second thief. Your home.

"Of course, we all assumed the responsible party was an adult. We had no idea that it was really their child who had stolen the data chip. A child who then destroyed it by throwing it into a lake."

Red's hands shook and hot tears poured down her cheeks. "You sent them. You. My mother, my father. I watched them die! I was twelve years old, and I watched my parents die, because of you."

Smith offered Red a handkerchief. She stared at it, her eyes burning, her jaw clenched. After a moment, Smith withdrew the handkerchief and tucked it back in his pocket.

"Earlier, you expressed disbelief that I might understand how difficult this is for you. There is one more piece of information that may help you understand. I knew your parents, before this incident with the data chip. I knew them quite well, in fact. Your grandmother too. You see, Richard Darkling and I were brothers."

Chapter 45

Red felt like she'd been sucked out of an airlock. She tried to speak, but she had no breath. "What . . ." she managed to whisper.

"Richard was my older brother. He was three when I was born. Our sister, Susan, was five. Our father—your grandfather—died shortly thereafter. I have no memories of him. As children, we were all three very close. I struggled to maintain the relationships when I began pursuing my criminal career. This turned out to be impossible.

"Susan was the first to cut me out of her life, when I was sixteen and she was twenty-one. My mother asked me to leave a year later, though frankly it was long overdue." Smith clenched his jaw. "Though they abandoned me, never once did I abandon them. I have ensured not only their safety these many years, but provided for their financial comfort, with no expectation of repayment, gratitude, or even acknowledgment. I am careful to leave no trace of myself in these matters. Neither one would willingly accept help from me."

"Granny's lawn service," Red muttered.

"Among other things, yes. Richard held on the longest. I didn't lose him until you were born. I was twenty-five then, and already controlled the criminal circles in several systems. Despite everything, I believe he still loved me, just as I loved him."

"Like hell you did," Red snarled. Smith spread his hands, then continued.

"When I learned that the data chip had been tracked to Richard and Lacey's home, I was faced with a dilemma unlike any I had encountered before. My moral code, the rule by which I live, the doctrine which protects me, requires that I show no mercy to those who oppose me. But this was my brother, his wife. My own blood."

He paused, staring into his mug. "In the end, I chose to follow my code. After all, Richard and Lacey might have wanted that information for their own purposes. It was no secret that Richard disapproved of my choices, and I had to consider the possibility that he was attempting to take me down."

"If he did, he would have been a hero."

"To some, yes. Krysia described morality as—"

Red slammed her fist on the table. "Shut up about your damn poets and philosophers!" she shouted. The room got quiet. People stared at them, and Red didn't care.

"Red, you need to control yourself." Smith's voice was deadly calm.

"Or what, you'll have me killed too? Is that how you deal with all your problems? Just call Limey Jim and give him a file?"

"I am a patient man, but even I have my limits. I will only say this once, so pay attention: restrain your temper or the conversation is over. You wanted truth, I am giving you truth. You seem to be under the impression that truth is easy, or simple. It is neither. If you cannot handle these truths, it is best you do not hear them at all."

"You sound like my father."

Smith gave her a strange look. "Indeed. Shall I continue, then?"

Red's back ached, her head throbbed, and mental, physical, and emotional exhaustion threatened to overwhelm her. All she wanted to do was crawl back to the *Pit* and disappear into space with a bottle or two of strong, cheap whiskey to help her make sense of all this. Or, help her forget.

She rubbed her temples, trying to block out the noise of the coffeehouse. This was what she wanted, wasn't it? To know the truth? And Smith wasn't done yet. It scared her know that whatever Smith had left to say would probably be even worse. It scared her even more to realize she still needed to know.

"Go ahead," she sighed. "I'll behave."

"Thank you. Let us return to the night your parents died."

"Were murdered."

"Yes. As I said, at the time, we assumed Richard or Lacey responsible for the theft. We did not realize our error until hours later, when a search of the house failed to produce the data chip. Only then did my thoughts turn to you. Joey Pockets confessed that he and his partner had been assaulted by two children in the marketplace. By the time we located you, the chip was at the bottom of the lake and you were with your grandmother.

"Here, another dilemma presented itself: what to do about you. My heart was still in turmoil from my decision to terminate Richard and Lacey. You were only a child, though admittedly even then you demonstrated formidable skills that could easily turn dangerous. I should have terminated you . . . yet, with the data chip destroyed and you ignorant of its contents, there was little need for vengeance. Besides, you had escaped to the protection of my mother, a formidable woman in her own right.

"For these reasons and others, I broke my own code and allowed you to live. I did not, however, want to take any undue chances. I monitored you carefully, utilizing every resource at my command. This became increasingly difficult as you matured. It was no coincidence you discovered Chuck's secret nature, you know. Nor is it coincidence that you have that ship."

"The *Pit*? I took that from some Andarian guy who shorted me on a job."

"Rolar was an employee of mine, tasked with making sure you ended up with that ship. He took some liberties with the plan, though, resulting in his untimely castration." A smile twitched at the corners of his lips. "Suffice to say, that was the last time Rolar and I did business together."

"But if you wanted me to have a ship, why couldn't you make it a nice one? You've got the money."

"Indeed. However, an expensive ship would have drawn undue attention to itself. You might have wondered why a man like Rolar would have such a ship. You might have traded it for a lesser model and pocketed the difference. Plus, I already knew you well enough, albeit from a distance, to know how much a ship like this would appeal to you, to your sense of self-identity. And I wanted very much for you to have an emotional attachment to this ship."

"Why?"

"Because I didn't want you to sell it, or abandon it. That would have defeated the purpose. You see, that ship contains hidden surveillance and tracking systems that have allowed me to monitor your movements and actions for years."

"Are you—" Red lowered her voice and leaned over the table. "Are you telling me that you rigged the *Pit* to spy on me?"

"Essentially, yes. I have access to your navigational systems, your vidchats and messages, even your musical selections. That particular model of ship, in its current condition, provides many opportunities to conceal modifications one does not want noticed."

"I suppose next you'll tell me Bonk is reporting to you on my bathroom habits."

He laughed. "No, I assure you, the cat is none of my doing. Though I admit I was relieved to see you had acquired a companion. The galaxy is a lonely place. It is not good to be alone."

"All right, all right. It's creepy as hell to know you've been watching me all the time, even in my own ship. But I knew someone had to be, ever since that shit that went down with the Guild."

"Yes. I monitored you, and occasionally arranged for a fortuitous circumstance to befall you, but mostly I left you to your own devices. As a man who built his own empire, I admire self-reliance and resourcefulness—both characteristics you possess. I wanted to see what you could do.

"However, the Guild overstepped its bounds. Sloane was vying for power, trying to cut into my business in my home territory. They kidnapped you and my mother in an effort to pressure me into signing some disadvantageous contracts. They could not be allowed to succeed, of course, but I dared not reveal myself directly. So, I pointed your friend Mr. Woodman in the right direction, and trusted you to do the rest." He paused. "I should thank you for removing Sloane from the equation. His death threw the Guild into chaos, from which they have yet to recover."

"Don't thank me, asshole. You used him, us, to do your dirty work."

"I confess, I did use Mr. Woodman to retrieve you, though I would never have done so if I had thought there was any real chance he would be at risk. Despite what you may think, I do not kill unless circumstances require it. And, for the record, I would have been more than up to the task of eliminating Sloane without your intervention. That was serendipitous, no more."

"So why didn't you send in the cavalry when we ran into that baega?"

"If you remember, your navigational system was down. I could not locate you until you made contact with her through the messaging system. By the time my sources managed to track you down, you had already escaped—on your own, I might add—with a fortune in goods."

"Fat lot of good it did me. Damn poachers stole the lot out from under me before I'd turned a single credit in profit."

Smith's eyes shifted away. Wait a minute.

"Did you set that up?" she demanded.

"You must understand, it was in your best interest, as well as mine, for you to remain, ah, financially limited."

"In my best interest."

"Yes. If you were suddenly thrust into a life of financial ease, you would not have continued to develop your skills. Hunger is, as they say, the finest whetstone."

"Grumshit. I earned that loot. I deserved it."

Smith shrugged, but said nothing.

"What else have you done to hold me back?"

"Hold you back? Petty crime, scraping for every credit, weeks spent idle, drifting uselessly. I hardly consider you in need of holding back."

Red's anger flared. "It was you! You blocked all my jobs. You told all my contacts that—told them who knows what? Just so I'd be desperate enough to come to this stupid planet, so you could impress me with your library and take me cloud walking."

"Again, you have proven yourself quite perceptive. But this is all merely logistics. We have, as they say, bigger fish to fry."

Red rubbed her temples. "Fine. Okay, so, I think I know what happened with Exley. Chuck saw me leave with him and sent you after me. Yeah?"

"One of my associates, but yes. That was when I began to worry. You may remember that I considered you reckless. Your impulsive streak has always been your greatest failing, though prior to the Exley incident it had remained innocuous enough. But when you allowed yourself to be drugged by a stranger in a bar, I had serious doubts about the direction your life had taken. I was no longer sure that you could be trusted."

"Trusted? For what?"

"To do what I have been grooming you for since you were twelve years old: to join me in my business, with the goal of taking over when I eventually retire."

"You're not serious."

"Indeed, I am very serious."

"Why the hell would I want to be a—a—a gangster?" Red sputtered.

"You have all the characteristics that I value in myself. You are resourceful and self-reliant, as I have already explained. You are also intelligent, clever, and perhaps most importantly, you do not shirk responsibility for difficult yet necessary tasks. I was impressed when I learned how you dispatched the baega with your own hand. Pity and mercy may seem like virtues, and perhaps they are in art and religion. But in the grim, gritty universe in which we toil, pity and mercy leave you vulnerable."

Red considered this. She'd never looked at herself this way. Most of the time, she felt like she was stumbling through life with a broken leg and no map. And she couldn't ignore the intoxicating idea of all that money and power. There was no reason she couldn't take over his business, get rid of all the criminal stuff, get someone to manage the legit businesses, and live fat and happy in her own beach villa. It would be tricky, and she'd have to make sure to do it all the right way, but oh, that beach villa . . .

"Even if I did want to join you—which I don't—but if I did, I still don't understand why you'd want me. You must know a thousand other people who'd be better."

Smith picked up his empty mug, swirled the cold dregs around in the bottom, then set it back down.

"What? Suddenly you're all out of truth?"

He looked tired. "'And here we stand, at the edge of reason, hands entwined, about to leap.'"

Red waited impatiently for him to stop blabbering poetic nonsense.

Finally, he sighed. "There is one piece of information you lack. This will illuminate all: why Richard cut me from his life, why I could not bring myself to order your death, why I followed you all those years, why I have protected you from harm, why you possess so many of the characteristics I admire in myself, why I have groomed you to succeed me in my business.

"Mildred Darkling, you are not the daughter of Richard and Lacey Darkling. You are my daughter."

Chapter 46

Red burst out laughing. She drew more stares, but was oblivious. She laughed until her sides ached and her cheeks were again wet with tears. Smith let her finish.

"Oh my god, I'm such an idiot," she gasped, wiping her face with a napkin as the laughter turned to hiccups. "You really had me going there. I almost believed you. Holy shit, you should go into acting, seriously."

"I am not acting. Everything I have told you is true. I am your father."

"I'll buy the criminal mastermind bit. The rest of it, though? I mean, dude, this 'I am your father' stuff is straight out of some lame-ass novel."

"I know this is a shock to you, but please, if I may continue—"

Red pushed herself out of the booth. "Thanks, but no. I've wasted enough time on this crap, and I'm sure you've got better things to do than sit here and tell me fairy tales all day."

He stood and reached for her. Before she knew what was happening, blood was leaking from a cut under his eye, and her face was pressed to the linoleum floor, arms bent painfully behind her back by a cursing Patrick.

Smith dabbed his wound with a napkin. "I warned you about your temper, Red." He nodded at Patrick. "Get her out of here."

Patrick yanked Red to her feet. Her left shoulder flared in hot pain as he dragged her across the restaurant. "That was stupid," he muttered under his breath, then shoved her out the door into the bright midmorning light.

On her way back to the *Pit*, Red replayed the entire conversation in her head, trying to pick out the facts from the fictions. Except for that crap about being her father, it all made at least some kind of sense. The criminal stuff was so obvious, she kicked herself for ever doubting it. She should apologize to Granny about that. The rest was ridiculous. Even seeing Joey Pockets and Limey Jim didn't mean anything. Hit men would work for anyone with the credits to pay. By the time she jerked open the ship's hatch and climbed on board, she was laughing again over the whole thing.

"Hey, Bonk," she said, flopping into the captain's chair and switching on the nav. The cat, laying in the copilot's chair as usual, switched off its energy conservation mode and blinked. "You wouldn't believe my morning. What d'you say we head over to Albicon 8 and check out the used ship lots? I'm thinking we could use an update."

Bonk's tail twitched.

"That's what I thought, too." She tapped in the coordinates and the ship rose. Red felt better once the sub-light drive kicked in, propelling them ever further away from Crysallia and its damn clouds.

Red's stomach growled. Dinner at Cloudtop was ages ago. She grabbed a can of duoofish, some crackers, and a beer, then headed back to the cockpit. She shoved a cracker in her mouth and pinged Granny.

She had to share this story with someone, and Granny was the only one left who'd talk to her. At least, Red hoped she would.

The pingback came in just a few minutes later. Red washed down a mouthful of crackers with a swig of beer and switched on the vidscreen.

"Why, Mildred, I haven't heard from you in so long. I've been worried sick! Is everything all right?" Granny twisted a ball of blue yarn in her hands.

"I'm fine, Granny. Sorry I didn't ping you before, I've been kind of busy. What are you knitting?"

"Oh, just another scarf for one of the ladies at the senior center. What have you been busy with? Work? Maybe you've met someone special?"

Red laughed. "No, nothing like that. I did see that John Smith guy again, though."

Granny tutted. "I do wish you'd stay away from that man."

"You don't have to worry about that anymore. That's why I pinged you: to tell you that you were right about him being a criminal."

"What! Mildred, what happened?"

"He wanted me to visit him at his house on Crysallia. I didn't have any work, and I hadn't been to Crysallia, so I figured what the hell? He kept talking about this business meeting he had, all mysterious, wouldn't tell me what he was up to. So I followed him, right? Turns out he was ordering a hit on someone. From a crappy coffeehouse!"

Granny's hand flew to her face. "That was so dangerous! Why would you do such a thing?"

"Wait, that's not all. Then, he starts telling me all these stories about how he got to be this big crime boss, like I'm supposed to be soooo impressed. And he says he wants to train me to take over his business when he retires because—get this—he's my real dad. Jeez, can you believe that I almost fell for that? It would be hilarious if I wasn't so embarrassed about . . . hey, what's wrong?"

Granny sighed heavily, twisting her yarn. "I think you should come home, Mildred. We need to talk."

"Granny, what is it? Is it about Smith?"

"Just come home. Will you come?"

"Of course I'll come. It'll take me a day or two."

"That's probably best. It will give me time to . . . prepare."

"Prepare? Prepare for what? Granny, what's going on? Whatever it is, just tell me now."

Granny smiled sadly. "Just come home." The vidscreen went dark.

"Shit!" Red spat, and stormed out of the cockpit.

In the copilot's chair, Bonk registered the crashing and cursing from the other parts of the ship. It analyzed the patterns, checked them against its database, and determined they did not match any known pest activity. It extended its neck hydraulics until its head panel was flush against its exhaust valve, thus completing the circuit that reengaged its energy conservation mode.

CHAPtER 47

Red eventually settled down enough to reprogram the nav for Granny's house on Sept Magossii. The travel time was eighteen hours, but she bumped the engines up to their limit and cut it down to twelve. She'd take her chances with the galactic cops.

She lay down on her new and gloriously hole-free mattress, trying to catch up on her sleep. But every time she closed her eyes she saw the flash of the blasters, heard her father hit the floor, and watched the life leave her mother's face. She gave up and polished Bonk within a micron of its circuitry. By the time she landed in Magross, the cat looked almost like new—if new meant dinged up but mostly rust-free.

Granny answered the door, her eyes red and puffy. "I'm so glad you're here," she said.

Red kissed her cheek. "I am too."

"Would you like some tea? Coffee?"

"No thanks, Granny. I really just want to know what's going on."

Granny nodded and led her into the living room. Photo albums covered the sofa. Granny picked one up and ran a hand over the letters pressed into the cover. "'Memories,'" she read. "As if life would let you would forget."

She opened the album and handed it to Red. "Do you see that photograph?" She tapped one of the pictures. "That's your grandfather and I, right after our wedding. Ernie wanted to take me to Glor for a honeymoon. A beautiful place for his beautiful bride, he said. But I was already pregnant with your aunt Susan, so we bought this house instead."

Red peered at the couple in the photo. They grinned at the camera, his hand on her slightly swollen belly. She had her arm around his waist and seemed truly happy.

"The next page, that's when Richard was born." Red sat cross-legged on the floor and turned to a photo of her grandfather holding a bawling baby wrapped in a blanket. Granny, looking exhausted, lay in a hospital bed with a curly haired toddler girl tucked in her arm.

"Ernie's heart was already acting up," Granny said, sinking carefully into her rocker. "He couldn't carry his own daughter to the playground without resting every five minutes. He was so young, though, we didn't think much of it." She waved a gnarled hand at the pile of albums. "Now take that one. No, the one with the napkin sticking out of it. Yes, that one. Open it."

The album fell open to the same photo she'd seen Granny looking at months before, the one with the mystery baby. "Ernie died just a few days after that picture was taken. His poor heart just gave up on him. I still wonder if that wasn't the reason things turned out this way. Maybe I wasn't strong enough on my own, without Ernie . . ." She trailed off, holding a handkerchief to her face.

"Granny, who's that baby?"

"That, Mildred, is John. I called him Johnny."

"John who?" Red asked, though she already knew the answer.

"John Darkling, my youngest son. He goes by the name John Smith now, thank the Fourteen."

Red shook her head. "This doesn't make sense. How come you never told me I have an uncle?"

"Mildred, dear, John isn't your uncle. He's your father."

Red dropped the album with a thump. "No. That isn't true."

"Oh, I should have told you years ago." Granny's hands twisted together in her lap. "But I thought he was out of our lives forever. I thought we were all finally safe . . ."

"I don't understand. How can he be my father? Were he and my mom—"

"Heavens no!" Granny rocked in her chair. "Johnny got himself involved in all that crime business when he was still just a boy. When Susan left home, she and Johnny got into a big fight about it. She told him she never wanted to see him again. As far as I know, he's honored that.

"I thought I could bring him around, make him give all that up. I let him live here, fed him, washed his clothes, all the while trying to make him see that what he was doing was wrong. I was a fool. One night he killed a man on the street, right there in front of our house. That was when I knew he was lost to me. I told him to leave and never return."

Red hugged her knees to her chest.

"He honored that too, at least for a while," Granny continued, picking up the album Red had dropped. "I worried so much about him. He was my baby boy. I felt I'd failed him, having to be both mother and father." She stroked the album's cover with shaking fingers. "Then one day he showed up at the door with a baby of his own. Mama, he said, don't you want to hold your granddaughter? I looked at that baby—you, Mildred—and I knew what he was asking me. He didn't want a baby. I asked about your mother, who she was, begged him to give me even a name. He refused. In the end, Richard and Lacey took you to raise as their own. They had only one condition: that Johnny would never have anything to do with you, or them, ever again."

"He didn't honor that one, did he?" Red whispered.

Granny shook her head. "That has always been the thing about Johnny. He can make you believe promises you know are lies."

"Did he . . . did he kill my parents?"

Granny rocked a moment, her eyes distant. "The night you showed up at my door, I knew that he had broken his promise. I didn't know what he'd done, and even now I have no proof, not the kind you are looking for. But only Johnny could cause that the kind of pain I saw in your sweet face that night. The kind I see in your face now."

Red leaned over and took her hand. It was cool, soft, just like it always was. Granny smiled at her, though Red could see she was crying.

"Oh, Mildred, your mom and dad loved you so much. They wanted you to have everything, and above all, to be safe. If they knew Johnny was in your life now, I don't know . . ."

"He's not, Granny. Not anymore."

"I'm sorry I never told you any of this before," Granny said, smoothing Red's hair. "Always the fool, me. Trusting that things would work out for the best all on their own."

"You're not the fool, Granny. I am." Red wiped her nose with the tissue from the photo album. "I'm the one who should be sorry. You tried to warn me about him, but I didn't listen. I didn't listen to anyone. I knew best, ha. I was too stupid, too . . . too grumheaded to listen. I thought, this was my big chance, you know? To get away from who I was. To be somebody, somebody important. He made me feel special." Red picked at her fingernails. "It all sounds so silly when I say it out loud."

"It's not silly to want to feel special or important," Granny said. "We all want that. Don't feel stupid. Johnny has a way of making people do what he wants. You're not his only victim, dear."

Red snuffled and dabbed at her nose with her sleeve. "Granny, do you think I could stay here for a while? Here, in the house? There are some things I need to take care of."

"You never have to ask, my darling Mildred. Now, I think I need a cup of tea. How about you?"

Red nodded. "I love you, Granny."

"I love you, too."

CHAPTER 48

That night, Red stared at the familiar ceiling of her girlhood bedroom, going over things with a clarity of thought she'd not had since, well, maybe ever. She worked things over in her head until she was satisfied, sometime around midnight, and slept dreamlessly.

She woke, refreshed and determined, early the next afternoon. She got dressed, washed her face, and went downstairs to find Granny who was, of course, in the kitchen.

"Good morning!" she chirped, grabbing a zuranfruit from a bowl on the table and plopping into a chair.

"Good morning yourself," Granny said, smiling. She poured Red a cup of coffee. "You are in a good mood today. Did you sleep well?"

"Slept great," Red said around a mouthful of zuranfruit. She washed it down with a swig of coffee. "I *feel* great. It's weird, don't you think? Considering everything?"

"You're a strong person, Mildred. You're like, well, you're like your father that way."

Red considered this. "Yeah. I guess I am. I don't think he knows that. Not really. But he will."

Granny sat across the table from Red and squeezed her hand. "It sounds like you have something in mind. You will be careful, won't you? He's a dangerous man."

"Don't worry, Granny. Woodman and I have a saying: do it right, do it careful, do it smart. I haven't exactly been following that lately, but it's time I started again."

"What about Mark? I know you two had a falling out. Was it about this business with Johnny?"

"Yeah, it was." Red smiled sadly. "Of course it was. I owe him a huge apology. I owe a lot of people a lot of apologies, actually. But first I have to deal with Smith."

~ ~ ~

In the *Pit*, Red pulled up the number and sent the ping. She thunked her boots on the control panel and lit a cigar. "Well, Bonk," she said to the cat sitting in the copilot's chair. "Now we wait."

She didn't have to wait long.

"Ms. Darkling," Claudia said with a touch of sneer. "Mr. Smith is in a meeting. Would you like to leave a message?"

Red blew a stream of smoke toward the ceiling. "Nah. Get him on the screen."

"I'm sorry, I don't—"

"Look. Claudia. You know who I am, right?" The assistant scowled. "Thought so. Now. Tell Daddy that his beloved daughter wants to talk to him."

The SmithCo logo flashed on the screen.

"You know," she said to Bonk, taking a draw on the cigar. "I don't think she likes me very much." Bonk's eyes flashed.

Claudia left her on hold long enough to finish the cigar and light a second. When the logo did pop off, it was replaced by Smith.

"Red, this is unacceptable." His cold eyes glared at her from the chipped vidscreen.

"Shut up and listen. I thought you'd want to know that I've thought about your offer."

Smith sighed impatiently. "I simply do not have time for this right now."

"Make time. How soon can you get to Magross?"

"You cannot expect me to—"

"I expect you to be here tomorrow afternoon. Two o'clock. I'll send the coordinates to Claudia." She disconnected before he could respond. She simply did not have time for him right now. She had shit to do.

Chapter 49

Red spent the rest of the day shopping. She hated dropping money on big ticket items, but she managed to find what she was looking for and didn't walk away feeling profoundly ripped off. Sure, she'd spent the rest of the money from Smith, plus some she borrowed from Granny—which, when she thought about it, was probably also from Smith. Red found this deliciously ironic.

Spending Smith's money gave her an appetite. She ate a huge roast darna dinner with Granny, and went to bed early feeling fat and happy. She slept well for the second night in a row.

The next morning, Red got to work and stayed busy until lunchtime. Darna sandwiches on mushy white bread with lots of mayo had never tasted so good. Afterwards, she finished up a few things just in time to go meet Smith.

Granny came out to the ship with her. "Will you be all right?" she asked.

"I'll be fine. I'm already fine, actually." Red hugged her. "I'll be back in an hour or so."

"All right, dear. What is it you said, be careful, be smart?"

Red smiled. "Do it right, do it careful, do it smart. I will, I promise." She hugged Granny again and climbed up into the ship. The engines fired up with only a tiny cough. Red stayed on manual control for the short trip to the rendezvous point.

She landed on the street and sat there a few minutes, engines idling, staring out the viewport.

Time had not been kind to her childhood home. Even in the few years since she'd seen it last, the weeds had gotten taller and the peeling paint revealed more bare spots. Red didn't remember the holes in the roof before, or the graffiti on the front door that said DEATH HOUSE. Neighbors must love that. She wondered why it had never been torn down.

Red got out of the ship and walked around back. She kicked at the weeds under her bedroom window, stubbing her toe on the stump of the homona tree. The basement window had been boarded up, along with the kitchen window and a few others. A stout padlock hung on the back door. Red examined it, then pulled a small plasma cutter from her jacket pocket. The tool made short work of the lock, and Red entered the house for the first time since she was twelve years old.

She walked among the debris that covered the kitchen floor: broken dishes, splinters from the blasted cabinets, food containers emptied long ago by the rodents who left only their teeth marks and droppings behind. She squatted to clear away a pile of shattered coffee mugs, revealing a dark stain on the wood floor.

She traced it with her fingers and closed her eyes. She saw her father, her real father, a crumpled heap in her mother's arms, her lips gently pressed to his forehead.

She crossed to the room to the wall with the ankle-high vent cut into it. Another dark stain here. Red knelt beside it and peered through the vent, imagining what her mother must have seen as her life slipped away: Red's own tear-streaked face looking back at her.

"Interesting choice of location." Smith's sharp grey suit and immaculately styled hair clashed with the destruction and decay of the kitchen.

"I thought it was appropriate." Red stood, her eyes quickly scanning the room. "You alone?"

"My associates are waiting outside. I would prefer they did not have to wait long."

Red crossed her arms and leaned back against the dusty countertop. Showtime. "Let's get down to business, then. About that offer . . ."

Smith narrowed his eyes. "Are you considering it?"

"Hell no," Red laughed. "After all that stalking, you should know me better than that."

His mouth tightened. "If you were not considering my offer of employment," he said in a strained voice, "then why are we here?"

"Maybe I'm going to kill you."

Smith tensed, then shook his head and laughed. "Congratulations, Red. You had me convinced, if only for a moment."

Red shrugged and kicked at a rusted soup pot. "I could do it, you know. It's just you and me in here."

"I suppose you could," he said, spreading his hands. "Though I am afraid your victory would be short-lived. My associates would need only one shot."

"Maybe. But you'd still be dead."

"True." He brushed imaginary dirt off his jacket. "So, shall we prepare ourselves for death?"

"Oh, I'm not actually going to kill you."

He smiled slightly. "To what do I owe this generosity of spirit?"

"Don't get me wrong. I thought about it. I think I'd even enjoy it. But I won't. Because you're wrong about me, Smith. You said I'm just like you, but I'm not. I don't kill family."

"Ah, so you have accepted the truth."

She ignored this. "Stay away from me, stay away from Granny, and stay away from Woodman."

"'And lo, the pillars of history spiral ever downward into the ravenous maw of despair.' Vladmir IV knew, as I do, the cruelty of family." He sighed and shook his head. "I will do as you ask. This I promise you."

"Uh uh. You can keep your promises. I know how little they mean to you. If there's promising to be done here, I'll be the one to do it." She looked him in the eye and pointed a finger at him. "If you so much as think about coming after us in any way, I promise I will find you and make you regret it."

"Your threats are unconvincing. Only a moment ago, you claimed you do not kill family."

She raised an eyebrow. "I wouldn't have to kill you."

A smirk spread across his pale face. "You actually believe you could hurt me in any way?"

"I'm your daughter. You tell me." She smiled. "Consider this goodbye, Smith."

"Are you sure you will not reconsider my offer?" His eyes flashed. "You know what happens to those who cross me."

"Yeah, I do. But you know what? I don't think you'll be calling your goons on me."

"And why not?"

Red brushed off her hands. "Because you didn't kill me when you found out I stole your data chip, and you didn't kill me when I bloodied your pretty face at Scarpio's. It's a safe bet you won't kill me now."

"Oh, but—"

"Don't interrupt me." Her voice was cold and hard. "I was going to say, I don't need safe bets when I've got insurance." She reached into her jacket pocket and pulled out a book. She tossed it to Smith, who caught it deftly.

"Vladmir's copy of *The Seven Discourses*," he said quietly, turning it over in his hands. "This was a gift."

"A great gift, actually. So much more than just a book." Red held up a small piece of paper.

Smith frowned. "What is that?"

"Found this tucked in the pages. You should invest in a real bookmark, you know." Red examined the paper. "At first I thought you wanted me to find it. Some kind of twisted psychological grumshit. Self-destructive tendencies, you know? I bet Exaius has something to say about that."

"Red—"

"But it's obvious you don't remember. Huh." She tutted. "Maybe your mind starting to slip, Smith. Have you talked to your doctor? There's no shame, you know, especially at your age."

"I assure you, my mind is not slipping."

Red shrugged. "Dude, fine, if you insist. But that means you're the single stupidest criminal who ever lived. And that's saying something. There's some pretty stupid people out there."

"You know I am far from stupid."

"Actually, I don't know that at all. I mean, not only did you commit this to paper, in your own handwriting, but then you left it in a book? A book you gave away! To me, of all people. That's colossal stupid. Galactic stupid."

Smith wrinkled his brow and fell silent for a moment. "This is madness," he finally said. "Tell me what is on that paper!"

"No. If you can't remember, that's your problem. Not mine."

Smith's jaw clenched. "I am losing patience with you, Red. Give me that paper." He took a step toward her.

Red drew her blaster casually. "I don't think you want to do anything *else* stupid. See, I haven't told you my plan."

He stopped. He was gripping the book so hard that his knuckles were white.

"Good boy. This isn't the original, of course. That's very safe. This is only a copy—one of many copies, in fact, ready to flood the galaxy. Every cop, every reporter, everyone will know about it. If anything happens to me, this goes public. If anything happens to Granny or Woodman, this goes public. If I so much as smell you around me or anyone I care about, *this goes public*."

Smith snorted. "I own more than enough policemen, lawyers, and judges to avoid prison."

"Yeah, I figured. But this would still be out there." She waved the paper. "Every crime lord from here to Orgulla will know you're either stupid or losing it. That you're weak. How long before the first one makes his move? The second? The third? How long before your own people betray you, the way you betrayed Farzod when you were a kid?"

Smith was silent.

"Have I made myself clear?"

"You are bluffing." But his voice had a slight tremor.

"Am I?" Red smiled sweetly and tucked the blaster back in its holster. "Maybe I am. But maybe I'm not. Are you willing to risk everything on that chance?"

Smith's face flushed with anger. "You bitch," he spat.

Red stuffed the paper in her pocket. "I'm my father's daughter." She pushed past him and walked out the door. She didn't look back.

CHAPtER 50

It wasn't until she was halfway back to Granny's that Red let the tears come, fast and hot. She landed on a random street to ride it out. When the waves finally subsided, her shoulders ached and her eyes were raw—but it felt good. She was lighter, purged, almost like a good puke after too much booze. She took the crumpled paper from her pocket and smoothed it out.

It was blank.

She went to the bathroom and scrubbed her face with cold water. She leaned against the sink, dripping, eyeball to eyeball with her mirrored self. Behind the puffy redness, behind the puckered scars, behind the lines beginning to creep up, she saw something new, something like acceptance. And that felt good too.

Back in the cockpit, she typed up a message for Woodman:

> >>>I'M SO SORRY. YOU WERE RIGHT ABOUT
> EVERYTHING. IF YOU'RE STILL IN MAGROSS,
> I'LL BE AT THE AQUEDUCT TONIGHT. MAYBE
> I'LL SEE YOU THERE. I MISS YOU. RED.

Sending the message made her nervous. But even that, in some weird way, felt good.

Granny waited for her on the porch. She stood when she saw Red's ship land. The knitting in her lap fell to the ground, forgotten.

Red hugged her, hard. "It's over," she whispered through fresh tears.

Granny hugged her back, filled with questions she would never ask. Instead, she simply said, "Good."

~ ~ ~

That evening, Red sat on a chunk of concrete, waiting. Pebbles bit into her ass. Her breath hung in the air like normal clouds in the dying light of the day. The sun's final rays, golden but cold, threw long shadows. Somewhere, a ship's engines roared, then faded.

Red shifted on the concrete as the shadows melted into night. Woodman still had not come. A broken streetlight flickered briefly to life, then went out. The last insects of the season buzzed weakly. Ghosts of her childhood whispered from the graffitied walls around her.

And then he was there. "Hey," she said, standing up quickly.

"Hey." He didn't quite meet her eyes.

"You got my message."

He shoved his hands in the pockets of his jeans and looked away.

She took a step towards him. "I'm so sorry, Mark. I've been so wrong about so many things, but about you most of all."

"You really hurt me, Red." The streetlight blinked back on, and she saw his cheeks were wet. "All I ever wanted was for you to be safe. I looked into that Smith guy, you know. He's straight-up evil."

"I know. I was—" She spat in the dirt. "No. I wanted to explain, to make you understand, but that's grumshit. It's all just excuses." She took another step. "All I can do is tell you I'm sorry. But that's just words, isn't it."

Woodman didn't respond. A breeze played with his hair, the unsteady light outlining his profile against the darkness.

Red shivered and pulled her jacket tighter around herself. Waited.

"I still care about you, Red. But . . ." He ran a hand through his hair.

"It's okay," she said, putting a hand on his arm. "I care about you too."

He pulled away and walked over to her ship. He cleared his throat. "This yours?"

"Sure is."

"What happened to the *Pit*?"

Red smiled sadly. "I had to disintegrate it," she said. "Long story."

"Shit." Woodman shook his head. "End of an era."

"It was time anyway. It was good ship, but it just wasn't me anymore. I dunno. That probably doesn't make any sense."

Woodman ran a hand over the hull. "Looks pretty solid. Does it have a name?"

"Not yet," she said. "I was thinking I'd see how it grows on me."

"You make it sound like a wart."

"Maybe that's it," she said. "The *Wart*. What do you think?"

"I think you'd actually call it that."

They laughed. It was wonderful.

"Hey, it's cold," Woodman said. "Let's get inside somewhere. Want to get something to eat?"

Red nodded. "Yeah. Anyplace but Shellchuckers, though."

"Ha, no. I was thinking someplace quieter, where we can talk. Really talk."

"Perfect," she said, opening the *Wart*'s hatch. "You mind if we take my ship? I'm still breaking it in."

"After you, darlin," he said, gesturing to the open hatch.

But she didn't go in. Instead, she took Woodman's face between her hands and put his lips to hers. He resisted for only a moment, then pulled her close. The kiss lasted an eternity. When it broke, she patted his cheek.

"More later, maybe," she said. "If you still want to after hearing about my father trying to hire hit men to kill you and recruit me into his life of crime."

Woodman's jaw dropped. "Hit men? Me? What . . ."

Red put a finger on his lips, took him by the hand, and led him into the ship.

Special Thanks

Writing the book was easy. Thanking everyone who made it happen? Impossible. And yet, I must express my deepest gratitude to David, for never getting tired of kicking my ass to get this book out. I hope he doesn't hate me for the character I named after him. Heaping piles of thanks to Jason, who brought Red to life with almost no help from me. And I can't forget the WPaD crew, whose brains I shamelessly picked for all things publishing. Finally, a big sloppy kiss of thanks to my husband Michael. Not only did he encourage me to slap together a bunch of stories and make a book, he surfed the waves of my self-doubt like a champ.

About the Author

Lea Anne Guettler is a freelance technical writer from Illinois. *Red Darkling* is her first novel. Her short fiction and poetry have appeared in several anthologies, including Wicked Women in Words' *Run Over By . . . An Omnibus.* Portions of this book appeared in slightly different form in the anthologies *Circuits & Slippers* and *Strange Adventures in a Deviant Universe*.

Follow Lea Anne at www.facebook.com/authorLeaAnneGuettler/

Made in the USA
Middletown, DE
02 July 2022